Inheritance

Landscapes of Love

Inheritance

Landscapes of Love

PHILIP TYLER

© Philip Tyler, 2023

philip@landscapesoflove.com

Published by Pickhill Publishing

A CIP catalogue record for this book is available from the British Library.

ISBN 978-1-7399815-4-9 (Paperback)
ISBN 978-1-7399815-5-6 (ePub)

Book layout and cover design by Clare Brayshaw

Cover photograph Sunset in the Al Ula Valley – Saudi Arabia – photograph by Thamim Zain/iStock

Prepared and printed by:

York Publishing Services Ltd
64 Hallfield Road
Layerthorpe
York YO31 7ZQ

Tel: 01904 431213

Website: www.yps-publishing.co.uk

Dedication

This book is dedicated to the Park Rangers who risk their lives every day to protect the mountain gorillas in Virunga National Park and the rhinos in the National Parks of Kenya.

In the year ending March 2021 alone, twenty young Park staff in Virunga were murdered in a 'ferociously violent and sustained attack' by armed poachers.

Mountain gorilla and baby in Virunga

"If we do not do something to prevent it, Africa's animals, and the places in which they live, will be lost to our world and her children forever."

Mandela

Contents

Artists and Photographers

Chapter 15	Page 333	Baby Mountain Gorilla – photograph by Goddard Photography /iStock
Cover photograph		Floating over Africa – photograph by Chao-Feng Lin / iStock

Chyulu Hills – Kenya – West Africa

Daniel slowly opened his eyes, after the operation to repair the muscles in his left thigh. The AK-47 bullet had torn straight through his leg but fortunately missed hitting the femur. His vision was blurred but he could see two figures, one on each side of him. He was disorientated and did not know if he was still in the forest with the dead Somali next to him, drenched in blood. Although the smell of the putrefying rhino carcass had gone, as had the buzz of the swarming flies around his legs.

"You are in Elizabeth's hospital at Mtito Andei. You were seriously injured but you're safe now my darling," comforted Charlie, holding his hand and giving it a gentle squeeze.

"I thought I was dead. I heard a second bullet," mumbled Daniel, still not sure what had happened to him. He tried to move but the pain in his leg was intense, even though the anaesthetic had still not fully worn off.

"Don't try and move my love. Just lie still and we will explain everything when you're feeling better," assured Charlie.

"Is Annie, OK? Is she alive?" Daniel started to panic. "Where is my darling Annie. Please tell me she is alive?"

Charlie looked a bit shocked and glanced across at Annie on the other side of the bed. Ann Marie looked back at Charlie and smiled reassuringly.

Ann Marie took Daniel's other hand. "I am here with Charlie. We are both here."

"I thought I was dead!" reiterated Daniel slurring his speech and losing consciousness again.

"He said that in Chocorua!" Charlie grinned at Anne Marie.

"We could send him there to convalesce and I will look after you!" offered Anne Marie with an even bigger grin on her face.

At that point, Karen, the senior doctor who ran the clinic for Daniel, came into the room to check on her patient.

"How's he getting on?" she asked Charlie.

"He's still a bit delirious and confused, but he is slowly coming round."

"He was very lucky the bullet missed the bone or he could have been in for a very long recovery," confided Karen. "But he's a tough nut and will be back on his feet in no time. Just don't let him go off on some other hare-brained adventure until the stitches are out and the wound has healed up properly."

"How long do you think he will be in for?" asked Anne Marie.

"I would like to keep him in for a week, but you know Daniel. If we get past tomorrow, I'll be surprised!"

* * *

Daniel arrived back in camp the following day.

"You are still meant to be in hospital," admonished Charlie at his surprise arrival. She gave him a hug and kissed his cheek.

"I was bored and I needed a decent cup of tea. What's been happening here? Have the police sorted out the dead Somalis? Is the rhino cow and calf down at the Springs, OK?"

White rhino and calf

"Yes, everything is fine," assured Charlie. "Just sit down before you fall down and Nzinga will make you a cup of tea."

The whole team had heard the news of Daniel's arrival and gathered around him to celebrate his rescue from being killed.

"So how did you two know the Somalis were going to ambush me?" asked Daniel smiling at Anne Marie and Charlie who had saved his life by killing the poachers.

"You've got Eshe to thank for that," said Anne Marie. "A few minutes after you left to find the rhino carcase, Eshe said that the white rhinos never go down as far as Utu. So, Charlie and I were suspicious, grabbed two AKs and jumped in the Land Rover. We only just arrived in time. He was about to shoot you again!"

"Come here Eshe and give me a big hug," offered Daniel and Eshe obliged, happy that she had helped save the life of the man she idolised.

"Jahir and I have some news for everyone," blurted out Eshe. "We are getting married next week!" Everyone cheered and congratulations flowed from every direction. "Will you give me away please Daniel. Please?" pleaded Eshe.

"Of course. It will give me the greatest pleasure in the world, Eshe. I wondered why you wanted to save my life!"

CHAPTER ONE

The Serengeti Ecosystem – Tanzania

Although Eshe and Jahir were both raised in the orphanage at Kilmana run by Father Peter, Eshe had worked so closely with the Maasai over the last few years that she considered them as her family. All the women folk in the local village were excited about the wedding of their adopted daughter and they were determined to organise a traditional Maasai wedding ceremony. Having both spent a lot of time away from Tsavo, in England getting their further education, Eshe and Jahir were sort of planning a more modern Christian ceremony. The women folk won!

"As long as I don't have to have my hair shaved off and lamb fat smeared on my head!" declared Eshe, at least rejecting that part of the traditional festivities.

"And we don't want any cows or goats as presents either," laughed Jahir.

Undaunted by these restrictions the women set to work and started making the elaborate and colourful costume for Eshe to wear. Hundreds of colourful beads were threaded and a decorative wedding collar lovingly created.

Charlie and Anne Marie were in charge of the preparation of the feast, consisting of roast beef, a sort of soup that was a mixture of cow's blood and milk, and a honey-based creation for afters. Charlie was not sure about the blood and milk but Daniel assured her it was delicious!

* * *

The morning of the wedding arrived. The sky was cobalt blue without a cloud in sight. Kilimanjaro rippled in the heat-haze drifting up from the savannah and the white-starred robins were twittering in the black ironwood trees. Eshe had spent the night with the women folk at Kambu, one of the local villages. They had spent the previous evening explaining to her how to be a good wife to Jahir and how to give him many children. Eshe entered into the spirit of the evening and did not let on that they had been living together for some while. She did however pick up one or two things about men that she had never thought was possible!

Meanwhile Jahir had spent the night with Daniel, Bomani and Thulani and definitely needed a black coffee for breakfast. The wedding ceremony was to take place on the special rock overlooking Kilimanjaro which meant so much to everyone at the camp. Father Peter, from the orphanage, had agreed to officiate, in conjunction with the Maasai elders, who would bring a traditional element to the ceremony. Jahir had decided to wear his pilot's uniform from his days at RAF Cranwell but the elders insisted that he wore a cow skin covered in coloured beads on top. This symbolised his wealth and standing in the community, so the bride and her family would be impressed.

Charlie fussed around Jahir, making sure his tie was straight and that the cow skin didn't hide too much of his pilot's wings.

"You look very handsome, Jahir. Eshe is a very lucky young lady," assured Charlie. Jahir smiled nervously and shuffled his feet self-consciously. Daniel appeared in his best linen suit and white shirt. No tie.

"How's the condemned man this morning?" Daniel asked with a smile.

"Have you got the rings?" asked Jahir tentatively.

"I had them somewhere last night. I will find them eventually," joked Daniel, pretending to search through his pockets.

"Don't wind him up any more," replied Charlie. "He is nervous enough as it is!"

* * *

The joy of the approaching bridal family could be heard a mile away as they ascended the red dusty track up to the camp. The intensity of the laughter and singing increased as the milling throng got slowly nearer and nearer. A thin cloud of ochre dust drifted amongst the bushes and tumbled down the hillside into the vast grasslands below. Finally, the party danced into view, with brightly coloured dresses billowing with exuberance and fun. Eshe, hidden at first by a multitude of happy smiling faces, finally appeared from the chaos in her magnificent red dress. Charlie ran over and gave her a big hug.

"You look absolutely stunning Eshe. Your dress is amazing, and all those beads. It must have taken them a year to sew all those together!"

"Are you sure I look OK?" whispered Eshe. "I couldn't see what they were doing."

"You look fabulous. Come and hold my hand I will take you to Daniel."

As they walked across the camp to find Daniel, Eshe turned to Charlie and whispered again, "I just wanted to thank you Charlie for taking me on that flight in the helicopter to Kilimanjaro with Jahir. If you hadn't done that for us, I would probably never have had the courage to kiss him."

"You are clearly very much in love with each other and I am sure you will have a wonderful life together," smiled Charlie as they found Daniel finishing a phone call.

"Good morning Eshe; you look different!" joked Daniel and Charlie gave him a quick dig in the ribs.

"Don't you think she looks amazing?" suggested Charlie, scowling at Daniel.

"Jahir is a very lucky man, Eshe. You are incredibly beautiful and I wish I was twenty years younger."

"So do I," blushed Eshe, revealing her fantasies about Daniel but added quickly, "you have Charlie and I think you are very lucky too."

Daniel took Eshe's hand, gave it a soft kiss and led her out into the cheering Maasai families. The tufts of savannah grasses, tied to Eshe's shoes to symbolise a plentiful supply of food for their cattle, flicked up little clouds of ochre dust as they walked across to the stone outcrop overlooking the plains of Africa. Jahir turned to look at Eshe, his eyes filled with joyous tears. Their eyes melted into one vision as they became man and wife under the midday sun.

* * *

"You may kiss the bride," said Father Peter and Jahir took Eshe in his arms and gave her a long passionate kiss. The cheering echoed around the camp and the party began.

"So, who was on the phone?" Charlie asked Daniel, as they collected their first glass of Dom Perignon Champagne from Bomani's rustic bar.

"What phone? I thought it was a lovely service," replied Daniel trying to avoid the question unsuccessfully.

"I knew you were up to something! So come on, what's going on?

"Just doing a favour for a friend."

"Which friend?"

"You'll see in a minute. That's his helicopter," smiled Daniel pointing to a tiny speck in the sky, swooping down the front of Kilimanjaro and across the plain towards them. As the drone from the blue and white Super Puma grew in intensity, the eyes of the party lifted to the skies. It circled the camp and hovered above the small landing pad next to Jahir's helicopter, throwing up a curtain of dust hiding its occupants. As the dust started to clear, a tall figure dressed in a pure white flowing thawb with a red and white checked keffiyeh walked towards the mesmerised gathering. In his right hand he held a small gift wrapped in gold foil.

Nzinga, who was standing next to Anne Marie, grabbed her arm when she recognised Prince Fahd.

"I can't believe it's him. Am I dreaming? Why is he here in Chyulu?" Nzinga was confused and elated at the arrival of her special friend from Saudi Arabia.

"I was only talking to him last night and he said nothing about this!" exclaimed Nzinga.

"I think you might have Daniel to thank for this but let's see how things pan out. Play it cool my dear. Don't blow it," advised Anne Marie.

Daniel walked across to the prince and they embraced as old friends. Fahd's eyes flashed around the gathering looking for Nzinga. Their eyes met and they smiled at each other with no hint of their real feelings.

"Did you have a good trip my friend?" asked Daniel.

"Thank you for inviting me, Daniel. I cannot wait to see how your rhino project is going. But why are you limping so badly?"

"Long story, but the girls killed the other guy!" laughed Daniel. They walked across to Eshe and Jahir, and Fahd presented them with his wedding gift. It would buy a lot of goats!

* * *

The champagne was starting to work its magic. The music got louder, the dancing more colourful and the white-starred robins were long gone. Charlie had a long conversation with Fahd about Rashieka and her continued recovery from her kidnap. She and Prince Khalid were back running their busy lives: he running endless meetings about oil production and Rashieka enjoying her daily shopping expeditions. Still no sign of any children though.

"Where are you staying? asked Charlie.

"I have hired the Safari Lodges in the Serengeti and I was hoping you would all come and stay as my guests whilst I am here?"

"That would be wonderful. I assume Daniel knows about this already?"

"Of course: he organised it all for me!" laughed Fahd. "I thought Jahir and Eshe could have a quiet lodge on their own and enjoy their honeymoon whilst we all go on safari!"

"I am sure they will enjoy the peace and quiet after all this excitement; it's very kind of you Fahd and it will be great fun to spend a few days in your company. Now I am sure you will want to see Nzinga on your own whilst everyone else is preoccupied with the festivities?"

"Do you think she will forgive my surprise arrival?"

"I am sure she will mellow with a kiss!"

"But…"

"You're a long way from Saudi here Fahd and amongst friends. Daniel would not have invited you if he thought there was a problem. Just enjoy your time with Nzinga; she talks about you all the time. Tomorrow is another day. If you walk across to the outcrop where the wedding ceremony was, on your own; I will bring her across to you in a few minutes," smiled Charlie.

* * *

Charlie found Nzinga talking to Anne Marie, took her hand and asked her to come for a walk.

"Has he gone?" asked Nzinga with a worried expression on her face.

"No, he is waiting for you over at the rock. You only have a few days together so make the most of it," advised Charlie.

"But Annie said to play it cool?"

"A prince from the Saudi royal family has flown two thousand miles to be with you Nzinga, now is not the time to be cool!"

Nzinga walked slowly through the confusion of colour and music and out to the rock. Fahd was looking out across the savanna and turned to face Nzinga when he heard her footsteps.

He smiled and held out his hand. "This is going to be incredibly complicated."

"I don't care," said Nzinga returning the smile, "I have never felt like this with anybody before and I am so pleased that you could come."

Fahd took her into his arms and kissed her softly on the lips. Their lips parted and they looked deeply into each other's eyes. Fahd lifted her off the ground in his arms and kissed her again, passionately.

A tear of joy trickled down Nzinga's cheek, "I don't care how complicated it gets. I only want to be with you."

* * *

The following morning, they climbed aboard the two helicopters and headed for the Safari Lodges in the Serengeti. Bomani and Thulani had agreed to stay behind and watch over the rhinos and Max had headed back to the airport to keep a birthday party appointment with his two goddaughters in Los Angeles.

It was early May and the long rains were coming to an end but the humidity was still intense and the daytime temperatures were over thirty degrees. The prince had reserved the whole site so they could relax in privacy and not be worried about the scourge of social media intrusions. Charlie and Daniel had their own lodge near the natural pool and Jahir and Eshe had theirs, a discreet distance at the far end of the group. Anne Marie had the lodge next to Charlie's and Fahd had booked a separate lodge for Nzinga, next to his, as he did not want to make any assumptions about their relationship.

After the frenetic activity of the previous day's wedding, they all decided to have a relaxing evening by the pool, overlooking the vast lands of the Serengeti. As the crimson sun drifted down to the distant horizon, the evening air cooled and a distant lion roared in preparation for his evening's sortie. The attentive staff at the lodge lit a fire to prepare an alfresco meal and filled the crystal flutes with Krug Clos d'Ambonnay to complement the smoky flavours of the chargrilled vegetables.

Daniel and Fahd were stood next to the firepit when Charlie appeared wearing her favourite long floaty dress made of fine Egyptian cotton. She had put her hair up and was wearing the long gold earrings her grandfather had left her. She looked incredibly sexy as the flames from the fire reflected through the fine material. Fahd kissed her on her cheek and Daniel just smiled in anticipation.

Charlie glanced at the flute in Fahd's hand but looked away quickly.

"It's only fizzy grape water!" he suggested without much conviction and they all laughed.

Jahir and Eshe wandered slowly along the path, hand in hand, towards the gathering, smiling and chatting to themselves, clearly happy to finally be together without creeping about in the dark.

"Now then you two, how was the first day of married life?" asked Daniel.

"This is just such a romantic place to spend our first few days together," replied Eshe. "We will always be indebted to you Prince Fahd and thank you for such a beautiful present."

"You make a wonderful couple and I am sure you will be very happy together. And please drop the prince bit. Just call me Fahd."

"Have you been to Africa before?" asked Jahir.

"Only once, to an oil conference in Nigeria, but it has always been one of my ambitions to come to this part of Africa and see all the wildlife that you are all doing such a fantastic job of protecting. We have similar conservation problems in Saudi and I am looking forward to comparing notes with you Eshe so we can learn from each other."

"Where are Annie and Nzinga?" enquired Daniel, looking at Charlie.

"I think Annie is doing Nzinga's hair? She wanted it to look special for you tonight Fahd. She is so pleased you have come all this way to see her."

"I came to see the lions," joked Fahd, unconvincingly. At that moment Annie and Nzinga appeared from Annie's lodge. Nzinga looked stunning in her long bright blue silk dress and her hair looked beautiful, tumbling around her shoulders in waves. Fahd took her hand and kissed it softly again. Nzinga could not believe this was happening to her.

"Daniel. How do you manage to surround yourself with such beautiful intelligent ladies in the middle of nowhere!"

"Everything is beautiful in Africa!" smiled Daniel. "Now let's get something to eat before the sun sets."

* * *

The following morning everyone was up early, at five o'clock, for a hot-air balloon ride in the clear blue skies above the Serengeti. The team from Arusha were already unpacking the green and gold balloon and inflating the Nomex envelope with the gas burners generating the hot air. The balloon slowly took shape as the hot air filled the inside of the envelope and lifted it vertically above the traditional wicker basket. The tension in the ropes holding the basket to the ground grew taut as the balloon strived for its freedom from the dusty African soil. The senior pilot was called Oscar and he had been flying hot-air balloons all over the world for over twenty years, including winning his category at the Championships in Rio Claro in Brazil 2014. Whilst he was completing his pre-flight checks, he got into a deep conversation with Jahir about air currents and the safety features of the balloon compared to Jahir's helicopter.

"Come on you two – enough of the techy stuff; these ladies want to see some wildlife before all the lions go for a midday siesta," admonished Daniel.

They all climbed into the creaking basket, Charlie with her Canon camera fitted with a long zoom lens, Anne Marie with a picnic hamper and Fahd with the obligatory bottle of champagne to toast the safe landing – hopefully. Oscar gave the envelope on the balloon one final burst of hot air whilst Daniel released the straining ropes allowing the party to accelerate into the cool morning skies above the Serengeti.

"Wow, it climbs really quickly," exclaimed Anne Marie.

"That's why we like an early start," advised Oscar. "The difference in temperature between the ambient air and the hot air in the balloon gives you a big advantage in the length of flight you can achieve with the gas we have on board."

"Where are we heading?" asked Fahd, getting enthusiastic about his first flight in a balloon.

"We are in the hands of the Gods," smiled Oscar, "but the air current should take us north-west along the Grumeti River basin towards Lake Victoria. The large herds of wildebeest and zebra will be chasing the grasslands on their annual migration up to the Masai Mara and we should get to see some of the early herds crossing the river which is pretty spectacular."

"Do you find the balloon frightens the animals?" asked Anne Marie.

"Only if you fly really low over them," replied Oscar. "The short burns on the gas sometimes startles the gazelles but the larger animals seem pretty immune to it."

Daniel was leaning on the edge of the basket with Charlie resting her head on his shoulder. He smiled at her and gave her a quick kiss whilst the others were preoccupied with the vivid reds and scarlets of the sun rising above the distant horizon, lighting up the magnificent scenery as far as the eye could see.

"You'd better get the camera fired up if you don't want to miss the sunrise," suggested Daniel, "and try not to fall out of the basket!" he laughed referring to Charlie's fall off Mount Chyulu in New England. Charlie grinned and dug him in the ribs. "I'll make you pay for that later."

"Quick Charlie," gesticulated Anne Marie. "There is a group of zebras over here with two babies."

By the time Charlie had got her camera set up, they had drifted past the group and the moment had gone.

"Can we go back?" joked Anne Marie to Oscar.

"Err no! We don't have steering I'm afraid," he smiled. "There will be plenty more."

The warmth of the early morning sun was welcome after the cool start, and as it heated the vegetation below, the pleasant aroma of the acacias drifted up to them in the basket. The smell of the distant herds hung in the passing air and the acrid scent of lion clung to the nostrils. This was Africa at its magical best. The huge scale of the landscape. The kaleidoscope of colours. The birth place of mankind. The endless peace. A place to love and be loved.

Charlie noticed that Fahd was holding Nzinga's hand and she smiled approvingly at Daniel. He nodded towards Jahir and Eshe who were similarly attached. Anne Marie was leaning over the edge of the basket on her own scanning the verdant grasslands for more zebras. Charlie crossed the basket and put her arm around her waist.

"Have you seen anything yet?" asked Charlie, in excuse for her friendly squeeze. Anne Marie turned and smiled.

"I have often dreamed of what it would feel like to float along above the trees and savannah of Africa. I have watched it so many times in films but the reality is a million times better. It's just wonderful Charlie. I can't thank you enough for inviting me."

"I think it was your idea to come to Africa and help Daniel to find the poachers – and we ended up saving his life! It should be me thanking you," smiled Charlie giving Anne Marie another affectionate hug.

Oscar gave the burner another short burst and the flames flickered into the balloon as it gained altitude to cross a hillside covered in trees. As they breached the summit, Anne Marie pointed frantically at a small expanse of water below, surrounded by eleven elephants and three calves. Two teenagers were rolling in the muddy waters covering their rough skin with the brown mud. One of the mother elephants was pawing at the water's edge trying to encourage her calf to make the treacherous descent of the bank into the water. The calf kept moving its front feet over the edge of the bank but then retreating in fear. The three-foot drop must have looked frightening to such a small calf for the first time. But slowly, with its mother's encouragement, it reached further and further down the slope until its back feet lost hold and it slid down the muddy slope into the water with a small splash. Charlie was ready this time and her camera whirred away as it took multi-shots of the infant's adventures.

"Did you catch that, Charlie?" asked Fahd. "I must have a picture of that on my office wall!"

"Of course; I will send you all a WeTransfer file when I get back so you can look through all the photographs I have taken of the safari. They will all be over five meg so it's the easiest way to send lots of photographs."

"You will have to come back to Riyadh and take some photographs of our Vision 2030 research programme for the Arabian leopards in the AlUla mountains for me," requested Fahd.

"We would love that, wouldn't we Daniel? It will be really exciting to see the new facilities you have built."

"It might make ours look a bit Heath Robinson!" joked Daniel.

"I think we might be able to work together on that one. Of course, it will mean I will have to come to Chyulu a lot," smiled Fahd, looking towards Nzinga whose heart leapt at the idea.

The elephant family continued with their muddy bath, and as the balloon drifted westwards, another small group of elephants were wending their way through the trees in curling, trunk-to-tail lines. The mothers were flapping their enormous ears and making squeaking noises to encourage their calves to keep up.

As the balloon moved out onto the dry savannah grasslands, punctuated only by the occasional flat-topped vachellia tree, a vast herd of wildebeest came into view. The swarming lines of animals looked like soldier ants from above as they moved relentlessly towards the Grumeti River; another hurdle in their relentless search for fresh grazing. Nzinga spotted a late calf being born but it stood no chance in the open plains against the voracious hyenas.

"Most of the calves are born in February on the plains south-east of Seronera which are rich in grasses after the short rains in November and December," explained Oscar. "After the end of the long rains, around the end of April, they start to move on their annual 800-kilometre migration with their calves. Many calves are killed by the predators along the way including the lions, leopards and of course the scavenging hyenas which none of us really like much!"

"Does the annual migration happen at exactly the same time every year?" asked Fahd.

"It depends on the grazing available in each area of the cycle," Oscar replied. "So, it is quite difficult to predict when the trek will start and how quickly it will progress but it always takes the same route, passed down from one generation to the next."

"I have decided I hate hyenas!" grumbled Anne Marie as the last of the calf disappeared down the throats of the hyena pack.

"I think they come into the same category as poachers but when did you last see a big game hunter, like Ernest Hemingway, sat on a dead hyena!" observed Daniel cynically.

The burning sun was now well above the distant horizon and the curved horns of the wildebeest were reflected on the ground beneath their ever-moving hooves. The enormous herds of zebra were interspersed with the wildebeest like black and white minstrels, braying donkey-like to their own youngsters to keep them in the safety of the herd. Those trailing behind were soon hunted down by the efficient techniques of lionesses.

Pair of Zebra

Nzinga spotted a female leopard resting in a wild date palm tree with her two cubs wrestling on the ground beneath. They rolled, fought and chased each other around the tree until an ominously large wildebeest approached. The leopard quickly jumped to the ground and rounded-up the wayward youngsters, carrying each in turn softly in her mouth, to the safety of the higher branches.

Each waterhole was surrounded by thirsty mouths and impatient crowds awaiting their turn. Giraffes with their golden mosaic skins, stooped to get fresh water; their front legs flexed apart so their long necks could reach. Thompson's gazelles, eland and waterbuck nervously sipped at the water's edge, constantly on lookout for the next predator to ruin their day.

Oscar pointed out the winding green belt of vegetation lining the Grumeti River ahead of the balloon, as the call of the baboons echoed from the dense treetops. The herds of wildebeest were growing denser as they backed-up from the dangerous river crossings filled with hungry crocodiles, looking for an easy lunch. As the balloon crossed over the river, they could see the huge hippos floating in the green tainted water, immune to the crocodiles. The impulse of the wildebeest to find new grazing overwhelmed their fear of the crocodiles and en masse they leapt into the turbid, boiling waters, thrashing their legs in frantic panic to reach safety on the far bank before the grip of the enormous carnivorous teeth sank into their limbs and dragged them to their final demise.

"I have read about these crossings many times but to see the reality of this primeval drive to get food is mesmerising and hypnotic," observed Fahd. "It's nature at its most cruel, horrific and saddest."

"But everyone who comes on safari wants to see the spectacle," said Daniel. "It's real, it's nature at its most primitive level and it could be mankind fighting for the last remnants of food on the planet if we don't look after the place."

"Before philosophy totally ruins the day, I think it's time for lunch," laughed Oscar. "I am planning to land in that clearing on the far side of the river so hold on tight when we hit the ground."

With great expertise, Oscar slowly released the hot air from the envelope and the basket touched the ground as softly as a butterfly on the buddleia in an English garden. The balloon gently deflated and fell to the ground in a long straight line away from the basket, for which he got a respectful round of applause from his passengers.

At that moment two Mitsubishi pickups appeared from a track through the trees with the recovery crew on board.

"How did they know where we would land?" asked Anne Marie, her head still full of hungry crocodiles.

"GPS!" laughed Oscar.

"You wouldn't think she can fly jets!" smiled Daniel patronisingly.

With the baboons burbling in the background and the odd vervet monkey screaming at a rival, they settled down to Anne Marie's picnic basket and Fahd's champagne, which was rather warm – but a nice thought anyway.

* * *

The long drive back to the lodges was hot and dusty. The tracks were rough and the back seats of the pickups cramped and uncomfortable. From the freedom of the skies to terrestrial transport was a sharp contrast and they were all pleased when the camp came into view.

"It was an early start, so I suggest we all have a rest for a while. I will arrange a meal by the pool later on and we can all have a relaxing evening enjoying the sunset," suggested Daniel. No one disagreed!

* * *

Charlie and Daniel walked down the path to the natural pool at about four-thirty and Anne Marie was already swimming up and down the pool vigorously, the silver

18

water droplets skimming down the black skin on her back. She didn't notice them arrive and continued her exercise whilst they relaxed on one of the rattan sofas covered in voluminous white linen cushions. An attentive member of staff magically appeared with a silver tray of gin and tonics. Charlie was wearing Daniel's favourite white silk and gold chain bikini hidden under a long white chiffon kimono for modesty.

"When did you two sneak up on me?" smiled Anne Marie, finally noticing their arrival and resting her chin on her arms at the water's edge.

"Oh, ages ago," lied Daniel. "Are you practising for the Olympics!"

"I just felt like some exercise. It gives me a buzz to push myself to the limit sometimes," replied Anne Marie lifting herself out of the water. Daniel's eyes glanced up and down her beautiful slim body for a fleeting moment. Charlie noticed with a tinge of jealousy. She let the kimono slip off her thigh as a distraction for Daniel.

"I love your kimono, Charlie; where did you buy it?" asked Anne Marie, her eyes beating Daniel's to the exposure.

"Riyadh actually. Princess Rashieka bought it for me as a present on one of our many shopping trips. This is the first opportunity I have had to wear it."

Anne Marie collapsed onto the sofa next to Charlie, curled one leg under herself and grabbed a G&T from the table next to her. "Cheers! That balloon flight was the most wonderful journey I have ever experienced. I just loved the baby elephants in the mud pond. I hope you've got lots of pictures for our book."

"I thought you had forgotten about that project?" said Daniel ruefully.

"I never forget an opportunity to work with Charlie," grinned Anne Marie.

Before that potentially complicated conversation developed, Jahir and Eshe wandered across from their lodge at the far end of the complex. Jahir had his arm around Eshe's waist and she briefly looked up at him, smiled and they kissed.

"Hi you two. How is the honeymoon going?" asked Anne Marie in a blunt but amicable American way. Eshe blushed and Jahir smiled!

"We are having a lovely time together," replied Eshe, regathering her composure. "Isn't this such a wonderful and peaceful place? We are so lucky Fahd invited us."

"Pull up another sofa and help yourselves to a drink," suggested Daniel, just as Fahd arrived wearing his bright red swimming trunks. Charlie had never seen him undressed before and was struggling to take her eyes off his extremely attractive physique. His naturally brown skin flattered in the evening sunlight.

Daniel stood up to welcome him but fell back onto the sofa as his injured leg gave way.

"Too much gin already?" laughed Fahd.

"He should be taking more rest after being shot but you know what he's like!" reprimanded Charlie.

"I'll give him a massage later. That'll fix it," said Anne Marie with a sly grin.

"Whose coming for a race up and down the pond then?" suggested Fahd. The words were hardly out of his mouth when Anne Marie leaped up and dived elegantly into the cool water.

"I'll take that as a challenge then!" said Fahd and followed her with a determined dive of twice the length. Charlie followed his lithe torso through the air and followed his body as it slid into the water without a ripple. He caught Anne Marie up before the first length.

"How many lengths then?" challenged Fahd.

"As many as you like!" replied Anne Marie.

"One hundred. One, two, go!"

"What happened to three?" shouted a surprised Anne Marie but Fahd was nearly one length ahead and pretended not to hear. Anne Marie set off in hot pursuit as Nzinga appeared from her hut adjacent to Fahd's.

"What are they up to – is it some sort of competition?" queried Nzinga.

"I think they are as competitive as each other but I doubt he has raced a woman before!" said Daniel.

As the two swimmers raced up and down the pool, Eshe got up from the sofa and walked across to Nzinga to talk to her dearest friend quietly on their own.

"So how is Jahir in bed now you are married?" asked Nzinga, coming straight to the point.

"Well, you know we have been together for a while," whispered Eshe, "but he has become incredibly romantic and wants me all the time. He makes me feel so special and is very considerate but we made love four times last night!"

"The women in the village did warn me about African men's libido but I did not expect quite so much enthusiasm," smiled Eshe. "Anyway, have you and Fahd done it yet?"

"Not yet. He is being very polite and kisses me so sensitively. He makes my tummy turn over."

"So are you going to let him?"

"I don't know what to do. I really want him. My body aches for him when he touches me but Anne Marie warned me not to be too keen because of the situation, with me not being from Arab royal blood."

"It's an amazing feeling when they are in you. I know we have never talked about it in detail but I am married now and feel I should help you. You are my best friend in the whole world!" smiled Eshe, hugging Nzinga.

"The truth is I am still a virgin," confided Nzinga, "and until I met Fahd, I never really thought about sex much; but now my whole body is on fire for him and I want him to want me."

"Look there is no rush. Apart from who he is, he also seems to be a gentle honest person to me. If you get close to him wanting you, explain that you have never been with a man before and that it is something very special for you. You will be able to tell from his reaction if he has sincere long-term feeling for you," advised Eshe thoughtfully.

"Thank you Eshe. I love you like a sister. Let's see what happens in the next few days."

The two of them re-joined the group who were now on their feet, noisily cheering on Fahd and Anne Marie who were on lap eighty-five. Anne Marie was catching Fahd and was now only a few strokes behind. Fahd was clearly getting tired but so was Anne Marie, who had already done a few hundred meters before the challenge commenced.

"Come on Fahd," shouted Daniel. "Don't let the men down!"

"Annie is going to win. She is catching him! Come on Annie!" called Charlie.

Jahir put his arm around Eshe's shoulders and gave her a passionate kiss, whilst the rest were willing on their chosen competitor. "What have you two been whispering about?" he asked.

"Just girl's stuff," smiled Eshe.

"Have they done it yet?" he breathed into her ear.

"How did you know what we were talking about?" said a surprised Eshe.

"Did I get a good rating?" enquired Jahir smiling.

"More practise needed," laughed Eshe. Jahir looked into her sparkling eyes, took her hand, and they ran back to their lodge, giggling.

"Ninety- nine," shouted Daniel, as Anne Marie and Fahd struggled up the last length, both completely exhausted.

"Come on Fahd!" screamed Nzinga, distracting him and Anne Marie just managed to touch first. Charlie grabbed a towel and helped Anne Marie out of the pool. She had never seen her so tired and completely burned out. Fahd jumped up on the side and helped Charlie lay Anne Marie on the sofa and got her a drink of water.

"Did I win?" asked Anne Marie, slightly disorientated.

"Yes Annie, you won," confirmed Charlie, "but you nearly killed yourself."

"You are an amazing lady, Annie. May I call you Annie?" asked Fahd, very concerned about her exertions.

"Of course, Fahd. It has been an honour to do battle with you," smiled Anne Marie, weakly.

Nzinga took Fahd to one side. "Are you OK? I was worried you were getting too tired," said Nzinga.

"I am fine. Don't ever tell the others but I thought she deserved to win. She is extremely competitive and fights like a man to get whatever she wants."

"So, you let her win?"

"Let's have drink before I die of thirst," he said, avoiding the question.

Daniel put a drink in Fahd's hand and toasted his swim. "Cheers. That was fun. Now let's have something to eat before it gets incinerated."

They all sat round the crackling fire as the glowing sparks floated into the sultry evening air and the blood-red sun made its way lazily to the distant horizon. The antelope meat was delicious from the firepit and the Leleshwa wine from the Rift surprisingly refreshing after a long hot day. Anne Marie found her strength again after the meal and laughed and joked with Fahd about women's role in modern Saudi, which he took in good spirit. He was more interested in when they could see the mountain gorillas. Charlie chatted to Nzinga about the latest camera technology and artificial intelligence. Fahd joined in the conversation, being really interested in the recent developments.

They had got so deeply into the benefits of quantum computing in high resolution photography that Charlie hadn't noticed that Anne Marie had started to give Daniel's leg the promised massage to ease the pain. Daniel was lying on his back on the sofa next door, and Anne Marie was stroking some sort of oil along his thigh around the gunshot wound. Daniel's shirt was undone and Charlie was smiling to herself about his strong masculine chest and how it was more attractive than Fahd's. Charlie then realised that Anne Marie's fingers were sliding higher and slowly firmer, towards the frayed edges of Daniel's shorts. He had his eyes shut and was clearly enjoying the feeling. Charlie tried to ignore what was going on but then caught Anne Marie's glance and she was smiling at Charlie, whilst her fingers sought further pleasure for Daniel. Anne Marie was playing games with Charlie and Charlie knew it, so she tried to ignore her and returned to the computing discussions with Fahd and Nzinga. Anne Marie was frustrated at the lack of response from Charlie and started to rub the oil into Daniel's chest, casually catching his nipples with her long fingernails. His body was responding when Charlie glanced back. She still refused to give in to the temptation.

The next time Charlie glanced over Fahd's shoulder, Anne Marie had undone the top four buttons on her white safari shirt which left nothing to the imagination. Charlie was left with no option. She stood up, cast aside her beautiful kimono to reveal her sensual body clad only in the miniscule silk and gold bikini that Anne Marie had given her in Chocorua. Charlie knew that would distract her, because Anne Marie loved to see Charlie wearing it. Charlie dived into the pond and Anne Marie immediately jumped up and dived in after her. They swam around each other, laughing and splashing each other until they came together. Anne Marie threw her arms around Charlie's neck and kissed her romantically on the lips. Charlie's body responded like never before, even though she knew others were watching.

Nzinga looked at Fahd and whispered, "Did you see that?"

"Oh, Annie and Daniel go back a long way. The three of them seem to make it work." Dismissing the query as a matter of fact.

"Would you like to come back to my lodge for a lemonade or something," Fahd smiled at Nzinga.

"The something sounds wonderful."

CHAPTER TWO

Mount Bisoke – Virunga – Rwanda

The distant roar of a lioness carried on the wind into Charlie's lodge and she woke up from a deep sleep with a start; not realising where she was for a split second. Daniel was nowhere to be seen, so she pulled the white Egyptian sheet around her and walked over to the door. It was still dark and the Milky Way blazoned across the night sky like an enormous firework. Daniel was stood at the far end of the veranda, leaning on the rough wooden pole that supported the thatched roof, in deep conversation with someone. His tone was sombre and his face lined with concern.

"When did they see the Isuzu?" he asked. "Where was it headed?"

Charlie could not hear the replies and grew increasingly concerned about the conversation. She walked along to Daniel and sat on the veranda rail next to him. He didn't acknowledge her, so she knew it was serious.

"OK, Wamwarav, I will fly up at dawn in the helicopter and meet you at the usual place. If you get any more intel before I get there, please ring me on the satellite phone."

"What's happened?" asked Charlie.

"One of Wam's friends, in the DRC, saw a white Isuzu truck coming out of a mountain track on their side of the border. The plates had been changed but his friend is sure it's one that has been used in the past for criminal activity over in Virunga, where our gorilla bands are foraging."

"Did the friend see anything in the truck?"

"No, it was dark and you don't get too close to these people if you want to carry on breathing."

"What are you going to do when you get there?" enquired Charlie, worried that Daniel had only just partially recovered from being shot by the Somali poachers.

"We need to check up on our groups of gorillas first and make sure none are missing. It's really difficult at this time of year because they roam over big distances in difficult terrain. The vegetation is too dense to use drones and it is impenetrable by pickup. You saw how difficult it was when I took you up there last time."

"If we all come and split into groups to search, it will make it much quicker," suggested Charlie. "If we have a tracker who knows the terrain for each group, we should be safe enough. If they have taken anything they are unlikely to return quickly."

"Sounds like a good plan but if Annie and Fahd want to opt out, we must not force them to come."

"Do you honestly think that Annie will give up on an opportunity like this?" smiled Charlie. "I don't think so!"

"I suppose you are right but Fahd has bigger things to worry about," suggested Daniel.

"I don't think he is going anywhere. His passion for conservation burns as brightly as ours and anyway he is not going to run away now he has finally got Nzinga into bed!"

"There is that I suppose!" laughed Daniel affectionately. "Can you round everybody up for a quick discussion about what we are planning to do?"

"But it's four-thirty in the morning and they will all be asleep!"

"Except Eshe and Jahir who will be .... anyway, it's imperative we get there asap if we have any hope of finding the truck."

* * *

"Annie are you awake?" asked Charlie, tentatively knocking on Anne Marie's door. A bleary-eyed Anne Marie opened the door but her face lit up when she saw Charlie.

"You've changed your mind about Daniel!" she said hopefully.

"Er no. Daniel has a problem with some poachers. Are you up for chasing them across Africa?" asked Charlie putting an adventurous spin on events.

"You try and stop me! Give me ten minutes to get dressed and I will meet you by the pool.

"Thanks Annie. I will round up the others," said Charlie heading for Fahd's lodge. Another tentative tap on a door. Nothing. Strange thought Charlie but moved on to Jahir and Eshe's lodge at the other end of the pool.

Eshe answered the door and looked a bit shocked to see Charlie.

"Is everything OK?" Eshe asked.

"Sorry to wake you up but we have some information from Wamwarav that a poacher's vehicle has been seen leaving Virunga on the Congo side and Daniel wants to fly up there asap to check that all our gorillas are OK," relayed Charlie.

"Oh my God! I hope they haven't taken one of the young infants. Jahir get up now!" she shouted back into the room.

"What's wrong, it's the middle of the night?" came the mutter from under the crumpled sheet on the bed.

"Charlie is here and there are poachers killing all the gorillas!" exaggerated Eshe to get some action from Jahir.

"What?!" he shouted leaping out of bed.

"I didn't exactly say that," said Charlie, "but Daniel wants us to fly up to Virunga asap, to see if all our bands are OK. Can you two be by the pool in fifteen minutes for a briefing?"

"No problem, Charlie. We will be there," replied Eshe.

Charlie walked back to the sofas, left from the previous night's frivolities, where Daniel had got some mugs of coffee organised.

"I can't get any response from Fahd and Nzinga. I am not sure what's happening there," said Charlie, mystified.

Daniel had just finished pouring the coffee, when two figures appeared in the distance walking towards the gathering.

"We saw the lights going on and wondered what was happening," said Fahd. Nzinga had her arm in his and looked very content.

"Where have you two been in the middle of the night?" asked Charlie.

"Leopard spotting," smiled Nzinga. "I heard one down at the watering hole with a kill and we both really wanted to see it. Fahd had never seen an African one before and with his interest in leopard conservation in Saudi, it was too good an opportunity to miss."

"Strange people, conservationists," laughed Daniel referring to their first night together. "Right, we have a potentially serious problem over at Virunga," and he repeated the Isuzu sighting and Charlie's plan to check up on all the gorillas in the project.

"Fahd, there are too many of us to fit in our helicopter. Can we use your Super Puma?"

"Of course. I will get the pilots to get it ready whilst everyone sorts themselves out. How long will it take to get there?"

"About two and a half hours in a Puma with his foot down," interjected Jahir, getting excited at his first trip in the world's most expensive helicopter.

"You can sit up front if you like?" offered Fahd.

"That would be amazing, thank you," smiled Jahir. Eshe smiled too, knowing she could not compete with a Super Puma!

"It will start getting light about six, so can we all be on board ready to go at five-thirty. I will brief Wamwarav about the plan so he can organise some trackers for us and also send off some of his team to locate the bands."

"Will we need guns?" asked Anne Marie excitedly, having already helped Charlie kill one poacher, saving Daniel's life.

* * *

The Super Puma touched down on the usual clearing, at the foot of Mount Bisoke in north Rwanda, where Wamwarav was waiting with two pickups.

"Things must be going well to buy a Puma," laughed Wamwarav.

"Not that well!" smiled Daniel, embracing his friend. "Can I introduce Fahd and Anne Marie who are spending some time with us to celebrate Eshe's wedding." Fahd had agreed with everyone that he would keep the 'prince' bit quiet for now.

"What have you found out?" asked Eshe, desperate to know how all her gorillas were and if any were missing.

Mountain gorilla and baby

"We managed to do a quick scout round some of them yesterday before it got dark and we found the two new infants with their mothers, so they are OK. It got too late to go any further so there are still three more groups to find."

"Shall we go up to base camp, Wam, and get some breakfast and then we can plan who is going where and how?" suggested Daniel.

"The ladies have already got the bushpig bacon on the grill. Not quite Riyadh, but tasty nonetheless," said Wamwarav, winking at Daniel.

"How did you know about Fahd?" asked Charlie.

"As I said before Charlie, we might live in the jungle but we are not as rustic as we appear!" joked Wamwarav, shaking Fahd's hand with a huge smile. Fahd enjoyed the lack of formality.

When they got back to camp, they were overwhelmed with the welcome from the tracker's families. Daniel was surrounded by the men who were keen to know all the news from Chyulu and how he was shot. The women scooped up Eshe and took her off, to get an update on how the honeymoon was going. Nzinga tried to keep her distance from Fahd and their relationship a secret but one of the women-folk saw them looking at each other across the cacophony, so that secret was not going to last long either.

After all the voluminous welcomes and the smoky bush pig they settled down to plan the day.

"So, tell us in detail, Wam, what your friend actually saw," asked Daniel.

"Well, not a lot really. He works as a ranger on the DRC side of the mountains so he knows what he is looking for. He recognised a white Isuzu FTR 850 truck coming out of a track that winds its way over to this side. You can't get all the way across in a vehicle, so it is effectively a cul-de-sac and therefore anyone coming out on it must have gone in for a reason. The truck had a new number plate OU62 CKZ but it had a rusty scratch on one of the doors which he remembered from when it was last used for poaching. It had two drivers but he was too far away to recognise them."

"Which way did it go when it came out onto the road?" asked Daniel.

"They headed south on the RN2 towards Goma on the edge of Lake Kivu. We don't know where they went after that or even if they had taken anything."

"OK. Well, I think the first thing to do is to find our other three research groups and make sure they are all well. Have you any idea where they are?" enquired Daniel.

Eshe was finding the whole thing overwhelming and burst into tears. Jahir put his arm around her shoulders and gave her a hug. He tried to console her but the thought of losing one of her treasured gorilla infants and years of observation material was very upsetting. Anne Marie also gave her a hug and told her not to worry. "They will probably all be fine Eshe. Let's go and see if we can find them."

Fortunately, Wam had seen all four groups in the last two weeks and they were feasting on the galium vines that covered the closer slopes on the Rwandan side of the mountain. The weather was also being kind which would make the trekking easier. Daniel issued the instructions for the hunt.

"Wam, can you take Nzinga and Fahd up to the highest group. Jahir you go with Eshe and Annie along the north ridge with Wam's colleague to find the second group. I'm afraid my leg will not let me walk far but Charlie and I will take the nearest group which should be close to the one Wam saw last night."

"Take care up there," advised Wamwarav. "It may be fine now but the weather can change rapidly in the hills. We have packed waterproofs and everything else you will need in the backpacks, including radios. If you see anything, positive or negative, ring Daniel and he will let the rest of us know what's happening. Don't take any risks and don't get too close to any silverbacks."

The three groups set off on their allotted tasks. Daniel, Wamwarav and his colleague were carrying rifles just in case of any problems. Charlie and Daniel set off last and took it steady because of the gunshot wound in Daniel's thigh.

"Are you sure you can manage the climb up to the top of this next ridge?" asked Charlie, worried about his leg.

"Not sure to be honest. It's bloody painful today and I don't know why. I didn't do anything strenuous yesterday," replied Daniel. They eventually got to a small clearing at the top but Charlie noticed some blood trickling down his canvas trousers and made him sit down on a large rotting tree root.

"Let me have a look," suggested Charlie. Daniel undid his belt and pulled his trousers down. The wound had burst out at the bottom and was leaking blood.

"It's nothing," said Daniel, "it will heal up."

"Don't be ridiculous; you can't go any further or the wound will pull right apart. Here, put my handkerchief on it to stem the flow and I will ring Wam for some help."

"Over my dead body. Let them get on with the hunt; we need to know if the bands are all OK. I will sit here for a while until we hear something from them."

"You're impossible!" Charlie sat next to him, in the silence of the Hagenia forest. It was a cloudless, still day as they looked out from the clearing over the verdant vegetation. A bright green, scarlet tufted sunbird landed on a vine stem next to them and seemed oblivious to the human invaders. Charlie held Daniel's hand. "I love you, my darling," she said and kissed his cheek affectionately. "I wish we were here under better circumstances. I adore being alone with you in such a wonderful landscape."

"You've forgotten your camera!"

"I know. We left in such a rush I forgot it. Anyway, I have the image in my head forever." At that moment Daniel's radio sprang into life; it was Jahir.

"We have found our group," he whispered. "Eshe says they are all here and well. Annie can't believe how close we are to them, munching away without a care in the world. I think she wants to cuddle one," he laughed. "How are you two getting on?"

"My bloody leg has let me down, I'm afraid. We got to the top of the first ridge over here but I can't get any further. Can you take the girls back to camp and come up here and give me a hand back down?"

"Of course. It will take a couple of hours at least. The last few hundred yards were pretty hard going before we found them. The vines had blocked the path, but fortunately Eshe knew where we were and found a way through. Have you heard from Wam and Nzinga?"

"No nothing yet. They had a much more difficult climb so they will be a while. I will send you our location and hope to see you in a couple of hours."

Charlie and Daniel whiled away the time marvelling at the diversity of plants and insects that surrounded them; not as sexy as a band of mountain gorillas but equally as important in the complex integrated world of Virunga. Jahir finally arrived and helped Daniel back down to camp so Wam's wife could dress his wound properly.

"The gorillas were amazing!" smiled Anne Marie. "I was this close to them," she indicated with her outstretched arms.

"No signs of any disturbance or injuries then?" Daniel asked Eshe.

"No, they all looked fine and were as relaxed as normal. The two new infants are growing on well and their mothers seemed very attentive and caring. Have you heard anything from Nzinga and Fahd?"

"No not yet but they had the longest trek so they may not have found them." replied Daniel.

"What about the band we were looking for?" asked Charlie, "There is still time to find them if the rest of us set off now."

"I think we should," said Eshe enthusiastically. "According to Wam they are not that far away."

"OK if you are up for it," suggested Daniel, "but you all take care and if they have moved further away, call it a day and we will try again tomorrow."

Daniel sat by the small fire, whilst the women folk fussed around him with endless cups of coffee and various potions to help his leg feel better. He was just about to shoot himself out of sheer frustration at being confined to camp when his phone rang. It was Jill, Anne Marie's housekeeper back in Yorkshire.

"Hi Daniel, sorry to bother you. Is it OK to talk?"

"Sure, what's going on?"

"I don't want to worry you but there has been a suspicious Russian gentleman asking questions in the newspaper shop in Leyburn."

"What sort of questions?" enquired Daniel.

"He was asking if they knew of anyone in the Dale who travelled abroad a lot and knew anything about tractors and slurry tankers. I thought it was really strange and I was worried they might be looking for you?"

"They?"

"Sorry. There is only one so far."

"Well at least that's a relief! I hope we will be coming back in a few days but we have a problem out here with poachers and we are trying to hunt them down. Can you keep me informed if they turn up again anywhere else in Wensleydale?"

"Will do. Better not tell Annie that I rang. She will only worry," suggested Jill.

"I agree. I will arrange to meet up with you as soon as I get back."

No sooner had Daniel put the phone down, when it rang again.

"Hi it's Nzinga. We are struggling to find our band anywhere. Fahd and I have stopped for a rest and something to eat, whilst Wam has gone further on to reconnoitre the next hillside."

"Have you seen any signs that they have been in the area?" asked Daniel.

"Yes, we saw some nests about an hour ago and there were faeces nearby. Wam thinks they were a couple of days old."

"OK keep me up to date. I have had to come back to base camp because of my bloody leg, so the others have gone off to find the fourth group. Keep me up to date with progress. If you get too far to walk back maybe Fahd could get his pilot to airlift you out from a clearing somewhere?"

"He has already suggested that and his pilots are already briefed to be on standby," said Nzinga, proud that her new lover was one step ahead of the boss!

Daniel sat back in his canvas chair drinking yet another cup of coffee musing on what Jill had said. How did the

37

Russians work out where to find him after he had blown up their new hacker facility near the Ukrainian border? There was no noise on any of the intelligence networks about who had carried out the sabotage or even which country was responsible. He knew he was on his own and both the US and UK would deny any involvement, but he was used to that. Their intelligence was obviously very weak and they were fishing for clues. He decided to ring Sebastian, his computer-genius accomplice in the Cayman Islands, who helped him set up the hit.

"Hi Seb, how is Marika?"

"She is expecting puppies next week."

"Who's the father?"

"Not sure. She was out on the tiles a few weeks ago. Could be interesting if it was a Yorkie!"

"It couldn't reach!" laughed Daniel referring to the great Dane's height.

"Sex is a great leveller! What's up."

"Is there any noise on the Russian front. We have a weasel at home?"

"Not a dickie-bird but I will have a closer look. Can I ring you back on this number?

"Yes. I am in the jungle looking for poachers."

"Blow their fucking heads off for me!"

"Will do. Speak later."

* * *

Just as the light started to fail, Charlie, Anne Marie, Eshe and Jahir trudged back into camp looking tired and hungry.

"They are all alive and well," reported Eshe, "but it's not the group with Didi, the older infant. That must be with Nzinga's band. Has she rung in yet?"

"About an hour ago," replied Daniel. "They had found some recent nests but no sign of the band. Wam had gone off on his own to look a bit further but I guess they are running out of daylight now. Come and sit down and have a cup of coffee. The ladies have started cooking some sort of jungle recipe for supper. Smells delicious!"

As they were drinking the coffee, the Puma helicopter took off further down the valley. "Fahd was going to call them in if they had got too far to walk back," advised Daniel. "Hopefully they will be back before too long. One of Mav's lads will drive down to the landing site in the pickup and fetch them back up to camp."

When they arrived back in camp Nzinga and Fahd were frustrated that they had been unsuccessful in finding the band but were beaten by the failing light.

"Where is Wam?" asked Daniel.

"He insisted on staying out tonight so he could get an early start at daybreak. He thought he had picked up some gorilla tracks and was following them over the next ridge," replied Fahd. "I wasn't happy leaving him on his own but he insisted he would be OK and would ring in later."

"He won't take any risks," said Daniel. "He has lived here all his life and knows what he is doing. Let's have some supper and have an early night."

* * *

Daniel's satellite phone rang at six-thirty in the morning. He was already up and dressed and sitting at the small table at the end of the hut. Charlie sat up in bed with a start when she heard the phone. "Is it Wam?" she mouthed silently to Daniel. He nodded affirmatively.

"Are they all there? Shit. No sign of them. Are any of the others injured? I suppose that's a blessing. OK. How far are you from where the helicopter took off from? Christ Mav you shouldn't have carried on in the dark. Is there anywhere we can land the Puma near to you? OK. We will be with you in an hour. You rest till we get there. I need you fit to track when we arrive."

"Have they taken the Didi?" asked Charlie.

"She's missing along with Kesia, her mother. They either managed to run off or the mother will be dead somewhere and the infant exported."

"Christ Daniel, Eshe will be heartbroken if they have gone."

"I know. I will round the others up. Can you get Wam's wife to knock together some coffee and provisions for the day? I have no idea how long we will be gone."

* * *

Within twenty minutes they were all in the pickups racing down the track to the helicopter. There had been rain over night and the track had turned from dust to thick mud but it was no trouble for the Mitsubishis. The helicopter was already powered up and the downdraft was swirling the surrounding vegetation like a hurricane. They ran, stooping below the rotors and boarded inelegantly through the cabin door. It slammed shut behind Daniel and they were away before they could get sorted. Eshe was crying in Jahir's arms, Fahd was instructing the pilots with the rendezvous coordinates Daniel had given him, and Charlie, Nzinga and Anne Marie were studying a map of the mountains, that Wam's wife had given them.

"We think that if they have taken Didi in the Isuzu, they will have taken this narrow track around the ridge where Nzinga was last night," said Charlie, pointing at the map, "and then down to this wider track which leads to the road. It looks like they could get a truck to within a mile or two of the narrow tracks."

"OK, said Daniel, "let's see what Wam says when we get there and see if his thoughts are the same.

* * *

The Puma pilot flew along the ridge, indicated by the coordinates Fahd had given him, until he saw Wam waving his arms in a small clearing next to a rocky outcrop. He slowly lowered the helicopter into the tiny space with only a few feet of clearance for the rotors on each side.

"Your pilot knows what he is doing," remarked Daniel respectfully.

"We have lots of jungle in Saudi!" joked Fahd.

They all climbed out of the helicopter and collected their rucksacks with the provisions for the day.

"What's the situation?" Daniel asked Wam.

"I have had a good look round and there is no sign of Kesia or Didi. The others all look fine and have drifted off foraging on the opposite hillside. There is evidence of some vines having been slashed with a machete over there," said Wam, indicating a dense group of vines at the far side of the rocks.

"Let's take a look," suggested Daniel and they all clambered over the small boulders.

"You're right Wam, there has definitely been a struggle here, look at the flattened grass over there."

"I know," said Wam, "I feared the worst, but there is no sign of any blood or a carcase." Eshe held Jahir's arm tightly and Anne Marie looked horrified at the word.

"I suppose that's a good start, in a way, but I don't think this is going to end well," said Daniel solemnly. "Charlie has been looking at your wife's map and thinks they may have gone down a tiny track on foot and rendezvoused with the Isuzu truck further down."

Charlie got out the map and showed Wam the route.

"It's possible, but a storm last year washed away the vehicle track lower down, so they would have had to carry them down at least five miles. Kesia will weigh well over 100 kilos, so two men would not be carrying her that far."

"Could they have sedated her to get the baby and left her to recover on her own?" suggested Fahd hopefully.

"These guys are feral," replied Wam. "They wouldn't know what an anaesthetic is, and in any case, they wouldn't spend the money on it, when a machete does the job for nothing. We are dealing with vicious, uneducated trash here. They would kill you, for ten cents."

"Charming!" exclaimed Anne Marie. "I knew I should have bought a gun!"

"Where does the small track start Wam?" asked Daniel.

"Follow me down to the bottom of this next ravine and we can pick it up down there. Be careful; the slope is steep in places and very slippy after the rain last night."

They set off in single file with Wam in the lead. It was hard going and Daniel was struggling with his leg but kept it to himself. The wet vegetation brushed against their waterproofs and scattered droplets of water in their faces as the vines flicked back after each person pushed through the dense undergrowth. Jahir slipped on a muddy stone and skidded on his bottom ten metres, down the slope, but fortunately was able to save himself on a branch. His hand was bleeding from a cut on his thumb and Eshe wrapped a handkerchief around it.

"Are you OK?" asked Charlie.

"Yes fine. Just a minor cut from the thorns on the branch," replied Jahir.

"Be careful on the next bit," advised Wam, "There is a sheer twenty metre drop to your left."

They all carefully picked their way down the steep slope. Eshe kept looking over the cliff edge worried about falling off, and hung on to Jahir. Anne Marie was in front of Daniel and her fitness was a great asset in keeping a firm footing when he had to grab her shoulder to steady himself.

"What's that revolting smell I keep getting a whiff of?" asked Anne Marie, looking back at Daniel. His face was lined with concern.

"Wam?"

"I know. I could smell the stench of death from the top of the slope. I think we know what it is?" he answered seriously. Eshe burst into tears again and clung desperately to Jahir.

"You think it's Kesia?" asked Anne Marie. "The bastards!"

"I am afraid you are right Annie," said Wam. "I will look with Daniel when we get to the bottom of the ravine."

They continued their descent in silence. Each knowing the sad outcome of their search. When they got to the bottom, Daniel and Wamwarav left the others and backtracked along the foot of the cliff towards the source of the stench. They found the body of Kesia, covered in flies, sliced to a hideous death in front of her infant and thrown off the cliff to rot in the jungle. She had been decapitated and her head hung to one side; her gut oozing out from a slash across her belly and her breasts, full of milk for Didi, leaking onto the forest floor.

"I will make them pay for this," said Daniel in a calm deliberate voice. "Wherever they are, whoever they are, they will pay."

"Let's get back to the others," said Wam putting his arm around Daniel's shoulders. "There is nothing else we can do here."

Their faces told the story. There was no need for words. Charlie wept on Anne Marie's arm, Eshe was totally distraught and fell to the floor inconsolable and Nzinga looked up to Fahd who said, "If there is a God, we need him to help us now."

CHAPTER THREE

Russian Roulette – Wensleydale – North Yorkshire – England

The flight back to England was sombre and silent. Daniel and Charlie dropped Anne Marie off at her house where she got a hug from Jill, who winked at Daniel as he got back in the Range Rover. Charlie noticed.

"What was that about?" enquired Charlie, suspiciously.

"What was what about?" replied Daniel, trying to avoid his indiscretion.

"That was more than friendly wink!" said Charlie firmly. "What's going on now?"

"I'll tell you in the bath!" smiled Daniel.

"I won't let you out till you tell me," grinned Charlie, mischievously.

Daniel drove onto the gravel driveway of the old stone mill that Anne Marie had given them as a present. They were glad to be home, in the relative safety of England, with the cool evening breeze a welcome change from the heat and humidity of Africa. Daniel carried the bags in and dumped them on the kitchen floor. Charlie made a cup of Earl Grey and rescued some of Betty's gingernut biscuits from a round tin in the pantry. They sat round the old pine table for half an hour, winding down after the last few manic days, filled with joy and then disaster.

"Let's have that bath and forget about the real world for a while," suggested Charlie with a glint in her eye.

"Good idea," said Daniel. "You get the bath running and I will lock up."

Charlie climbed the stairs, passed the old mill wheel, still turning slowly as the energy from the water in the leat created the free electricity for their home. She felt a wave of relaxation inside her, as she walked around her bedroom, casually discarding her travelling clothes onto the stool by her dressing table. She walked into their bathroom haven, lit the candles that lived round the bath, and put on their favourite Mozart concerto; the Flute and Harp in C. She lowered herself into the warm water and the sandalwood bubbles covered her beautiful body as she closed her eyes in peace and contentment.

"Is there room for one more?" Daniel was standing naked next the bath; his muscular form flickering in the candlelight. Charlie liked his body, even if it was a bit battle-scarred. Charlie edged backwards in the bath, to make room, revealing her breasts, slowly appearing as the bubbles flowed downwards into the frothy mass.

Daniel lifted her legs over his as he sat down, and leaned back at the opposite end to Charlie. She felt sensuously vulnerable to his touch, but he made her wait. They laid there for half an hour, enjoying the peace and the touch of each other's bodies. Their special music filled their minds with thoughts of previous bath times and Charlie began to feel a slow tightening in her thighs and she stroked Daniel's leg with her fingertips. He opened his eyes and looked into hers. They were on the same wavelength. Charlie smiled and walked her fingers up his thigh, getting the response she had hoped for.

"Do you like that?" she grinned.

"Not sure yet: keep going and I will let you know."

Charlie tickled the bottom of Daniel's foot and he blew bubbles from his upturned hand in her face. Charlie pulled her legs back from his and kneeled in front of him, between his thighs. Her hands disappeared below the water and she held his manhood firmly. "So, what was that wink about Mr Daniel?" she asked with a smile.

"What wink?" he said dismissively.

Charlie closed her hands more firmly and pushed down. Daniel responded by arching his back and throwing his head back.

"This will only get worse if you don't tell me!" joked Charlie in the best dominant voice she could muster.

"I hope it does!" mumbled Daniel struggling to contain the pressure between his thighs.

Charlie pulled his legs down the bath, accidentally submerging Daniel's head. He came up spluttering, but Charlie had already lifted herself on top of him so she was sitting astride his hips. She pressed herself against him and she could feel his firmness beneath her. Her own body responded to the touch and her own passion leapt up three notches. She wanted him inside her, to feel his strong hands on her breasts and his lips on hers.

"And so – the wink?" she enquired again. "It will only get worse!"

"I think you were seeing things," Daniel laughed.

Charlie dug her fingernails into his chest, dragging them down across his nipples. She knew he could not resist that. Daniel arched against Charlie again, she lifted her hips and let him enter, whilst holding him inside tightly. She pressed down as firmly as she could and Daniel's whole body shook in ecstasy. He lifted himself forwards and kissed her lips sensitively.

"I adore you, Charlie. You are the most sensuous lover in the whole world."

Charlie held him tightly in her arm, moved her hips twice and came instantly against him.

* * *

They laid next to each other for a long time, listening to the Mozart and just enjoying each other's touch and being together. "I think we have heard this loop three times?" Charlie smiled and gave Daniel a long loving kiss.

"His concertos were always too short!" joked Daniel.

* * *

The following morning the collared doves were playing football on the roof as usual, so Daniel went down stairs to make some toast whilst Charlie surfaced slowly from her dreams. When he returned with the Earl Grey and Elizabeth's homemade marmalade, Charlie resumed the inquisition.

"So come on then, what is going on with Jill?"

"OK, but this is top secret and even Annie doesn't know."

"More intriguing by the minute? I thought she was just a housekeeper?" suggested Charlie.

"Well, she is now, sort of. Jill has always lived in the Dale and the locals think she was a cookery book writer, who travelled a lot to discover new recipe secrets from the chefs around Europe. She actually sold quite a lot of books but had to ease off because she was starting to get too well known. She was actually very good at getting secrets out of people in another way."

"What other way?" asked Charlie, mystified.

"She actually worked for British intelligence as an interrogator in Israel. She 'retired' after she accidentally killed one of her subjects," related Daniel.

"You know some really charming people Daniel! I thought she was a nice person."

"She is – and she makes excellent whipped soufflés."

"Very funny!"

"Seriously, she is actually a charming person," said Daniel, "and I knew she was looking for something more exciting to fill her retirement with. Anyway, I am meeting up with her tomorrow to get a proper debrief on a small problem we have."

"And what else is going wrong!"

"There has been a Russian gentleman looking for me, or someone like me, up at Leyburn."

"Oh my God! Not Novichok again?"

"Don't jump the gun. We know nothing about him. He might be looking for someone else," said Daniel unconvincingly.

"So, there might other men in the Dale that blow up Russian secret facilities as well!"

"There could be. How would I know?" smiled Daniel.

"It's not funny Daniel. What about mummy and daddy?"

"I will make sure that you are all safe. Stop worrying. Let me talk to Jill tomorrow first and then we will have a better idea of what we are up against."

"Talking of your parents, are we planning to go up to the Hall to see them later on?"

"We better had, before the next Russian intercontinental ballistic missile hits Leyburn!"

* * *

It was a beautiful Yorkshire morning as they drove up to the Hall. The trees were in full leaf and the birds in full song, as the open sunroof captured the fleeting sounds and smells of the rural countryside. As they turned into the deer park, two hinds with young fawns leapt up from the shade of an ancient oak and made a hasty retreat towards the lake. Daniel pulled into the stable yard where Mac was readying his mole traps.

"Now then you two, how was Africa?"

Charlie jumped out and gave Mac a hug. "It was wonderful thank you Mac. Eshe's wedding was beautiful and she was so happy. So where are Abbey and Misty? I hope they have been behaving themselves."

"Well Annie was up here at seven to fetch Misty home. I think she had really missed her. Annie gave her a big hug and I think I saw a tear in her eye. Made for each other those two."

"Is Abbey in the kennels?" asked Charlie.

"What do you think? She has lived in the kitchen all the time you have been away, chewed through my favourite old slippers and disgraced herself on the mat by the door, when I was just five minutes late letting her out one morning."

Black Labrador

"You're getting soft in your old age Mac," said Daniel.

"Boss's orders Daniel," replied Mac. "Sally said I had to train her whilst you two were away because she was eating your dresser!"

Sally had heard Charlie arrive and opened the back door so Abbey could see her mistress. She gambolled across the grass to Charlie who knelt down to give her young dog a welcome.

"So will she make a good gun dog?" asked Daniel.

"She might; when she is about twenty!" laughed Mac, "and if Charlie doesn't spoil her along the way."

"Would you like a cup of tea?" offered Sally.

"Thank you, Sally, but we haven't seen mummy and daddy yet, so we better go and find them. Are they in the kitchen?"

"I think so. Your father was talking with Mac about the new borehole up at Haggs Gill about ten minutes ago, and headed in that direction.

"OK. Can you hang on to Abbey for a bit longer whilst we go in and catch up?"

"Of course. She can stay as long as you like. She is a lovely dog and I know Mac regrets letting her go."

The wisteria was in full flower up the side of the stone wall of the Hall and the blue panicles cascaded downwards, filling the air with a dreamy fragrance. Charlie lifted her hand and let the blooms stroke her fingers as she walked past them. The hallway was cluttered with the usual homely pile of boots and thumb sticks.

Edward stood up from the old kitchen table and gave his daughter a long hug. Daniel kissed Elizabeth on the cheek and shook Edward's hand, when he had finished his paternal welcome.

"Now then you two. Tell us all about the wedding; did they have a vicar or a witch doctor?" asked Elizabeth.

Charlie fell into a deep conversation with her mother about tribal weddings and the joyous party afterwards. Edward was more interested in the borehole.

"So, we took up your suggestion Daniel and looked into the feasibility of a borehole and it was not as expensive as I thought, especially if we drill one up at Annie's lambing barn at the same time. I have got them down to £5000 each, but they are not squirming yet so I think I can still push them a bit more. We will need to dig the holding tanks ourselves but I know where we can hire a JCB for a few days."

"What about lining the tanks?" asked Daniel tentatively,

"I know a bricky up at Hawes who owes me a favour, so he can block them out."

"Sounds like you've got it all worked out Edward. When are you planning to start?"

"Tomorrow!"

"Nothing like getting on with the job," replied Daniel hesitantly, hoping for a few days to catch up on his own projects.

Charlie and Elizabeth had finished the rerun of the wedding and were busy over the Aga making some bacon sandwiches for lunch. Edward fetched in the plans for the borehole. Daniel winked at Charlie when her parents were otherwise engaged and she smiled back, enjoying being home with her family again.

* * *

The following morning, Daniel was up early to meet up with Jill. He left Charlie in bed and went downstairs to make himself some breakfast and let Abbey out into the garden. There had been torrential rain overnight and the rill was running too fast with the volume of water. He grabbed the ancient, rusty lever that operated the sluice gate and closed the gate down to reduce the water flow, so the mill wheel didn't turn too fast and burn out the generator. He pondered the irony of drilling for water later on, when he was dealing with too much in the rill and chuckled to himself as he made his way back across the wet grass. The rain started to fall again and the thick black clouds hiding the distant moors didn't bode well for the rest of the day.

Daniel had arranged to meet Jill on the gallops above Middleham so they could lean on the rails and watch the early morning strings being exercised, but the rain was lashing down and the trainers were obviously waiting for clearer conditions. Daniel dashed across to Jill's Suzuki and jumped into passenger seat.

"Lovely morning for spotting Saturday's favourite for Doncaster!" joked Daniel.

"I think that might be called off after this lot!" replied Jill. "How was Africa?"

"Good and bad. Eshe and Jahir's wedding was great. The Maasai had made a special effort for them and it was a simple service but very special for them. Everyone had a great time and the reception was colourful! Fahd finally got Nzinga into bed and Annie saw some elephants!"

"I know. She was exhausted yesterday but insisted on getting up early to go and fetch Misty. She loves that puppy; I think it's a bit of a child substitute. I wish she could find a partner to live with – she is such a nice lady."

"We are working on it!" smiled Daniel.

"She briefly told me about the poachers taking the baby gorilla and the horrendous way they disposed of the mother's body. I have dealt with some awful people in my time but they are really vile. Have you any idea where they have taken the infant?"

"No not yet. Fahd and Nzinga tracked the vehicle down to near the airport at Goma but their security cameras were useless and we don't know where the poachers went after that or where they sent the baby. But I will find them one day. So, tell me about this mysterious Russian."

"Not much more than I told you on the phone. He just turned up at the newsagents in Leyburn, bought a bar of chocolate and a copy of the *Yorkshire Post*. He then started asking about an old friend he was trying to find. He said he knew he lived in the Dale and travelled abroad a lot. He was involved in farm machinery, knew a lot about slurry tankers, and he also had a new cat! Random but that's all he seemed to know."

"What did he look like?"

"I know the lady in the shop really well but she said there was nothing special about him. He was dressed like a hill walker, medium height, clean shaven, grey hair and about sixty. She said there was something creepy about him. Oh, and he had wire-rimmed round glasses."

"That's a bit old for a Russian field operative," mused Daniel.

"That's what I thought. They obviously don't know much and are just fishing. I don't think he will be the one sent to finish you off!"

"Thanks! I will remember that with an AK stuck up my left nostril!"

"I am quite enjoying this. It's like old times," laughed Jill, as a flash of lightning lit up the leaden sky. "I miss the thrill of all the secrecy and intrigue. It's quite invigorating."

"You are well out of it, Jill and anyway you love your cooking."

"I know. I would never go back to my old life. I still see my last victim, his face screwed up in pain, just repeating his daughter's name again and again. I know he killed over a hundred of our soldiers with his filthy landmines and knew where the next trap was going to take place, but by going too far and not getting the answer, four more of our lads got killed the following day. I will never forgive myself."

"We all regret what we have to do sometimes," consoled Daniel. "But the world is a dangerous place and if people like us don't do the dirty jobs, the meek will not inherit the earth."

"I know, but it doesn't stop the nightmares," confided Jill.

"Do you think you could come up with some excuse to move in with Annie for a while, till we see what this Russian chap is up to?"

"Of course. They can rewire my cottage; it needs doing anyway."

"Don't let anyone get too close to Annie, she's a very old friend," said Daniel seriously.

"I know all about you and Annie in Morocco," smiled Jill secretively.

"How do you know about Morocco?"

"I am very good at finding out secrets!" she laughed.

Daniel felt his face flush slightly as he climbed out of the car, and said, "You look after yourself too!"

* * *

When Daniel got back to the Mill, Charlie was still in bed, not feeling too well.

"Can I get you something to eat or drink?" asked Daniel. He had never seen Charlie poorly before and was a bit worried.

"No thanks. I am fine, honestly. I think that egg and cress sandwich I had at the airport must have been off. I will be fine. You go and help daddy with the borehole. I will get up later and go and see mummy for a bit."

"If, you are sure. Give me a ring if you want me to come home later. I am sure they can manage without me."

"I will. Love you, tons."

* * *

Daniel drove up to the cattle sheds at Haggs Gill, to find the giant blue drilling rig already in place and making a loud roaring noise as it ground its way down through the underlying rock.

"How deep are we going?" Daniel shouted to Edward above the noise of the rig.

"Probably about 300 metres down, if the hydrologist is right, but they can go down to 400 if necessary. They assess the rock strata as they go down so they can decide on the strength of the rock layers and what support casing configurations they need," shouted Edward in reply.

"I see George has started on the reservoir tank. I thought he was the shepherd not a digger driver?" joked Daniel. "When did he learn to drive a JCB?"

"Yesterday!" shouted Edward, oblivious to the modern healthy and safety implications.

"How much water will it hold?" asked Daniel.

"About 50,000 litres but there is room for another tank a bit further down the bank if we need more capacity. It should keep us going through a long freeze next winter, if we ever get one again with global warming!"

"Are they doing the one up at Annie's sheep shed this week as well?"

"No, they say they are really busy with vertical ground-source heat pumps at the moment so they will come back in a few months to do that one."

At that moment a huge gush of water cascaded up from the borehole and covered everyone with a thick layer of slimy mud.

"I think they have found some water," laughed Edward, pleased that he didn't have to pay for another hundred metres of drilling.

* * *

Daniel decided to go home to get a shower and see how Charlie was. When he got home, she was nowhere to be seen, so he gave her a ring on her mobile. Charlie picked up straight away.

"I am up at the Hall with mummy."

"Are you feeling better; I was worried about you?"

"Much better thank you. Why don't you come up to the Hall for some tea?"

"OK. Give me half an hour to get a shower. Your father has hit gold!"

"I know. He has just brought half of Haggs Gill into the kitchen with him!"

* * *

Daniel walked into the kitchen to find Charlie, Elizabeth and Edward sitting around the old pine table drinking tea and eating homemade scones with Elizabeth's special raspberry jam. As he entered the room their conversation stopped dead and they all looked at each other very seriously.

"What's gone wrong now? Are you sure you are OK Charlie?" he asked, kissing her on top of her head. Elizabeth could not keep up the pretence any longer and smiled broadly.

"What have I missed? What's going on you three?" asked a now, very concerned Daniel.

"I am going to be a granny!" laughed Elizabeth.

"But I thought Charlie was an only child?" asked an even more confused Daniel.

"And …" Charlie got up and gave Daniel a hug. "You are going to be a daddy!"

"That is amazing… I mean it's wonderful my darling… But how…?" muttered a flabbergasted Daniel.

"I think we all know how that happens!" laughed Edward. "I am off to get a bottle of my special Pol Roger Winston Churchill. I think I still have some 2008 left."

Charlie sat on Daniel's knee and he kept kissing her and asking stupid questions.

"When did you find out you were pregnant?"

"This morning."

"How?"

"I got a test from the chemist in Leyburn."

"How does that work?"

"You pee on a stick."

"Are you sure it's safe?"

"Millions of women use them every day!"

"When will the baby, sorry our baby, arrive?"

"Not this month!"

"Good; we will have to get a cot," said Daniel, with his mind totally scrambled by the revelation. Edward reappeared with the champagne and flutes. He filled the glasses and proposed a toast.

"To Charlie! You have made us very, very happy my love. And your mother will now fill your house with enough baby clothes for the whole of Wensleydale!"

"I can't believe this," said Daniel thinking hard. "Why didn't you tell me this morning?"

"Because I wanted to do the test, just to be sure. I didn't want to get your hopes up."

"Are you sure you feel OK? You looked a bit grey this morning?"

"Charming! Just a bit of morning sickness. I feel fine now. Stop worrying," said Charlie, giving Daniel another hug.

"Another glass of bubbly my dear?" enquired Edward, elated at the news. "You have finally solved our inheritance dilemma!"

"Not too much drink now Charlie. There's two of you to think about," smiled Elizabeth protectively.

"Mummy, I've a while to go yet."

"I know, but you can't be too careful; and no more riding for you, young lady until after our grandchild is born."

"Yes mummy. I promise."

"And we had better book you in for a scan at the clinic to check everything is OK," instructed Elizabeth, taking over full control of everything baby related.

"Yes mummy!" smiled Charlie, raising her eyebrows in fun.

* * *

On their way back to the Mill, Daniel's phone rang in the car.

"Hi John. Did you manage to find anything out?" asked Daniel; it was Charlie's godfather, the lieutenant-colonel at Catterick garrison on the call.

"That's good I suppose. Hopefully he has given up and gone back to Moscow," suggested Daniel. "I suppose there were no travel details? Too much to ask. OK. Thanks for checking. Please let me know if you hear anything else. Thank you, and by the way, I am going to be a father. Yes Charlie! I will. Speak soon."

"Did you ask him to check the Russian out?" asked Charlie.

"Yes. I gave him a ring yesterday but they have heard nothing and seen nothing. Our friend seems to have disappeared without leaving a trace."

"Well, let's hope he's given up and gone for good," said Charlie, not really believing that would happen, and knowing the Russian culture for life-long revenge.

CHAPTER FOUR

Money for Nothing

The following morning there was a banging on the kitchen door at the Mill. Charlie and Daniel were still asleep.

"What time is it?" asked Charlie as she rushed to the bathroom to be sick.

"Seven-thirty. Are you OK? I will go and see what's up."

"Yes go!"

Daniel pulled on his bathrobe and ran down the stairs. As he opened the door, Misty shot through his legs and leaped onto Abbey in her basket; Anne Marie swept in and gave Daniel a huge hug and kissed him passionately on the lips.

"You've heard then," smiled Daniel. "Go on, who told you?"

"The postman, when he delivered the mail."

"How did the bloody postman know, I only found out myself yesterday!"

"It's fantastic news Daniel. Where is she? I can't wait to be a godmother!"

"She's being sick in the bathroom."

"Great. Tea and toast please!" called Anne Marie as she dashed up the stairs. "And let the dogs out!" Daniel's life was about to change forever.

"Oh! you poor thing," said Anne Marie, holding Charlie's hair out of the loo. "Is it awful?"

"I'll be fine, stop fussing."

"Can I be the godmother?"

"Of course," said Charlie. "Who else would we ask? How did you know anyway?"

"The postman told me. Your father told Mac and he told Sergeant Pickles, who dropped in for some dog food and he told the postman."

"So, the whole Dale knows within a day that I'm pregnant, before I've got used to the idea!"

"Pretty much! Anyway, it's wonderful news Charlie. I can't wait to buy you lots of maternity clothes and all those cute things for the baby. It's going to be such fun. We are having a baby!"

Anne Marie rinsed out a warm flannel under the tap, wiped Charlie's face gently and gave her a quick kiss on the lips.

"Now you must get back into bed and rest. Daniel is making the breakfast and I am going to look after you."

"Annie, I am pregnant, not ill!"

"That's not the point. I am going to look after you to make sure my goddaughter has everything she needs."

"It might be a boy!" smiled Charlie.

"No, it's definitely a girl; I can just tell by looking at you."

Daniel arrived with the tea and toast and the three of them sat on the bed debating the issue, whilst enjoying the good news. Charlie tried to steer the conversation away from babies for a while.

"So how are the new foals coming along?"

"I am so excited by the Into Mischief colt that George helped me foal on that foul winter's night. If it wasn't for George, we would have lost the mare and the foal. It was a red-bag delivery and George knew what to do because there was no hope of getting the vet and Aiden was trapped at home with no internet so he couldn't see what was happening on the cameras."

Thoroughbred Mare and Foal

"Are you going to sell him at Tatts or bring him on yourself and then get him trained under your colours?" asked Charlie.

"Oh, definitely keep him. It will be great fun going to the races together and watch him win lots of money!"

"They don't all win!" advised Daniel realistically.

"Ah, but he will. He is by the top-rated horse in America, who has already bred the Kentucky Derby winner in 2020 called Authentic and another son, called Mandaloun, who was second in the same race this year," replied Anne Marie confidently.

"Who will you get to train it?" asked Charlie.

"It's a bit early to say yet but there is a very good trainer in Middleham who might take him."

"Have you decided on a name yet?"

"Yes, I woke up yesterday and I was thinking about it. I wanted a nice positive name about the future, so I am going to call him Inheritance; Harry for short."

"That's a good choice Annie," approved Charlie. "Let's hope it's a good omen for the future of all of us on the planet."

"It's even got a royal connection!" joked Daniel. "Well, if you two are OK, I am off up to the borehole to see how your father is getting on."

"We will be fine. I am sure Annie will look after me," smiled Charlie looking across the bed at Anne Marie. "I thought we might give Annabelle a ring. She is due any day now and I might pick up some hints on coping with this nausea every morning."

"Good idea. See you later; give me a ring if you need me for anything." With that Daniel escaped any further baby talk, to deal with the man's stuff he was more comfortable with.

When he got to Haggs Gill, George was in deep conversation with Edward.

"How's our mother-to-be?" asked Edward.

"She is OK but a bit sick in the mornings."

"Elizabeth was like that for weeks when she was carrying Charlie. Must be genetic," said Edward.

"Anyway, Annie turned up at the crack of dawn and has completely taken over."

"Sounds like Annie!" chuckled George. "But Daniel, we have a bit of a problem up on Annie's moor. The bloody sheep rustlers have been back and taken about thirty Swaledale ewes. There is a shitty patch near Melmerby Beck, so I think they have built a temporary pen there and loaded them into a trailer or wagon."

"They must have some good sheepdogs if they can get them into a pen up there," said Daniel. "I assume they were all tagged and marked?"

"Yes, they were all checked at lambing time. There might be an odd tag missing but they all have chips in, so they can be easily scanned," replied George. "We had this problem last year and they took three lots off the moor but it is a vast area to cover and they always take them at night."

"Have we informed the police?" asked Daniel.

"Yes, I rang Sergeant Pickles a while ago and he is going up to the Beck to see if he can see anything but he didn't hold out much hope of catching them," replied Edward. "It's sort of become a regular problem in the Dales. They will just take them down a 'rat-run', avoiding all the cameras on the main roads, and the poor things will be dead by now and in a kebab, on some backstreet shop in Bradford. They are not bothered that it's taken a family, generations to build up a healthy flock that provides high-quality locally produced meat and keeps the moor naturally picturesque for all the tourists in the summer."

"We must be able to do something to stop them. It must stress the sheep to hell, herding them up in the dark and carting them off to have their throats cut like that." argued Daniel angrily.

"All the farmers on the moor keep an eye out for strangers doing a reconnaissance trip but there are so many hikers about it's difficult to differentiate between them," replied George. "Last year we even did a night vigil on the moor on a rota basis but we still couldn't catch them."

"Ok, let me have a think about what we could do to sort the bastards and then we can make a plan," said Daniel constructively. "Anyway, the new holding tank is looking good George; you've done a great job digging that out."

"Thanks. I think it should see us through the winters. It holds about ten times as much as the old one we have used for the last two hundred years," laughed George. "We'll get it blocked out tomorrow and rendered next week. We've got a concrete manhole to go on top, with steps, so we can get in to clean it out, if necessary, in the future."

"Come and have a look at the new control room for the borehole Daniel. It's very smart," said Edward, pleased with his new investment. "These ultraviolet filters take out all the impurities so we can feed the farmhouse as well as the bullocks. The flow of water is all monitored and tested automatically and the details sent back to the people who drilled the hole, so they can come out and fix any problems."

"It all looks a big improvement Edward," said Daniel, "and saves all that hauling water up from the river when it snows hard and freezes everything up."

"Yes," smiled Edward in a Yorkshire way. "And I got them down another 600 quid, because they didn't have to drill so deep as they thought!"

"Enough for a new pram then," joked Daniel.

Daniel had been drawing up a surprise plan for the sheep rustlers in the back of his mind whilst he was pretending to be a farmer. He leaned on the green moss-covered stone wall next to the storage tank and talked to Edward about lamb prices, a new tree-planting project for the red squirrel conservation area, and Annie's potential racehorse called Harry; but his heart wasn't in it. He made his excuses and headed off towards Bedale, turning off on the tank road up to Catterick. He arrived at the army barrack gates at about lunchtime.

"Could I see the lieutenant-colonel please?" he asked politely of the grim-faced armed soldier, manning the red and white barrier.

"I am afraid he doesn't see civilians without an appointment sir. If you visit our website, you can try there to get an appointment, but he is a very busy man as I am sure you understand."

"Yes, I do understand but this is a matter of national security. Could you possibly ring his office and say Daniel Knight is here on important business?" Daniel, realised he should just have rung John first but his brain was not working properly, with Charlie's news whizzing round in his head.

"I will try sir but I doubt he will have time today." The soldier returned to his post and made a call, whilst another soldier kept guard on Daniel's car.

The soldier returned. "They asked me to ask you for your wife's name?"

"Charlie," replied Daniel.

"Funny name for a lady!" smiled the guard. "I assume you know where his office is?"

"I think I can find it," replied Daniel, returning a lightening of the mood.

John met Daniel at the door to his offices and shook his hand firmly.

"You're going to be a surprise father, I understand. Congratulations old chap."

"It was a shock to me too; I haven't got used to the idea yet. How did you find out?"

"Edward rang me this morning. He and Elizabeth are over the moon. I think they had all but given up hope that Charlie would have any children. I think the baby might get slightly spoilt! Anyway, how can I help you?"

"This is a bit random, so say no if you can't help, but does your satellite surveillance of the garrison, that we can't talk about, cover Wensleydale?"

"You know I can't tell you that, because it doesn't exist. This is not Kenya and we don't have rhinos!"

"Point taken. But let's say a Russian agent was in the Dale and I knew where he was last night, could you tell me where his vehicle went to, if I knew the starting point."

"That's different. I might be able to help," said John formally. "Where exactly did he set off from and when?"

"We think near Melmerby Beck above Middleham. I can give you the coordinates. Sometime during darkness last night. Probably after midnight."

"I'll see what I can do. That's on Anne Marie's new estate, isn't it?"

"Yes, it is but she doesn't know anything about this," confided Daniel.

"Give me a couple of hours and I will be back in touch."

"Thank you, John. I really appreciate your help."

"You owe me a ride in that Ferrari don't forget, and this conversation never took place. Not sure Whitehall would approve of us tracking sheep rustlers!"

"How did you know… I know, you know everything!" grinned Daniel.

* * *

When Daniel got back to the Mill, he found Charlie asleep on the sofa with an empty coffee cup on the floor beside her. Misty was lying on the hearth rug guarding her mistress. Charlie opened her eyes slowly and Daniel leant over and gave her a gentle kiss.

"How are you feeling my love?"

"I am fine, just a bit uncomfortable down there. Annie and I went up to Annabelle's and had lunch with her. She is enormous but seems very well and is looking forward to having the baby in the next day or so. It was officially due yesterday but the doctors think it will be another couple of days yet. After the tragedy with the last birth, they are keeping a very close eye on her and mummy has paid for a midwife to be with her 24/7. Poor Tim is at his wits end with worry but we tried to calm him down. What have you been up to?"

"Oh, nothing much," he lied, not wanting to worry Charlie. "The new borehole looks great. Edward has done a super job of managing the project and it all seems to be going to plan. Did you get any tips on your morning problem?"

"Not really. Annabelle was very kind but she basically said it was just a phase and it would soon wear off. Mummy has booked me in for a scan in a couple of weeks, so maybe the nurse will give me some hints."

"I'll grab a sandwich and come and sit with you for a while," said Daniel sympathetically.

"Annie has made a casserole for supper so don't eat too much."

"I thought she might still be here actually."

"No, she went about half an hour ago. Something to do with a virtual board meeting with one of her publishing houses, in New York. She said she will be back in the morning to look after me tomorrow. She is a wonderful friend Daniel. We are so lucky to have her."

* * *

Daniel was just finishing his second beef sandwich when his phone went.

"Hi John, any luck?… Really, that's great. Where did they go then?… We thought they would go over the tops. Where did they finish up? That's just outside Keighley near Bradford. Is there any intel on the owner? OK. That's brilliant thank you. I owe you a long drive in the Ferrari, sorry Charlie's Ferrari! I will."

"What was all that about? Was it our John?"

"Yes. He sends his love. This beef is very tasty," said Daniel resuming his sandwich, in the vain hope Charlie would not pursue her first question.

"So, what are you up to now? We are meant to be having a break from intrigue and explosions!" grinned Charlie, knowing it was a forlorn hope with Daniel.

"Well, you mustn't tell anyone, especially Annie, but some rustlers stole thirty of her ewes off the moor last night and I asked John for a favour to see where they went. Anyway, he has come up trumps again and they ended up at an industrial unit just outside Keighley. It's evidently owned by a business man who is a 'pillar of the local community' and who owns some restaurants and Indian takeaways called Goddess of India. I'll do a reccy tomorrow and see what I can find out about the place."

"Be careful my darling, there will be cameras everywhere and we can't manipulate the police as easily in the urban areas. Half of them are in cahoots with the local business people anyway."

"A bit like Sargent Pickles and us you mean?" Daniel grinned.

"You know what I mean! I don't want to be bringing our baby into prison for visits."

"Good point! I will have to take extra care now I am going to be a father."

* * *

Daniel was eating his breakfast in the kitchen when Anne Marie arrived. She knocked once, opened the door and floated past Daniel with armfuls of magazines and shopping bags. As she hurried up the stairs, dropping a *Mother & Baby* magazine, she asked, "How is the patient today?"

"Thank you for the casserole!" called Daniel after the whirlwind had passed. No reply.

Daniel's plan for the day was to do a quick drive past of the sheep rustler's industrial unit, and try and find out more about who owned it and where they lived. He decided to follow the rustler's route and drove up to Wensley, the little hamlet that gave the dale its name, across to West Witton and then hard left over Kidstones Bank to Buckden. It was a beautiful sunny morning and he was enjoying being on his own for a while. The old, lichen-covered walls criss-crossed the vertiginous hillsides, dotted with horned ewes and their whiter frivolous offspring. A ruddy shepherd was busy looking around his flock on his red quad bike with two black and white sheep dogs hitching a ride on the back. Daniel dropped down to Rylstone on the Grassington road and skirted round Skipton on the bypass.

The urban landscape of the Aire River valley slowly overtook the beauty of the dales. The houses became duller and architecturally wanting. The backstreets off the main road were narrow and forbidding and the inhabitants were multicultural. Not that it bothered Daniel, having spent much of his early life in an African orphanage. He crossed the Leeds and Liverpool canal, which was slowly coming back to life, after years of neglect from its former glory as the wool waterway to riches. For some anyway. He followed John's directions and strangely found himself climbing out of the mundane and along a stone built 'millionaire's row', with well-kept landscaped gardens. He finally reached the identified property which was a magnificent 'Dallas type' edifice complete with balcony, outside swimming pool (ridiculous in Yorkshire!), and black metal gates. No eagles he noted. There was a side track leading around the back of the house to a large modern industrial unit with no windows and a closed green, roller-shutter door. A hundred yards further on he stopped to talk to the local postman delivering the letters in his red van.

"Good morning. Grand day," said Daniel hoping to kickstart a conversation.

"Are you lost?"

"Not really. Looking for a house to buy actually. It's quite nice up here."

"You won't find any for sale up here, they all belong to the big house you've just past."

"What all of them!" Daniel put on his best astonished expression.

"Aye. He's the local bigwig. Knows everybody. Can buy anything he wants, Mr Untouchable."

"You're not his best fan then," Daniel risked a joke.

"Arrogant bastard actually. He bought our cloth dyeing mill, promising to keep it going and then pulled it down and built a fancy restaurant that's too expensive to eat in. I was lucky and got this job but a lot of others never found another job and idle away their last days playing bowls on the social."

"So, what's in the big shed down the lane at the back?" asked Daniel.

"No idea. Vehicles come and go at night. Probably something to do with importing stuff I suppose?"

"Well, it was interesting talking to you. I don't suppose you know of any houses to sell with a bit of land?" asked Daniel, covering his tracks.

"I saw one the other day at Carleton-in-Craven. There's a sign on the road side. Five acres, I think. You can't miss the For Sale board."

"Thanks for the lead," said Daniel and he retraced his route back over the canal and down into Keighley. He stopped for a moment and googled local bowling greens, in the hope of finding more information from an ex-mill worker. He opted for Lund Park on Malsis Road, where there were two municipal bowling greens surrounded by stone-terraced houses. He parked outside the ornate stone gate pillars; the gates long since removed, presumably for the war effort many years ago. He walked down an avenue of trees, passed a derelict bandstand, an empty pond devoid of water, and the stone base of a neglected fountain, equally thirsty. He sat down on a green park bench, next to a young, unshaven man, smoking a vaping pipe, overlooking the bowling green.

"Do you play bowls?" asked Daniel, trying to open a conversation.

"I'm not that bloody old!" exclaimed the man, who got up and walked off, clearly hiding some misdemeanour. Daniel was just thinking he was wasting his time, when a white-haired Indian lady in a saree and pushing a pram, asked if she could sit down to rest. Daniel stood up and offered her the seat.

"Please stay. I did not want to disturb you but my granddaughter has fallen to sleep, at last, and I need a rest. I think I have walked twenty miles," she joked.

"It's a lovely day to sit in the sunshine and watch the world go by. You have a beautiful granddaughter," said Daniel, looking into the pram.

"She belongs to my eldest son and I look after her two days a week whilst his wife helps him at work. They work very hard so I am pleased to help. She is very good, most of the time!" she smiled.

"Have you lived in Keighley long?" asked Daniel hoping to find some common ground with the rich rustlers.

"I came here with my husband in 1947 from Jaipur near new Delhi. It was during the partition of India and Pakistan and life in India was horrendous, so we upped sticks and moved to Keighley. We were young and ambitious and thought we would have a better future for our family in England."

"I assume you are both retired now?" enquired Daniel.

"No, never! We will never retire. We have always worked very hard for what we have and we have a wonderful family to look after. You don't get money for nothing in this life!"

Daniel admired the old ladies work ethic and her ambitions for her family. If only everyone had her views on life, the world would be a better place. But then the bombshell dropped.

"We have built up a group of restaurants, called Goddess of India, which are very successful and are now run by my oldest son, Daksh and his wife Amala. They live next to us and so I am very lucky and see a lot of the four children."

Daniel was dumbstruck for once in his life and conflicted. He could not believe his luck, but equally this hard-working family were not what he was expecting his sheep rustlers to look like. He was thinking more like a stinking blood-soaked shed up some backstreet run by lowlife he could despatch with impunity.

"So do you live in the town?"

"No, we have a nice house up the hill, on the other side of the canal, near East Riddlesden Hall, owned by the National Trust. Where do you live?"

The question took Daniel by surprise so he lied. "Near Skipton. I am just here for a meeting."

"What do you do for a living?" The questions were getting a bit uncomfortable for Daniel so he made something up. "I work for Natural England on conservation projects. I am working on a red squirrel programme at the moment."

"There aren't many red squirrels in Keighley!" she laughed. "My husband is really into conservation and supports a project in Jaipur to look after orphan elephant calves that get left when their mothers are killed or die."

The conversation was getting surreal. There was no way these people were rustling sheep off the moors. Firstly, they seemed to have integrity and secondly, they obviously didn't need the money. So why were the sheep ending up in their barn behind the house? Perhaps John had got the intelligence wrong, or the satellite was malfunctioning?

"Well, I must be going. It has been a great pleasure meeting you and hearing about your family. I hope you enjoy the rest of your walk," said Daniel, as he rose to his feet.

"I've enjoyed our little chat and it was nice to meet you too. Maybe our paths will cross again one day?" she smiled again and resumed her grandmotherly duties, rocking the pram.

* * *

When Daniel got home to the Mill there was no sign of Charlie, so he made himself a cup of tea and cut a slice of Madera cake that Elizabeth had made the previous day. He gave Charlie a ring on her mobile and she picked up straight away.

"Hi darling. Did you have a productive day?" asked Charlie.

"Sort of; I will tell all about it later. Where are you?"

"I'm at Annie's house. Harry got kicked in the field this morning and she is really upset, because he is her big prospect to win some races when he grows up."

"Is he badly hurt?"

"The vet has been and Harry has had to have six stitches in the cut on his shoulder. The vet thinks it will be OK but he will have to stay on box-rest until the wound heals up."

"Why were they fighting? I thought that group were well established in the field."

"Just one of those things, I think. Annie seems to be a bit better now the vet has been. She is new to the practice and very attractive, with a blonde pigtail and very slim. I think Annie will need regular visits for weeks!" chuckled Charlie.

"When are you coming home? Shall I put something in the oven?" asked Daniel, having missed lunch and feeling hungry already.

"Mummy has invited us up for supper tonight so I will see you up at the Hall about six. I need to pick up some bits and pieces from Leyburn on the way back."

"Are you sure you are feeling, OK?"

"Oh! stop fussing. I am fine. See you in a while."

* * *

Daniel pulled up in the stable yard and met Mac, who was just getting out of his Land Rover wearing smart jacket and trousers.

"Hi Mac. Where have you been, all dressed up?"

"I've just got back from the hospital. Annabelle and Tim have just had a healthy baby boy."

"That's fantastic news Mac. Are they all OK?"

"Annabelle and the baby are fine. I am not sure about Tim though! I think we will have to open that bottle of Arran twelve-year-old malt whisky I won, at the gamekeepers shoot last month."

"I am so pleased it has worked out for them after the terrible disaster with the last birth. Hopefully they can settle down to a happy family life now."

"How's Charlie getting on?"

"She is fine. She will be here in few minutes; we are having supper with Elizabeth and Edward."

* * *

Daniel walked into the boot room and the delicious aromas of Elizabeth's cooking emanated from the kitchen. He met Edward in the main hall, who was holding a bottle of Brunello di Montalcino in his right hand and a Farmers Guardian in the other.

"Have you heard about Tim and Annabelle's baby?" asked Daniel.

"I have, it's great news for them. I've found a bottle of 2016 to celebrate with! How's Charlie doing?"

"Still being sick in the mornings and gets tired, but she seems fine. She'll be here shortly."

"Great. Come in the kitchen and we will try this wine. I know it should breathe and all that, but I'm thirsty," Edward smiled.

Elizabeth was busy over the Aga, with endless pans steaming away and the gravy simmering. Daniel leaned over and kissed her on the cheek.

"That smells delicious Elizabeth. I'm starving."

"Where is Charlie?" asked Elizabeth, slightly worried.

"She has been up at Annie's. Her favourite foal got kicked and they had to get the vet to stitch it up. She is on her way and will be here in a few minutes."

"It's brilliant news about Annabelle. I am so relieved it has all gone OK this time," said Elizabeth.

Edward poured Daniel and Elizabeth a glass of the red wine and they toasted the new baby.

"Has it got a name yet?" asked Edward.

"Give them chance! He was only born a few hours ago," admonished Elizabeth.

"I hope they pick a proper name and not one of these modern things, like Twitter."

"I don't think that's a name darling!" laughed Elizabeth.

"Well, you know what I mean!"

"What does he mean?" asked Charlie, appearing round the kitchen door.

"Your father thinks Twitter is a boy's name! Anyway, have you heard about Annabelle's baby?"

"Yes, Mac just told me. It's wonderful for them. I am so pleased for both of them; Annabelle has got something to cuddle at last and hopefully Tim will feel more relaxed when he is shooting."

"Hopefully he might miss a few more clays now!" joked Daniel.

They sat round the kitchen table and Edward carved the sirloin of beef. Elizabeth served the roasted King Edwards and Charlie helped with the tender stem broccoli and courgettes.

"So, did you manage to track the rustlers down?" asked Charlie.

"Well, it was all a bit odd really," replied Daniel and he related the story of the big house and the Indian lady in the park.

"So, what are we going to do about them now?" asked Edward. "They may be decent folk but Annie's sheep still ended up in their shed.

"I thought I might speak to Sargent Pickles and see if he has any contacts in the Keighley police station who might make some discrete enquires for us?" suggested Daniel.

"That's almost civilised!" said Charlie looking at Daniel, knowing that historically he would probably have just blown them up. Maybe, just maybe, becoming a father was starting to mellow his view of the world.

CHAPTER FIVE

Landscapes of Love and Loss

Elizabeth drove down to the Mill at ten o'clock to pick Charlie up for her scan at the local hospital, to check to see how the baby was developing. Charlie had been awake early and was feeling a bit apprehensive about the results of the scan. She got up to have a bath and took Abbey for a walk. Daniel was away in London on business and although he was getting used to the idea of becoming a father, he was not really into the whole 'sitting by the bed and holding hands' thing. He thought Elizabeth would make a much better job of it and left them to it.

Elizabeth opened the back door and called up the stairs.

"I'm here darling; are you ready?"

"Coming! Just packing my things."

"Where's Abbey?" asked Elizabeth.

"Oh, Annie came and fetched her first thing. She was dying to come with us to the hospital but I asked her to look after the dog instead. I wanted today to be just you and me. It's a very special day mummy and I wanted to be close to you in case there were any problems."

"Come here my darling and give me hug. It will be fine," They put their arms around each other and Charlie felt the warmth of her mother's love.

They arrived at the local hospital with half an hour to spare so they sat patiently in the deserted waiting room. Charlie picked up a leaflet on morning sickness but it didn't say much more than she had already found on the internet.

"Is it getting any better?" asked Elizabeth.

"Some days it's worse than others. I guess I am just getting used to it."

"It will fade away after about twelve weeks, although I was not feeling well till nearly twenty weeks with you!" smiled Elizabeth.

"Thanks, that's a big help!"

A rather large, young nurse appeared with a ruddy face and trainers.

"Charlotte Blaire-Fox?" she called out, seemingly oblivious to the fact that Charlie was the only pregnant lady in the waiting room.

"They weren't allowed to wear casual shoes in my day," whispered Elizabeth as they followed the nurse into the consulting room.

"Hello, my name is Mandy and we just want to see that you and your baby are progressing well and everything is on course."

"Is that cross-country or national hunt?" said Charlie, attempting humour to cover her nervousness.

"Yes," replied Mandy, clearly more conversant with mosh pits and rap music. "Now, how old are you?"

"Thirty-six."

"Ah, a mature mum to be. Have you had any children before?"

"Not that I have noticed," replied Charlie, slightly irritated at the implication.

"And when did your last period start?"

"They more or less stopped five years ago."

"So how many weeks do you think you could be, based on your sexual activity?"

Charlie felt like a prostitute. "About twelve weeks, I think."

"Ok. Well, let's jump on the bed and see what we have in your tummy."

Sounds like it might be an alien, thought Charlie.

"I expect you have seen on Google what will happen today but let me just explain what I am going to do and if you have any questions as we proceed, then please ask me. I have been a sonographer for over ten years so I know what to look for!" she smiled, alleviating some of Charlie's tensions. "If you just pull your shirt up so I can feel your tummy; I will then put some of this gel on the head of the scanner and on your tummy. The gel simply lets me get a good contact, so I can see a clear picture on the screen. It might be bit cold – sorry."

Elizabeth was trying to look over Mandy's shoulder to see the screen but her head kept getting in the way. Mandy showed no facial expression whilst looking at the screen, as she slid the probe backwards and forwards. She fiddled with the dials next to her keyboard and kept pressing various buttons.

"OK, so just listen to this," said Mandy, with a smile. The characteristic whoosh of the baby's heartbeat brought tears to Charlie's eyes and her mother joined in. Copiously.

"Can I see the baby?" asked Charlie.

"Of course." Mandy turned the screen towards Charlie and she could clearly see the white outline of the tiny baby on the black background. She was used to seeing the screens when the sheep scanner came every year to scan the ewes, so they knew which sheep were in lamb and how many lambs they were having.

"Does it all look OK?" asked Charlie hesitantly.

"I think you said you were twelve weeks, but it looks more like ten or eleven from my measurements. That would make the birth date around the fifteenth of February. We will be more definite when you come back for the twenty-week scan later. The baby looks fit and healthy and is well positioned in the uterus. I can't tell the sex at the moment because those bits are hidden but it's nothing to worry about. We can tell you next time if you want to know. Have you got any other questions?"

"Can we have a photograph of the baby please," asked Elizabeth.

"Of course. There is a small charge but they will sort that out in reception. Right, I will just clean off the gel for you and you can get dressed. I would just like to take a couple of blood samples to check that everything else is OK with you and the baby, so we have a base line to monitor your hormone levels etcetera."

* * *

Charlie and Elizabeth walked out into the sunshine, holding hands and gave each other a hug in the carpark, before they got into the car.

"I thought she was very nice, after a shaky start," said Elizabeth.

"Yes, I felt a bit guilty about my negative thoughts about her at the start too," replied Charlie. "I don't think she goes to York races much!"

"You'd be surprised my dear. They seem to wear anything at the Knavesmire these days!"

* * *

When they got back to the Mill, Elizabeth had to rush off because the man was coming to service her beloved Aga and she always liked to be there in case there was a problem.

"Give me a ring later darling to let me know you are all right," instructed Elizabeth.

"I will. I am going to make a cup of coffee and sit down this afternoon and go through some of my African photos. It's ridiculous but I do feel a bit tired after this morning."

"It will just be the excitement with seeing your baby for the first time," said Elizabeth, getting into her car. "And don't forget to ring Daniel. I know he's a man, but he will be eager to know that you are both OK."

Charlie sat down at the kitchen table with her coffee, looking at the scan photo of her baby, carefully placed in front of her leaning on the salt and pepper pots. She was uncertain how to feel. She felt strangely alone with her photo and put her hand on her tummy. This morning's revelation would change her life for ever. Would she have the same happy relationship with her child as she had with her mother? Would the birth go OK? Would the baby have any abnormalities? Could she cope with being a mother? Would she still be able to travel with Daniel and continue with her photography business? Would the child be interested in conservation or be a brain surgeon? Would global warming have devastated the planet? How would Daniel cope with changing nappies?

Charlie burst out laughing; there was no way on this planet Daniel would be changing nappies! She picked up the phone and gave him a ring. Voicemail.

"Hi darling. It all went well this morning. The scan looks amazing. I am sitting here looking at it and think of you. I can't believe it really. Hope you will be home soon. Give me a ring when you have a minute. Love you."

Charlie was just about to go and sit down on the sofa for a quiet afternoon when Anne Marie swept into the kitchen with a bottle of Bollinger champagne and two Labradors fighting over a piece of wood which Abbey had found on the drive.

"Hi darling. Where's the scan; I must see my baby girl?" She gave Charlie a kiss on the cheek and stared at the photograph. "Wow a baby! Where's the head? Is it a girl? Please say it's a girl."

So much for a quiet afternoon; but Charlie was really pleased that she had Anne Marie to discuss everything whizzing around her head.

"We don't know the sex yet; you will have to wait for the next scan." Charlie smiled and Anne Marie pulled a funny sad face. Charlie explained what the scan showed and the different parts of her baby.

"It's fantastic Charlie; we have to celebrate." Anne Marie opened the champagne much to the surprise of the dogs who piled into Abbey's bed in fear.

"I have to be careful now what I drink," said Charlie.

"Oh, come on one glass will do you good. We have got to get the baby used to the best champagnes!"

"OK but just a small glass. How is the foal coming on? Has that new attractive vet come out to see it again?"

"Good and bad news. The foal is doing really well and the cut should not affect how it races. The bad news is that the vet has a boyfriend!"

"Ah well, back to the drawing board," laughed Charlie.

"Anyway, I've got you and I am going to be a godmother, so I don't care," said Anne Marie, leaning over and kissing Charlie again. Where is Daniel? What is he doing in London? I thought we were having a break from work at the moment?

"It's something to do with Didi, the baby gorilla that the poachers took. One of his contacts picked up a lead about a private zoo in South Africa but it's all very complicated because the zoo is owned by an Indian man who works for their government and has diplomatic immunity. They can't just send in the police because that would create all sorts of other issues."

"Well, I hope Daniel finds the bastards and kills them. I still wake up at night and think about Didi's poor mother, hacked to death on the floor of the jungle."

"It just takes time Annie. If you don't catch them red-handed at the time, it's really difficult tracking these people down. They are usually criminals or very, very wealthy, so they know how to avoid detection," said Charlie.

"I know. I don't understand why these people do it? Anyway, what's the plan for this afternoon?"

"I thought I might go through some of the photographs I took in Africa and select some of the good ones for my clients over there."

"That's a great idea. I will carry everything down to the sitting-room for you, if you show me where things are. We can choose the ones for your new book at the same time," suggested Anne Marie.

"I thought you had forgotten about that project now Aurora has found another girlfriend."

"She would have been useless anyway," retorted Anne Marie, curtly. "My team in New York will make a much better job of it."

They spent the afternoon reliving the African trip. The photographs Charlie had taken from the hot-air balloon were spectacular. The vivid colours and pure light, a dream. The focus from the new Canon camera was unbelievable, considering the size of the zoom lens and the movement of the balloon basket. By the end of the afternoon, they had enough images to fill three books. Now all they needed were the words!

Hot air balloon ride over Kenya

Anne Marie had to leave at five for some business meeting or other and Charlie needed to take Abbey for a walk. She put her on the lead and wandered along the lane enjoying the fresh air, after having been inside all afternoon.

Tim's Range Rover pulled up alongside her and he put the passenger window down.

"How did the scan go?" asked Tim. "It can be a bit nerve-wracking!"

"All good thank you. Feels a bit odd being pregnant! How's Annabelle and the new baby doing?"

"Annabelle is being amazing. She's breastfeeding, so that makes my life easier!" he joked. "Although sleep is a thing of the past! When is Daniel back? I need to talk to him about some new butts up on the grouse moor."

"Sometime tomorrow I think, but you know what he's like."

"OK, can you ask him to give me a ring when he finally appears? "

"Will do."

"Enjoy the rest of your walk. Have a look at the stone wall in Long Meadow. I think some walkers have knocked it over again."

* * *

The following afternoon, Daniel drove into the Mill driveway after his long trip from London. Charlie heard the car and opened the kitchen door. Abbey ran across to meet her master and he made a big fuss of her. He unloaded his bag from the boot of the Range Rover and walked over to Charlie and gave her a big hug.

"I love you," he whispered in her ear.

"Spooky! I love you too."

"Are you feeling OK?"

"I am fine. Still sick in the mornings but the rest of the day is good. How was the trip?"

"It was very productive… I think? I have found the location of the private zoo near Rustenburg, just to the west of Johannesburg. We know it has primates there but we are not sure about gorillas. It's a high security set up and this Indian guy that owns it is very secretive and also a diplomat, so we can't go wading in with machine guns."

"I am sure you will track Didi down eventually. Anyway, come in and I can tell you all about the scan and show you a picture of your daughter."

"So, we know it's a girl then?" queried Daniel, a bit surprised they knew already.

"Well not exactly, but Annie is convinced it's a girl, so we are going with that until the doctors tell us something different," laughed Charlie. "She's got a fifty percent chance of being right!"

They sat at the table in the kitchen, next to each other, holding hands and just looking at their baby on the scan.

"Sorry I wasn't there today with you; I should have been there to support you."

"I know you're busy trying to track down these awful people who took Didi. Mummy really enjoyed coming and we had a nice morning together. We think that Mandy, the sonographer, was into mosh pits!" joked Charlie, reminding Daniel of their sensual trip to Verbier in the Alps.

"We never talked about having children. I don't know why, I just thought it would never happen. But now it has, I'm so happy. I couldn't wait to come home and look after you."

"I love you, Daniel. Mandy said I am a mature mum, so that makes you geriatric!" Charlie smiled, and Daniel tickled her ribs. Charlie flinched a bit and held her shoulder.

"Are you OK?"

"Yes, I am fine. Must have pulled a muscle playing with Abbey earlier. Now what do you want for supper?"

"Oh, something simple so we can sit by the fire and enjoy planning the future for the three of us."

"Annie brought up a lasagne yesterday; I will put that in the oven for half an hour. What would you like to drink?"

"I think there is an Old Peculier beer in the fridge. That will do fine."

Daniel lit the fire and put *Cavalleria Rusticana* on the old CD player. He knew Charlie loved the intermezzo, and he thought it would help her relax. They talked and talked about the baby, their lives together so far, and what the future might look like for their child when it was grown up. Charlie laid on Daniel's shoulder and they watched the flames in the hearth slowly die, as the intermezzo echoed around the old oak beams of the Mill.

* * *

It was Sunday morning but Daniel woke up early; he crept out of the bedroom so Charlie could have a lie-in. He let Abbey out into the garden and made himself a cup of tea and some toast. He answered a few emails on his phone and sent Tim a text about the grouse butts. He got an immediate reply:

"Been up for three hours! Need an excuse to escape! Do you fancy a trip up to the moor to look at the butts this morning?"

"Let me check on Charlie and I will let you know."

Daniel walked quietly back upstairs and Charlie was in the bathroom being sick.

"Are you OK my darling?" Stupid question he thought, as the words came out of his mouth.

"Wonderful!" said Charlie, as she came out of the bathroom clutching a hand-towel to her face. "I am going back to bed for a bit. My shoulder really hurts. I don't know what I've done to it?"

"I'll get you some ibuprofen from the bathroom cabinet." Daniel put the tablets and a glass of water next to the bed.

"Tim has asked me if we could go up and have a look at the butts this morning. Do you think you will be OK?"

"Yes, I am fine. I just need to rest for a couple of hours. Annie said she would come round a bit later for a coffee."

"If you are sure. Just give me a buzz if you want me to come back."

"Oh, go on and stop fussing."

"OK see you in a while. I will take Abbey with me so she doesn't bother you. I will make us something for lunch when I get back."

Daniel kissed Charlie on the forehead, put Abbey in the car and sent Tim a text:

"Will pick you up from home in ten minutes."

Daniel got a 'thumbs up' in reply.

* * *

Annie arrived at the Mill at about half-ten, tapped on the kitchen door and let herself in. She put a tin full of teacakes she had made fresh that morning onto the table and called upstairs.

"Hi darling. I'm here, do you want a drink?"

No reply.

Annie ran upstairs. Charlie was not in her bed but there was blood on the sheets. She dashed into the bathroom. Charlie had collapsed on the white tiled floor and was barely conscious. She was gripping her stomach in excruciating pain and moaning incoherently

Annie fell to her knees next to Charlie, with tears pouring down her face in fear for her friend's life.

"Oh my God Charlie, what's happened?"

Charlie mumbled something but Annie could not make it out. She pulled out her phone and dialled 999.

"Ambulance. Dire emergency. Annie Macmillan. I have a pregnant mother bleeding profusely." Anne Marie gave the address details and as much information as she could. "I don't know, I have only just found her, please come quickly, I think she is going to die!"

Anne Marie grabbed a bath sheet and wrapped it around Charlie, who was beginning to shake. "Please Charlie hold on, the ambulance is coming."

Charlie opened her eyes but couldn't speak. She smiled weakly at Anne Marie, her eyes drifted upwards and her face lolled to the floor.

"No, no, no, stay with me," cried Anne Marie. She lifted Charlie's head onto her thigh and stroked her hair. "Please don't die. I love you."

Anne Marie rang Daniel on his mobile. Answer phone.

"Daniel this is Annie. Come home as fast as you can. Charlie is seriously ill. I have rung for an ambulance. Please, please, come quickly she is bleeding heavily. I think she is losing the baby."

She put the phone down and rang Charlie's mother. Elizabeth answered.

"Good morning, Annie. It's a lovely day isn't it."

"Elizabeth, Charlie is really ill and losing a lot of blood. I found her on the bathroom floor. I have rung for an ambulance. Can you come over, quickly?"

"I am on my way. Keep her warm and keep talking to her."

The 999-operator rang back.

"An early responder will be with you in ten minutes Annie and we are sending the air ambulance. We will take her straight up to James Cook Hospital at Teesside. How is she doing? Is her breathing steady?"

"No, it's very erratic and she is unconscious. Please tell them to hurry up. I think she is dying."

"It's Ok Annie, stay calm. You are doing a brilliant job. They will be there soon. Just keep talking to her. Put a towel firmly between her legs to try and stem the bleeding. I will stay on the phone now. Keep talking to me."

There was a screech of gravel on the drive as the first responder arrived. He dashed into the house and called upstairs.

"We are up here, please hurry," replied Anne Marie, in a broken voice.

"Hi I am Pete, what's the patient's name?"

"Charlie."

"Charlie, can you hear me?" No response.

"Is she dead?" cried Anne Marie, beside herself with worry.

"No, but she is very ill. Do you know how far on she is with her pregnancy?"

"She had a twelve-week scan yesterday and everything was fine. She brought a lovely photograph home with her. She heard her baby's heart beating."

He got on the radio to the 999-control. "Patient stats very weak she has lost a lot of blood. Suspected heterotopic. Have surgical team standing by."

The faint drone of the rotors got louder as the yellow Yorkshire air ambulance circled the Mill looking for a place to land. It put down in the paddock next to the house and three crew, dressed in green overalls jumped out and ran into the house. One was a doctor.

"Good morning. I'm Phil, the doctor on the air ambulance. What have we got Pete?

"Charlie Blaire-Fox, thirty-six years old, first pregnancy. Scanned yesterday. Normal scan. Baby in womb. Possible rupture of the fallopian tube. Possible heterotopic."

The doctor did a quick check of Charlie's stats. "Get the stretcher lads this needs to be quick one. Pete, confirm surgical team – category one."

They carefully lifted Charlie onto the stretcher and carried her out to the helicopter. She wasn't responding to anything.

"Can I come with her?" asked Anne Marie.

"Of course, jump in. Sit on that seat over there and belt up." The door slammed shut and they were gone.

The pilot radioed in to James Cook. "This is Whisky Charlie Oscar request permission to overfly Catterick garrison. Urgent shout to JC."

"Granted. Cleared with Leeming. Straight in, team waiting."

"ETA ten minutes. Give it all you've got James," the doctor called to the pilot.

* * *

Daniel and Elizabeth both arrived at the Mill at the same time, just after the helicopter had taken off.

"What's happened?" asked Daniel panicking. "I just saw the air-ambulance."

"I don't know where they are taking her," said Elizabeth, trying to hold back the tears. "Where were you?"

"I was up on the moor with Tim, when I got recorded message from Annie to say Charlie was seriously ill."

"She found Charlie on the bathroom floor. I think she is losing the baby, Daniel."

"Oh, Christ no! I thought they said everything was fine yesterday?"

"I don't know what has gone wrong Daniel but she is seriously ill. They wouldn't send the air ambulance unless it was an emergency."

"They can't land at Northallerton, my guess is James Cook. Jump in the Range Rover and we will head up there. You ring Annie and see if you can find out where they are."

Daniel turned the Range Rover round, sent a quick text, and set off at high speed towards Bedale.

"It is James Cook," said Elizabeth. "I've just got a text from Annie in the helicopter.

"That's good, they are brilliant there. Hold tight."

Half way up the A1, Daniel saw a blue light in his mirror. He slowed down a bit to ninety miles per hour and the police car shot past and pulled in front of him.

"About bloody time!" muttered Daniel under his breath.

A red-light message came up in the back window, 'follow me', and the MOD police car set off again, at over a hundred miles per hour.

"What's he doing?" asked Elizabeth totally mystified.

"Not sure," Daniel lied, "but he seems to be going our way."

* * *

The tyres screamed on the car as Daniel turned into the A&E car park and came to halt in the only free space, disabled.

"We haven't got a blue badge," said Elizabeth, climbing out of the car.

The question didn't register with Daniel, in his urgency to find Charlie.

They hurried into reception.

"My daughter has just been flown in on the air ambulance. Can you please tell me where she is?"

"If you follow the red line, it will take you to the A&E waiting area and a nurse will be able to help you." They ran down the corridor as fast as Elizabeth could manage.

Daniel took over. "My partner was just brought in by air ambulance can you tell me where she is. It's urgent."

"Is her name Charlie Blaire-Fox?" asked the nurse calmly.

"That's right. Where is she?"

"She's being prepped for emergency surgery sir."

"Can I see her?"

"She is already sedated sir. She is very poorly, we had to move quickly." Elizabeth burst into tears and Daniel put his arm around her.

"I know it's very stressful, but the most help you can be at the moment is to give us as much detail as you can about Charlie and her pregnancy."

"I really would like to see her?" asked Daniel, with a lump in his throat.

"Let's leave her with the surgical team sir. They are her best hope at the moment."

At that moment, Anne Marie came through a set of double doors with tears running down her cheeks.

"Thank God you are here!" said Anne Marie and threw her arms around Elizabeth and wouldn't let go. "I think she is going to die."

The nurse, holding a green file, came across to the three of them.

"Would you like to sit down so I can take some details about Charlie to give to the doctors. I understand she went for a scan yesterday and that you went with her?" she asked Elizabeth.

"Yes, I went with her because Daniel was away on business and we thought it was a just routine scan."

"Who was the sonographer?"

"It was nice lady called Mandy; sorry I don't know her surname."

"That's fine. I know who you mean. I will get the records shortly. Was there anything unusual about the scan?"

"No, it all seemed fine. I could see the baby on the screen and we could hear the heartbeat. They gave us a photo of the baby but Charlie has that at home. Sorry I didn't think to bring it. Elizabeth started to get upset again, so Anne Marie put her arm around her."

"Don't worry, we can get full copies of the whole scan straight away, to see if there was anything unusual."

"There was one thing," said Elizabeth, "The sonographer thought the baby was a little small for twelve weeks but Charlie was not sure about her period timings so Mandy didn't seem worried."

"Did she take any blood samples?"

"Yes, she did at the end. Is that significant?" asked Elizabeth.

"Not necessarily but it will help us with the diagnosis."

"I don't understand why she was fine this morning and then so seriously ill within a couple of hours. I shouldn't have left her on her own," said Daniel starting to worry that it may be his fault.

"I don't think this is anyone's fault, but let's just stick with the facts for now," said the nurse quietly. "So, was there anything unusual about Charlie this morning before you left?"

"No, I wouldn't have gone if there was. She was sick, as usual, first thing and then she said she was tired and wanted to have an easy morning in bed. We knew Annie was coming over during the morning, to be with her, so I was not worried. I thought she would just have a slow start to the day."

"I wish I had set off earlier now," pleaded Anne Marie," If only I had missed taking Misty for a walk, all this might not have happened."

"If you had not turned up when you did, Charlie might not have made it. She probably owes her life to you, so please don't feel guilty," confided the nurse.

"I've just remembered something else," said Daniel. "Charlie had a pain in the shoulder the night before which she thought was caused by her puppy messing about on the lead. It did seem worse this morning and I fetched her some ibuprofen. I am not sure if she took them though."

"I just need to see how the surgeons are getting on," said the nurse seriously. "I will be back in a few minutes."

"That was a bit abrupt," said Anne Marie. "Shouldn't she have taken the ibuprofen?"

"No, I don't think that's it," said Elizabeth. "What did the doctor in the air ambulance say Annie?"

"I can't remember, it was all such a blur; I was panicking and so worried about what was happening to Charlie."

The nurse reappeared with her green file. Daniel stood up.

"How is she. Is there any news yet?" asked Daniel. "Has she lost the baby?"

"The situation is very serious I am afraid," relayed the nurse solemnly. "Charlie has had a lot of internal bleeding in her abdomen and it will be a long operation to try and sort it all out."

"But she will be OK?" asked Anne Marie, desperate for a positive reply. She did not get one.

"She has lost a lot of blood and her internal organs are affected badly. They are doing their best in there but it will be a while before the surgeons can give you a full debrief."

Daniel went over to the window and looked out onto the courtyard with a bronze statue of Asclepius, partly hidden by a rambling Virginia creeper. His eyes filled with tears and his heart full of guilt. Charlie did not deserve this after everything else she had bravely overcome in her life. Elizabeth came over to him and put her arm around his waist.

"She will be fine, you'll see. My Charlie has always been a fighter, Daniel. She loves you very much. She will come back for you."

Daniel kissed Elizabeth on top of her head. "I hope you are right. I can't live without her."

* * *

Three and a half hours later, a surgeon dressed in blue hospital scrubs, pushed his way through the double swing doors into the waiting room.

"Are you Charlie's family?" he asked without expression.

"Yes, I am Daniel her partner, this is Elizabeth, her mother and this is her best friend, Anne Marie," replied Daniel. "Is she OK?"

"Charlie has had a very serious and very long operation. She had what is known as a heterotopic pregnancy. It is extremely rare and very hard to identify in the early stages of the pregnancy. She had conceived twins but one of the fertilised eggs had not made it down to the uterus, where it should implant to form a viable foetus. Instead, it implanted in one of fallopian tubes which normally funnels the eggs down to the uterus. When this happens, the fallopian tube cannot grow to accommodate the enlarging foetus and if it is not removed it finally bursts the wall of the fallopian tube and you get serious internal bleeding. There is still a long way to go but we hope we have manged to save Charlie's life. I am afraid the twins did not make it."

"Thank God she is OK!" said Anne Marie.

"Well, as I said, she is still very ill and it will take her a long time to recover."

"Why could we not see the other twin on the scan?" asked Elizabeth, clearly devastated by the whole situation.

"It is sometimes impossible to see the second foetus on the scan but the sonographer did take some blood samples to check. Unfortunately, the tube burst before we got the results. In this case we would have lost both foetuses anyway, because of the damage to the uterine wall, as well."

"Can we see her now?" asked Daniel.

"I am afraid she will not come out of the anaesthetic for a few hours. We will let you know when you can see her. If you want to go home for a while and get something to eat, we will contact you there."

"I'm not going anywhere," said Daniel firmly.

"I understand Daniel, but you need to keep your strength up. This is going to be a long haul. We will provide you with a lot of support and help over the coming weeks, but let's concentrate on getting Charlie through the next couple of days first, and then we can go from there."

"Thank you doctor for everything you have done for her," said Elizabeth. "If she needs anything, and I mean anything, please just ask. And please pass our thanks onto your team for saving her life."

"I will," smiled the doctor, "it's what we are here for." And the doors swung shut behind him.

Daniel put his head in his hands and wept. He had not cried since he went to his murdered wife's grave with Charlie, at Mzima Springs in Kenya. Where his wife had been hacked to death by Somali poachers. He did not know what to feel now. Anger, guilt, fear and frustration. Anne Marie put her arm around his shoulders and they wept together in total desolation.

CHAPTER SIX

The Long Road Back

Daniel reiterated his wish to stay at the hospital, to be as near as possible to Charlie. Elizabeth knew she could not see her daughter until later in the evening, so Anne Marie drove her home to explain to Edward what had happened. Anne Marie agreed to look after Abbey for a while and had to get back for a few hours to check on her own animals.

Daniel walked upstairs to the intensive care unit, where Charlie was to be looked after for her initial recovery period. He was not allowed into the private room but could see Charlie through a glass window. She was hooked up to an impressive array of monitors with moving waves of lights and constant beeps. Various tubes were keeping her alive and he took solace from the regular trace of her heart beat.

"Would you like a drink?" asked a passing nurse.

"Thank you. That's very kind of you," he replied.

"Why don't you sit down over there and I will bring you a cup of tea. Sugar and milk?"

"Yes please. How long do you think it will be before she comes round?"

"It varies a lot from patient to patient. She will come round very slowly and it's best not to rush it. She will probably not realise what has happened to her and maybe not even recognise you, to start with. I will give you a call when she opens her eyes and you can sit with her for a while. She will sleep a lot for a couple of days. Just try to comfort her and don't mention the babies at this stage unless she asks you. There is plenty of time for her to understand what has happened and we don't want her to get stressed. It's important that she knows that you love her and are going to look after her."

Daniel sat down on the chair and tried to take in the gravity of what had happened to Charlie, and how she might react to the situation. Although she had never mentioned having a baby, she seemed so happy to be pregnant. Her mother and father were delighted with the news, but that all now laid in ruins. How would she cope with constant well-wishers and reminders of her grief? Daniel knew from his own experience that it lasted for years. Old, long-lost friends and acquaintances that he met years after his wife, Elizabeth's, murder would ask how she was. It was like a razor-sharp knife opening a healed wound every time it happened.

"Here is your tea sir and a few leaflets about what has happened to Charlie and how we, and you, can help with her recovery. She'll need a lot of support and understanding over the next few months. And don't forget yourself in all this. You've got to come to terms with what has happened too. Men are notoriously the forgotten ones in this situation."

"Thank you for the tea nurse. I have lots of questions but the only thing I want at the moment is my Charlie back."

The minutes turned into hours and time dissolved into darkness. A new shift of nurses arrived and they floated in and out of Charlie's room at regular intervals, attending to the monitors and checking her progress. Nothing seemed to change. At eight-thirty Anne Marie and Elizabeth returned to see how Charlie was getting on and gave Daniel a hug.

Anne Marie lent on the glass window of Charlie's room and looked very sad.

"Has she come out of the anaesthetic yet, Daniel?"

"No, they are a bit worried about her temperature going up, so they are going to keep her heavily sedated until tomorrow. They will see how she is then and decide what to do."

"Did they say if she had an infection?" asked Elizabeth, very concerned.

"No but they are checking her every thirty minutes," replied Daniel.

"Daniel, you look really exhausted. Have you had anything to eat since you came into hospital?"

"No. I am fine. I don't want to leave her."

"I will stay with her for a while, whilst you go with Annie to get something at the canteen downstairs. We can't have you keeling over. That's no help to Charlie."

"Come on Daniel, I will treat you to a steak pie and chips; it will do us both good," smiled Anne Marie.

When they had gone down stairs, Elizabeth went up to the window and looked at poor Charlie covered in tubes and motionless. A tear trickled down her cheek and she wiped it away with a tissue.

* * *

Anne Marie and Daniel carried their trays across an almost deserted canteen, apart from an old man sitting in the corner with a half-empty cup of tea. His eyes were red with grief and he was staring, motionless, into his mug. Another life hanging in the balance perhaps.

Daniel didn't know how to feel hungry or anything else come to that. His mind was full of the devastating situation and he pushed the chips around the cold plate aimlessly.

"Come on Daniel, you must eat something," said Anne Marie sympathetically. She put her hand on his and gave it a gentle squeeze. "Charlie will be OK. We will both look after her and nurse her back to life again."

"I just feel so helpless and guilty, Annie. Why did I leave her alone when she was obviously ill? Why wasn't I more careful about getting her pregnant? Why didn't I go to the scan with her; I might have seen something that they missed?"

"You can't think like that Daniel. You love each other and made love together. Charlie didn't ask you to stay at home and I suspect she told you to go. She was perfectly happy to go to the scan with her mother and in fact, I wanted to go but she wouldn't let me. She wanted to go with Elizabeth. I blame myself for not getting to her quicker, but the reality is there was no way that I could have known she was that ill. If she had rung me, I would have dropped everything and been there much sooner. But she didn't. It was a catastrophic event and none of us could have seen it coming. We must pull together now and help her recover. It will be a long road back but we will get there together, eventually."

"I know you are right Annie. You are the best friend anyone could ever have. I really treasure our friendship."

"Anyway, I love her more than you do, so we are in this together," grinned Anne Marie.

"Nearly as much." Daniel managed a hint of a smile.

* * *

It was a long night after Anne Marie and Elizabeth had gone home. Daniel walked up and down the dimmed, windowless corridors like a caged animal. His life felt in limbo and he kept returning to the window of Charlie's room to check the monitors and looking for the faintest flicker of her eyelids. But nothing. He found a machine selling chocolate bars but had no money. A passing cleaner, carrying a bag of rubbish, lent him a pound coin from her nearly empty purse. In the days that followed, he never saw her again to repay the debt. No one seemed to know who she was.

* * *

The following morning at ten o'clock, one of the surgeons, a Mr Harris, appeared, surrounded by a team of junior doctors and a nurse with a green file bursting with patient notes. They entered Charlie's room and Mr Harris looked carefully at the paperwork and listened to the nurse's observations. Daniel waited patiently outside, not able to hear what was said. The doctors finally walked out of the room and the surgeon walked over to Daniel.

"I understand that you are Charlotte's partner?"

"Yes, I am Daniel Knight. Can you please tell me how she is doing?" asked Daniel.

"Charlotte is very lucky to be alive, Daniel. Fortunately, she was found quickly after the rupture happened, and with thanks to the speed of the air ambulance, we managed to rescue a desperate situation. As my colleague told you yesterday, Charlotte had a heterotopic pregnancy and the second foetus developing in the fallopian tube outgrew the capacity of the tube and it ruptured, causing severe damage to her reproductive organs. It also caused profuse internal bleeding into her abdomen which is concerning us now with a possible infection. We are controlling it with antibiotics but she is very weak and I want to keep her sedated for another twenty-four hours. I will review the situation again tomorrow and talk to you again then."

"Thank you. She will make a full recovery in time though?" asked Daniel tentatively.

"Let's take it one day at a time for now. We are doing everything we can Daniel."

* * *

Daniel sat around all morning, checking on Charlie every few minutes but there was no change in her condition. At two o'clock Elizabeth and Anne Marie turned up to see how Charlie was getting on. Elizabeth had brought a small posy of blue freesias which were Charlie's favourites.

"How's she doing?" asked Anne Marie, and Daniel relayed the news from the doctor.

"Why don't you go home for a while Daniel and get something to eat and have a rest. We will stay with Charlie all afternoon and obviously we will ring you straight away if there is any news," suggested Elizabeth.

"I don't want to leave her until I know she is going to be OK," replied Daniel, with guilt still in the back of his mind.

"You look terrible and smell worse," said Anne Marie bluntly. "Do as you're told and go home for a bit. We will take care of her."

Daniel reluctantly agreed and said he would be back at seven. On his way back to the Mill his mobile rang. It was Nzinga at Chyulu.

"I have just heard about Charlie, Daniel. I am so sorry. Is she going to be OK?"

"She is still heavily sedated, so she has not recovered consciousness yet. They say we have just got to take it one day at a time at the moment. Annie and Elizabeth are with her at the moment. I am just nipping home for something to eat."

"I am sure she will be OK. She is a tough lady. Give her all our love and we will have a video call with her when she feels a bit better."

"That's kind of you; I am sure she will look forward to that, when she feels a bit better. How are you and Prince Fahd getting on?"

"We are great thank you. He came over a couple of days ago because Wamwarav's friend, the ranger on the DRC side of the border, thought he saw the white Isuzu truck that was used to take Didi, heading into the Virunga mountains again."

"That's all I need at the moment," said Daniel frustrated that he could not go out there straight away.

"Don't worry Daniel, we have got it under control. Fahd has sent two of his men up there with a military drone that can see infra-red so we can track human bodies even under the vegetation. Anyway, Fahd and his team can't find any sight of the truck or the poachers, so it looks like they were only on a reconnaissance mission this time."

"Does Prince Khalid know his young brother is using his military equipment so he can come across to Africa to see you?" joked Daniel, forgetting all the problems with Charlie for a second.

"I am helping him with his leopard project in Saudi as well!" retorted Nzinga.

"As long as you two are enjoying yourselves. Keep an eye on that lot up in Virunga and tell Wam to check the gorilla bands every few days."

"He's on it."

"Sounds like you have it covered Nzinga. Well done. Keep me up to date with what's going on. I must go now. Thanks for ringing".

"Give our love to Charlie when she comes round."

* * *

Daniel felt much more positive after a hot shower and plate of homemade lasagne that Elizabeth had left in the fridge for him. He laid down on the bed and shut his eyes with exhaustion and did not wake up for two hours. He put on some chinos and the green Fynch-Hatton shirt that Charlie liked. He thought he better take some things into the hospital for her but had no idea what. He filled her washbag with a selection of small colourful bottles and brushes from the bathroom and Charlie's dressing table. He didn't know what any of them were but hoped some would be useful. He grabbed a nightdress and some boring-looking underwear from the drawer and put them into her small leather travelling bag.

He drove back to the hospital at a more sedate pace than last time and went upstairs to the ICU. Anne Marie was leaning up against the glass looking mournfully at Charlie, who was still in the same position as when he left.

"Where is Elizabeth," he asked Anne Marie.

"She had to go home because Edward was not feeling very well."

"Is he OK?"

"I think so; just a bit stressed about Charlie. She's his only daughter and he is very worried about her after everything that's happened," replied Anne Marie.

"Has she made any movements since I've been away?" asked Daniel hopefully.

"No. The nurses keep going in and checking on her but I think it will be tomorrow before she comes round. Was everything OK at the Mill?"

"Yes, all fine. I've brought a few things in in this bag for her. I wasn't sure what she might need. Perhaps when she comes round you could sort it out for her?"

"Of course, I will. I will get her everything she needs," said Anne Marie positively. "I can't wait to see her open her eyes tomorrow."

"The doctor said she might not realise what had happened to her straight away and that she had lost the babies. She only thought she was having one remember."

"I will explain it all to her," said Anne Marie. "She will find it very difficult to start with but we will get her through it. We will have to focus on some positive things, like her new book. We can work on that whilst she is convalescing."

"I hope you are right Annie, but I was reading some of the leaflets that the nurse gave me last night and losing a baby can have a bad effect on a lady even if it is early on in the pregnancy."

"I know it will be very hard for her, but she has both of us to lift her out of any depressions. We need to keep her mind on other things and help her as much as we can. I'll get us a cup of coffee each and then I must get back to take the dogs out for a walk."

Whilst Daniel settled into another long night on a very uncomfortable chair, he decided to ring Sebastian, his computer genius in the Cayman Islands, about the phone call from Nzinga.

"Hi Seb, how's things out there in the sunshine?"

"Apart from the odd tornado, we are both fine thank you. I was sorry to hear about Charlie. Is she getting on OK?"

"How did you know about Charlie?"

"Nzinga rang me up about the white Isuzu in Virunga, to ask me to keep an eye on any internet noise, and she told me then."

"It's a small world! I am with her now in hospital but she is still heavily sedated. They are hoping to wake her up in the morning, so we will know a bit more then. It's been a stressful couple of days Seb. She has been very ill; I just hope she comes through it OK"

"I am sure she will be fine, she's a tough lady Daniel."

"That's what Nzinga said. I am sure you are right. Anyway, have you picked anything up?"

"Nothing yet but I will keep a close eye on things and I have asked my friend in South Africa to keep her eyes open there."

"That's great thanks Seb. Give my love to Marika."

"She can hear you on speaker-phone but has got her mouth full of a rather large bone I bought for her yesterday. Look after yourself and give my love to Charlie when she wakes up."

* * *

At ten o'clock the following morning, Mr Harris, and his entourage, swept along the corridor like the Pied Piper. He went into Charlie's room with her dedicated nurse and looked at all the data from the monitors and charts. He gave instructions to the nurse and came out to speak to Daniel.

"Good morning, Daniel. I hope your night wasn't too uncomfortable. Well, I have some good news for you. The antibiotics are doing their job and Charlie's temperature has come down nicely, so we are going to try to bring her round slowly this morning. It will take a few hours and she will drift in and out for a while so don't expect too much too soon. The nurse will give you a gown and mask to wear and keep your hands clean with the gel provided so we don't get another infection. She will be disorientated at first so just keep reassuring her until she understands what has happened. She will drift off to sleep a lot but that is perfectly normal. If you are worried about anything, just call for the nurse who will come straight away. She will also pop in every fifteen minutes to check on Charlie's stats. Have you got any questions?"

"Can she have a drink if she asks for one?" The only practical thing Daniel could think of, amongst the million other questions about their future.

"Only small sips of water through a straw. Her throat will be dry because of the intubation of her trachea for the operation. The nurse will help you if she asks."

"Thank you for everything you are doing for her. We really appreciate it."

With a small smile, Mr Harris and his acolytes disappeared into another ward to rescue other poor souls. Daniel returned to his chair and waited. After two hours the nurse, called Shirley, appeared with a gown and mask for Daniel. She took him into Charlie's room and put a chair next to the bed so he could hold her hand, which was motionless next to her gown. It was the first time he was able to touch her since the morning before she collapsed. Tears trickled down his cheeks as he felt her warm hand under his. Shirley put her hand on his shoulder.

"She will be fine now Daniel. It will take time but she will be fine. She's a very lucky lady to still be here."

He looked up at Shirley's kind smile and wept some more.

* * *

After about half an hour, Charlie's hand moved imperceptibly at first and Daniel thought he was being wishful. But then again, her index finger moved against his hand. He squeezed her finger gently and it moved again. His heart lifted and he stared at her face looking for any movement. Her left eyelid twitched and Charlie made a small moaning noise.

"I'm here my darling. You are in hospital. I love you."

Charlie moaned again and tried to move. Her face grimaced at the discomfort she felt.

"Just lie still for a while my darling whilst you come round."

Charlie opened her left eye again but could not focus on Daniel. She laid motionless again and drifted off. Daniel pressed the buzzer for Shirley and she came in straight away.

"She is starting to come round but has fallen asleep again. Is she OK?"

Shirley checked a couple of things on the monitor and wrote notes on her iPad.

"She is following the pattern we expect for recovery from the sedation. Don't worry. I am keeping an eye on her on my monitor in my office. Would you like a cup of tea?"

"Thank you that would be good."

When Anne Marie and Elizabeth arrived for their visit, Charlie was still asleep, so Daniel came out to talk to them.

"How is she getting on?" asked Elizabeth.

"She is starting to come round but hasn't said anything yet. She opened one eye a while ago and moved her fingers."

"Can I sit with her for a while?" asked Anne Marie.

"Of course. The nurse is called Shirley. She will fit you up with a gown and mask."

＊ ＊ ＊

Anne Marie held Charlie's hand and stroked a wayward lock of hair from her face. Charlie opened both eyes and looked at Anne Marie, trying to focus. She tried to talk but coughed instead. The nurse appeared and gave Charlie a sip of water through a straw. Charlie tried to speak again, and Daniel rushed into the room and stood at the far side of the bed, taking her other hand.

"We are both here my darling; everything is going to be alright," consoled Anne Marie.

"I remember …" Charlie struggled.

"Don't try and talk my love, your throat will be sore from the operation," consoled Daniel.

"Did I lose our baby…."

"I am afraid so," whispered Anne Marie softly. "But the important thing is that you are going to be well again and we are going to look after you."

Charlie turned her head down to the pillow and a tear ran down onto the white pillowcase. Daniel held her hand firmly and kissed her on the cheek.

"I love you my darling," assured Daniel. "As long as we have each other nothing else matters."

"Is mummy here? I want to see her."

Anne Marie went out to Elizabeth and they swapped places. Elizabeth gave Charlie a kiss.

"I am sorry … Mummy. I couldn't stop it, I was in too much pain."

"I know my love. The only thing we want, is for you to be well again and back home with us."

"I …" Charlie drifted off again and Daniel gave Elizabeth a long hug and they wept together, partly out of sadness and partly out of joy that Charlie was back.

Shirley came to the door of the room. "I think you should all go and get a cup of tea, whilst Charlie has a rest. She is doing much better than I expected but we mustn't overdo it."

* * *

"She must come back to the Hall when she gets out so I can look after her properly," said Elizabeth.

"I think she would be better at home with all her things around her," suggested Anne Marie.

"Let's wait and see what she wants to do when she is feeling better," brokered Daniel, as he carried the not-Earl Grey tea across to the Formica table in the restaurant.

* * *

When they got back to the ward, Shirley advised them all to go home, now that Charlie was out of danger.

"Charlie will probably sleep now until tomorrow. The next few weeks are going to be hard work for all of you, so go and have a nice meal and a good night's sleep. Why don't you come back about ten in the morning Daniel and you can speak to Mr Harris then, and get an update on how she is doing."

"I really want to stay near her," suggested Daniel.

"I know, but you will be no use to Charlie, exhausted and hungry. She will want to see a happy smiling face so she knows you love her and she has done nothing wrong. It is typical in this situation for everyone, especially the mother, to blame themselves for what has happened. You will need to keep reassuring her that it was no one's fault and that the important thing is that she recovers quickly and you enjoy yourselves together again."

"If you promise to ring me if there is any change?"

"Of course. If you give me your mobile number, I will make sure the night team of nurses, have it."

* * *

Daniel and Elizabeth went back to the Hall and Elizabeth got a shepherd's pie out of the fridge and heated it up with some fresh peas and beans from the garden. Edward was clearly upset by what had happened to Charlie and was struggling to come to terms with it. Daniel gave him an update on how Charlie had woken up and was starting to speak again and that seemed to cheer him up a bit.

Anne Marie called into the florist in Bedale and ordered some flowers for Charlie to be delivered to the hospital the next day. The lady in the shop thought she might need a bigger van!

* * *

When Daniel got to the hospital at ten o'clock as instructed, he found Charlie sitting up in bed surrounded by flowers and Anne Marie chatting away to her as though nothing had happened. He didn't know whether to be annoyed or happy for them. He went for the latter. Mr Harris turned up as usual and was delighted with Charlie's progress.

"Charlie is an amazing lady, Daniel. You've got a good one there!" he smiled.

"Now then you two. I thought Charlie was meant to be resting," said Daniel looking straight at Anne Marie.

"We have lots of planning to do. We just can't wait around for men to turn up!" laughed Anne Marie.

Charlie smiled at Daniel and he gave her a kiss on the cheek. "You're looking much better today my darling. How are you feeling?"

"A bit tired and my tummy hurts but they are giving me some painkillers for that, so I am OK. Annie is keeping me busy with all sorts of plans for my book. She has got a specialist editor coming over from America to help us develop the book together."

"That's great, I am not sure where she gets all the energy from!" grinned Daniel looking sideways at Anne Marie. "Are you going to let Charlie and me have a few minutes on our own?"

"Of course. Give me a ring when you want me to come back. I'll go for a walk in the garden outside for a bit."

"I asked them to ring me when you woke up again," said Daniel.

"I know but I wanted to wash my hair and clean up a bit before you came in and then Annie arrived and surrounded me with all these wonderful flowers."

"It's fine as long as you are OK."

"I know we have got lots to talk about, but can we leave that till I get home. I just want to get better for you as soon as I can."

Daniel gave Charlie a kiss and sat next to the bed holding her hand.

"There is one thing I want you to do for me," said Charlie seriously. "I have spoken to the doctor about our twins and I want them to have a proper burial in the churchyard next to Thomas' grave, so he can look after them till we get to heaven. I only want you and me, and mummy and daddy to be there. I am sorry I couldn't bring them safely into this world for you Daniel, but at least we can put them into God's care."

"Of course, my darling," and they broke down and cried in each other's arms.

The Church of St Andrew, Kirkby Malzeard

CHAPTER SEVEN

The Power of Pain –
Democratic Republic of the Congo

Charlie had been in hospital for over a week and was making really good progress with her recovery from the operation. Anne Marie and Daniel visited every day, taking it in turns with the afternoon and evening shifts, although the hospital was very good about flexible times. Elizabeth called in when she could and cooked special little hampers of Charlie's favourite food.

One afternoon, Daniel was driving along the A66 towards Stockton-on-Tees on his daily run, when his phone rang.

"Hi Daniel, it's Fahd. My men have picked up the Isuzu with two men heading up into Virunga about an hour ago. What would you like me to do?"

"Does Wam know?"

"Yes, I have briefed him about the coordinates and he is heading over there with four armed men."

"Could your men block the road out, by felling a couple of trees across the track at a strategic point?"

"Of course. I will fly them up there myself now."

"I don't want you getting hurt or your brother will never forgive me."

"I will be careful; don't worry."

Can Eshe and Jahir fly up to base camp in Virunga and organise things from there. I can't come out to Africa at the moment because I am looking after Charlie. She is still in hospital."

"How is she doing?"

"Really well thank you. I am just off to see her now. Can you give me a ring later and let me know how you are all getting on?"

"Will do. Give Charlie our love."

Daniel was now completely frustrated and conflicted. He did not want to leave Charlie in case she relapsed, but he wanted to be out there tracking down the killers of poor Didi's mother. He thought about it but decided not tell Charlie about the situation because he did not want her to get stressed about it.

Daniel walked into Charlie's room. "Hi darling, how are you feeling today?" and he kissed her on the cheek.

"What's up then?" asked Charlie.

"What do you mean?" replied Daniel in a nonchalant manner.

"Come on, I can tell there is a problem from the look on your face."

"It's nothing, just work stuff."

"Now I'm really worried. If it was unimportant, you would tell me anyway! Come on, I like to know what is going on. It's boring sat in here all day."

"OK, but you are not to get stressed about it. Fahd rang me on the way in today and they have seen the Isuzu truck heading up into the gorilla feeding grounds in Virunga. Wam is on the way up there with some armed rangers and Fahd and his men are going to try and trap them in."

"What are they going to do with them if they catch them. Hand them in to the authorities?"

"Not until they have told us who they are selling the baby gorillas to."

"You need to get out there quickly Daniel or they will kill another female and take her baby."

"I can organise it all from here. Wam and his colleagues are perfectly capable of catching a couple of poachers. In any case I am not leaving you on your own again, until you are completely better. So there!"

"Well, if there is a problem you must go straight away. I am fine now and the doctors say I should be able to come home in a few days, once my stitches have healed up. Annie and mummy can look after me at home whilst you are away."

"So, you definitely want to come home to the Barn then, because your mother offered to look after you up at the Hall for a while if you wanted?"

"I love mummy to bits, but I just want to be back in our home and snuggle up in our bed with you."

Daniel held Charlie's hand and kissed her on the cheek again.

"I do still have lips available," smiled Charlie, and Daniel obliged.

"I love you," he returned the smile. "Now what have the doctors actually said about you coming home?"

"As long as the antibiotics keep any infections under control, and I promise not to lift anything for at least six weeks, they will let me come home. They recommend that I should always have someone with me for the first few weeks in case I have any problems, but I am sure Annie and mummy will be around when you are working."

"Did they ever say anything about the pain in your shoulder?" asked Daniel. "When you were brought into the hospital, the nurse rushed off when I told her about it."

"It's evidently a sign that your fallopian tube is bursting and that blood is leaking into your abdomen. The tip of your shoulder hurts for some reason. I never knew that or I might have gone to the doctors the day before. Anyway, they say the outcome would have been the same, so there is no point in dwelling on it. They had to do a total hysterectomy and take my ovaries out as well. The operation has a long name but I can't remember what the doctor called it. It means we can't have any more children, I'm afraid, but we have got all the children at Father Peter's orphanage in Tsavo and we can concentrate on helping them," said Charlie, positively.

"As long as I have got you, that is all that matters to me Charlie. You changed my life when I first saw you and I love you very much. We have got a million things to do to help our research programmes in Tsavo and Rwanda so hopefully we can make a difference to the planet that way."

Daniel put his arms around Charlie and they hugged each other.

"Now then you two, that's enough of trying to make me jealous!" Anne Marie had arrived with armfuls of books and magazines about publishing and training Labradors.

"Daniel might need to borrow your plane for a quick trip to Virunga," said Charlie. "Can you organise a pilot if he needs one, because I need you here."

"Er, yes. What's going on?"

"Those bloody poachers are back in the hillsides again looking for gorilla babies," informed Charlie.

"I haven't said I am going yet. I don't want to leave you, until I know you have fully recovered," said Daniel.

"Why don't you ask John if that nice lady Suzi is free at the moment," asked Anne Marie, with a hint of levity in her voice.

"Nice lady, eh? I knew you fancied her!" grinned Charlie.

"Well, I thought she was very intelligent and she did save our lives, Charlie," responded Anne Marie sheepishly.

"Pretty sexy body too, I thought!" said Daniel, joining in the joke.

"You two are impossible. I'm off to get a coffee," blushed Anne Marie.

* * *

Later that evening, Daniel was sitting in the kitchen at the Mill trying to do some washing. He had just worked out how the machine worked when his phone rang again. It was Nzinga ringing from base camp in Virunga.

"Hi Daniel, Fahd asked me to ring you with an update. Wam and his men managed to ambush the poachers before they got to the gorilla bands and there was a terrible firefight. There were three poachers this time, not two as we thought, and they were well armed with Uzi machine guns. Wam killed two of them but the third poacher managed to get away into the dense vegetation. They don't know if he was injured or not. Fahd has put up the infrared drone again and they are trying to find him."

"Are all Mav's rangers, OK?"

"One has a superficial arm wound but Fahd flew him back to base here and Wam's wife has dressed it for him."

"Thank God for that! These bastards obviously aren't frightened to kill people, so tell Wam and Fahd to be careful. The poacher will probably still be armed."

"Fahd is assuming that he will try and make his way back to the Isuzu truck so they are setting up another ambush there," reported Nzinga, proud of her new lover's tactics.

"Sounds a good plan. Ask Fahd, if they can possibly get the third man alive; we desperately need to find out from him, who his contacts are, where he is taking the baby gorillas to, and who is buying them. It won't be the end customer but it might lead us in the right direction."

"OK, will do. I will report back later or early tomorrow."

Daniel continued with unravelling the mysteries of their Bosch washing machine, but his heart was in Virunga. He urgently needed to find a lead to Didi, if he was going to get her back alive.

He didn't sleep much that night, thinking about poor Charlie in the hospital ward. He desperately wanted her back home, so he could look after her. He worried about poor Didi stuck in some cage somewhere for the pleasure of some wealthy plutocrat. He was angry at the greed and cruelty of the poachers and dealers who were tearing apart the beauty and delicate balance of nature in Africa. But most of all he was angry at himself for not doing enough to protect all three. If he couldn't have his own children now, he would dedicate his life to the children of Africa and their inheritance.

* * *

"Max, what are you doing today?" asked Daniel on the phone to his friend in America.

"I was going to have peaceful day riding out in the autumn sunshine but I guess I'm not now!"

"How do you fancy helping me track down Didi tomorrow in Africa?"

"Let me check the flights and I will get back to you. Will Nairobi do?"

"Perfect. I will get Jahir to pick you up in the helicopter and fly you up to Virunga. I'll try and be in Nairobi at roughly the same time so we can fly up together."

"I thought you were in Yorkshire?"

"I am at the moment but I will fly out later today."

"Is Charlie coming too?"

"No; but that's a long story. I'll explain when I see you."

"OK. Give her my love and I'll give you a bell with an eta later."

Daniel had just put the phone down when it rang again. It was Fahd.

"We've got him Daniel."

"Is he still alive?"

"He's alive alright but he's a nasty piece of work and we can't get anything out of him. He just reckons he is going to kill us all, even though we have tied him naked to a tree!"

"Don't worry, we will get something out of the bastard when I get there. Ask Wam to round up a couple of bush pigs and some Dorylus."

"What are Dorylus?"

"Wam will explain. Max and I will try and be with you sometime tomorrow, we are flying into Nairobi. Tell Jahir I will need him to pick us up when we land. I will text him an eta landing time. Don't give the bastard poacher any food or water."

"Don't worry. He's not getting any home comforts from us."

* * *

Daniel put the phone down and rang Anne Marie.

"Hi Annie, can you do me a favour?"

"The flight plan is already filed and Suzi is on her way up to Teesside now."

"But how did …?"

"Charlie said there was no way you would not go and to contact Suzi and get my plane ready. Charlie knows you too well Daniel!"

"Promise me you will look after her whilst I'm away. I should only be a couple of days."

"Of course. Nothing would give me greater pleasure. I will spoil her rotten!"

"Thanks Annie. You're a star. I will give her a ring when we land in Nairobi."

* * *

Jahir was waiting on the tarmac at Nairobi with the rotors turning. Max was already on board. Daniel threw his bag in through the open door and jumped in next to Max. They belted up, Jahir took the rotors up to full power and they were on their way to Virunga.

"Thanks Jahir; I will catch up with Max and then come and have a chat with you. Is Eshe OK?"

"She is fine thanks, but obviously a bit upset about what's going on at the moment with the poachers."

"I know, but hopefully we will make some progress now we have one of them to give us some information."

"Good luck with that. He's an arrogant little bastard. We can't get anything sensible out of him."

"Now then Max, how are the Godchildren getting on?"

"They are amazing Daniel. They pick things up so quickly and come out with some really funny stuff they have seen on their iPads."

"How old are they now?"

"Seven and nine but going on seventeen. I asked them if they would like to go to see a baseball match and the reply was – 'We will have to consult our schedules. We are very busy you know!' Jahir has told me about Charlie, I am really sorry she's had to go through that. Is she recovering, OK?"

"She is feeling much better now thanks. It was touch and go for a while but the surgeons did a fantastic job. Annie is staying with her in hospital. I didn't want to leave her but she insisted I came out here, to try and get a lead to Didi, and this poacher might be the best chance we ever get."

"Do you think we can get anything out of him?" asked Jahir.

"If nobody else is looking!" said Daniel, with a cold, hard expression on his face.

* * *

Jahir landed the helicopter in the usual place, near the base camp, and Nzinga and Fahd were waiting for them, in one of the pickups. Nzinga put her arms around Daniel's neck and whispered in his ear. "I am so sorry to hear about Charlie. Is she making a good recovery?" Daniel knew everyone meant well but every time somebody asked after Charlie, the pain and the anger kept rushing back. He replied softly and positively on the outside.

They drove up to the camp but the usual colourful welcome was subdued. Wam's wife came across from her rustic kitchen and offered Max and Daniel a drink before the meal, she had lovingly prepared. Fahd and Nzinga briefed them about the poacher and his vehicle. There was not much to go on but there was a note on the dashboard of the Isuzu with a mobile number and a time written on it."

"It may be nothing," said Fahd, "but it's all we have so far. Nzinga is trying to track down the number."

"OK, well it's going to get dark soon so why don't you radio Wam and say that Max and I will fly up in the morning, as soon as it's light. It's probably best that you and Nzinga stay here and keep an eye on the track up into the gorilla feeding grounds on the DRC side. If the poachers send in any reinforcements, you can warn us, well in advance."

Fahd knew what that meant and agreed he would keep Nzinga out of the way of any unpleasant happenings. They all sat round the fire, eating chikwanga, a local dish based on cassava chips and a hot pepper sauce. Nzinga and Fahd told Daniel about all the improvements they were making to the leopard project in Saudi by using drones and getting students to monitor the pictures. Daniel thought it was a brilliant idea and perhaps they could maybe discuss applying it to the rhino project in Tsavo in due course.

* * *

Daniel was up early the following day and raked over the glowing embers in the fire, left from cooking the evening meal. He filled the smoked-blackened kettle and put it on the fire to make a cup of coffee. After fifteen minutes Wam's wife arrived and made some breakfast for Daniel and Jahir. She had also made up a bag with some food for a couple days for Wam and his fellow ranger up in the forest.

"When do you think you will be back?" she asked Daniel.

"Two days at the most," replied Daniel confidently. "I need to get back home to see Charlie as soon as possible. If you need Wam back here to go and see any of the gorilla bands, just radio him and Jahir can bring him back in the helicopter."

"Thanks Daniel. Do you think you will get anything out of the poacher? Wam has tried but said he was a bit of a nutcase."

"I will do my best," smiled Daniel.

"If you don't have any success, let me have a go!" she laughed.

* * *

Jahir landed the helicopter in a small clearing close to the track where the Isuzu was parked. Wam guided him in, because the trees were very close to the rotors. The down draft flattened the tall grasses and Daniel could see the poacher standing with his back to a small tree with his hands tied behind it.

Daniel threw his bag out to Wam and jumped out. Jahir pushed the rotors back up to full speed and disappeared over the tree canopy. Daniel deliberately did not talk to the poacher or look at him. He walked out of earshot and sat down on a rock with Wam, to get an update on how the interrogation had gone so far.

"He's a complete fanatic. Religious, mental and genetic," relayed Wam. "I've beaten him up a bit and not given him any water but he won't say anything much apart from blasphemous remarks about how we are ruining his life and treating animals better than his family."

"Does he speak any English?"

"I think he does but only talks in the local Congo dialect. It's not a problem because I can understand him pretty well."

"Did you get the pigs and the Dorylus?"

Bush pig

"Yes, the pigs are over there behind that big rock in a crate. The ants are in a bag next to them."

"OK, we will just ignore him for a couple of hours, whilst you make some stew with the meat and veg your wife has put in the bag. I'm going to be nice to him for a bit first to confuse him. Can you sit behind him and jot down anything he says no matter how trivial? It might all mean something at some stage."

"Ask your mate to sit over by the rock. If the poacher tries to escape, he is to shoot him in the legs. Don't let him kill him whatever he does."

When the stew was ready, Daniel walked over to the poacher who was semi-delirious with dehydration. He was leant forwards against the pressure of the ropes binding his hands behind the tree.

"Good afternoon," said Daniel in his calmest voice, even though he was seething underneath. "Would you like some lunch?"

"Fuck off. Do you think I am stupid?" slurred the poacher.

"That's good, at least we speak the same language and can understand each other," replied Daniel winning round one. "You can stay tied to this tree for a week, till you die of thirst or you can come and have a chat with us."

"Fuck off!"

Daniel walked back to Wam and sat down next to the cooking meal and took a long drink of cool water from a flask in the bag.

"That's all I got out of him," said Wam, stirring the pot.

"Just fetch the pigs round and put the basket in front of him and say nothing," instructed Daniel.

"What the fuck are they for?" mumbled the poacher with sweat pouring down his body through the filth. Daniel didn't reply; he just focussed on the stew pot.

The poacher stared at the pigs and then blinked repeatedly as the salty sweat stung his eyes. The midges had bitten his face in the morning and now, in the heat of the day, the red blotches were starting to irritate him but he could not reach his face to relieve the itching. Daniel took another long drink ensuring the captive could see. A pig squealed, the poacher jumped in fear and the rope cut into his wrists. His bare back dragged down the rough thorny bark and it lacerated his skin.

Daniel and Wam started eating the stew and the poacher's eyes widened, the hunger pains gnawing at his empty belly.

"I don't know anything," he groaned. "I am just the poor sod that does the dirty work."

"Would you like a drink and some stew?" asked Daniel nonchalantly. "We're all just workers paid to do the shitty jobs. We will never make any real money. The big guys make the cash."

"You don't fool me with your stupid talk. You arrived in a bloody helicopter. You must be rich."

"Wish it was mine. Belongs to my boss in Mombasa. He deals in ivory out to China," lied Daniel.

"My boss used to do that but baby gorillas are worth more these days," slurred the poacher.

"Fetch him over here and give him a drink," said Daniel to Wam, who got up and untied the poacher. Not believing his luck the poacher looked around deciding whether to run but he saw Wam's colleague with a gun on the rock and thought better of it. He stumbled over to the fire and grabbed the flask from Daniel's hand and took a long swig. The water spilled out of his mouth and down his chin, in his desperation for water. Daniel offered him a bowl of the hot spicy stew and he bolted it down, coughing as the spices caught on his throat.

"So how many baby gorillas do you get each month?" asked Daniel casually.

"About five or six, mostly the lowland ones from down in the river Congo basin. They are easy to catch and no one misses one or two. We only come up here for special orders that my boss gets for the mountain gorillas. I think they are a bit rarer and the collectors like them."

"We need some good people up here to help us get into the gorilla trade," lied Daniel again.

"I thought you were from the government lot," said the poacher ramming some more food into his mouth.

"Well, we work both sides!" laughed Daniel. "We get ten times the money from Mombasa than we do from the useless monkeys that run the ranger service."

"How much do you get paid for each baby you catch?" asked Daniel, feeling he was making some progress.

"Twenty US dollars for a good one. Sometimes more for females."

"If you worked for us, we would give you twice that and a hundred for a mountain one," offered Daniel. The poacher's eyes lit up.

"Ah, my boss and his henchmen know where I live, if I worked for you, he would kill me and my family. They are evil bastards. Money is the only thing that means anything to them. I hate them, but they rule the world where I live and the police turn a blind eye to their trades."

"So where do they send all the gorillas?" asked Daniel pushing his luck. The poacher was starting to get a bit suspicious of all the questions.

"I dunno really. I just take them to a barn on a farm and they pay me cash," he lied. His eyes flashed around. He saw a gap in trees and he ran for it. He stumbled over a galena tree root and fell to the ground. He scrambled to his feet and tried to run again. Daniel pointed to the poacher and a shot rang out from the rifle of Wam's colleague. The bullet smashed through the knee of the poacher and he screamed, crumpling to the ground. Daniel walked slowly across to the agonised heap on the ground and stood over him.

"You have got two options my friend. I can finish the job and bury you with those pigs over there in a deep hole, or we can fix you up and you can tell us all about your boss."

"Fuck off you bastard!"

Daniel dragged the bleeding poacher back to the tree and retied his hands behind the tree.

"You'll not get any more out of me. I'd rather die," he mumbled

"Your death is for certain, you little shit. The only question is how slowly," said Daniel staring him directly in the face. "I want to know who your boss is and where you take the baby gorillas to.

"You've got ten minutes to change your mind or I get the Dorylus."

"Who the fuck are they."

"Siafu to you; Safari ants to eat you alive. It will take five days for you to die in the most excruciating pain possible and then I'll bury in a grave with those pigs so you will go to hell. So, fuck you – the gorillas are starting to fight back," shouted Daniel with fierce aggression in the poacher's face.

Wam was taken aback. He had never seen Daniel so emotional and he was starting to feel uncomfortable with the whole thing. Killing poachers with a gun was one thing, torturing them to death was another, but he kept his thoughts to himself. He knew Daniel was upset about Charlie and that he was frustrated about not being able to track down Didi.

After about ten minutes Wam wandered over to check on the poacher. Blood was leaking from the gunshot wound and he was delirious.

"I think we better give him a drink and stop the bleeding or will lose him before he tells us anything," Wam suggested.

"OK, you do it, but only enough to bring him round."

Wam held a cup of water to the poacher's lips and he took a sip and coughed it out. He took another gulp and seemed a bit revived. Wam tied a piece of cloth, from the food bag, around the knee, to stem the bleeding but the poacher screamed in agony. The bullet had obviously smashed the knee joint into fragments. Wam walked back to Daniel.

"I don't think we have got much longer. He's deteriorating fast."

Daniel walked over to the poacher, with the bag of safari ants in his hand.

"So, what is your name, so I can tell your family how you died?"

"Musango," he muttered, grimacing in pain. "Please don't kill me. I have a wife and three children to look after."

"Where do you take the gorillas to?"

"Goma."

"Where in Goma?"

"I don't know," he lied in defiance.

Daniel slowly opened the bag and scattered the ants over the poacher's body and the insects started to bite into his flesh. The poacher screamed again as the intensity of the pain intensified.

"A big green warehouse… on the Avenue du lac opposite the hospital," he muttered, nearly losing consciousness again.

"And whose is the phone number on the piece of paper in your van?"

"It's the… boss…" His head fell to one side and he lost consciousness completely.

"Radio Jahir and ask him to pick us up," Daniel asked Wam. "I think we are done here".

* * *

The helicopter touched down and Jahir slid open the door. He glanced across at the slumped, bloody body of the poacher now infested with ants.

"Did you get anything out of him?" asked Jahir, as Daniel climbed into the co-pilot's seat.

"Enough," replied Daniel seriously.

As Wam's colleague climbed aboard, a rifle shot rang out and Daniel looked back to see Wam with his rifle at the poacher's head.

"You should have left the bastard to die, like he left poor Didi's mother," said Daniel in a fiercely, revengeful tone.

"That would make us like them," retorted Wam; and he shouted at Jahir "Get us out of this bloody hellhole."

CHAPTER EIGHT

The Route to Retribution –
Johannesburg – South Africa

They arrived back at base camp, as Wam's wife was serving lunch, and they sat around the rustic table discussing how to use the information they had extracted from the poacher.

"So, we have the location they use for the transfer of the baby gorillas but we don't know whether it's owned or rented by the so-called boss or even who he is?" said Daniel.

"Well, we have a stroke of luck there," replied Nzinga. "Seb managed to track down the mobile phone number, from the piece of paper in the Isuzu, to a Mr Van Hoebeek who is a businessman based in Goma. He is involved in the export of timber. He appears to be legitimate, although there are rumours that some of the wood he exports, comes from illegally felled trees in the protected areas of the forests."

"That's great. Do you think you could find out if he is associated with the green warehouse opposite the hospital, that our friend told us about?" asked Daniel.

"I can do that," said Fahd. "We have all the company data from around the world. I will make a call back home and get it checked out."

"Thanks Fahd, that would be great. In the meantime, Max, could you and Mav drive down to Goma and do a reccy of the warehouse and see if you can pick anything up about when they are open etc., so we can plan a break-in to see if we can find anything useful," suggested Daniel. "It may be a red herring but I picked up a lead to an Indian guy near Rustenburg who owns a private zoo. It's west of Johannesburg so keep an eye out for any documents sending stuff in that direction. If this Van Hoebeek is into exports, his staff should speak good English, but Wam can pick up any local dialogue."

"You need to get back to see Charlie," suggested Nzinga. "We can take care of everything at this end for now. I can ring you with an update every day."

"I will have to get back to Saudi too," said Fahd. "I have several meetings this week about our new solar power plant and I can't miss those because they are too important to my country."

"Of course, Fahd. You have been a fantastic help tracking the poachers. We couldn't have done it without you," thanked Daniel.

"I will leave the drone pilots here for now, until my brother sees they are missing," laughed Fahd.

"Jahir, can you take Fahd and me back to Nairobi tonight in the helicopter? I will ring Suzi to get a flight plan booked for Annie's jet back to the UK."

"Will do. I'll get the helicopter serviced whilst it's at the airport and get Bomani to pick me up and take me back to Chyulu until I hear from you."

"Can you stay here Nzinga and coordinate things? Jahir can come and fetch you if Eshe has any problems at Chyulu."

"No problem. I can keep an eye on the gorilla bands with the rangers and talk to Fahd's drone pilots if we need them."

"Good. That's all sorted then. Let's aim to leave about three. Max don't you and Wam take any risks in Goma. It's an information gathering mission. Don't blow anything up – yet!"

* * *

Daniel managed to get some sleep on the flight back and didn't wake up until Suzi touched the jet down at Newcastle. She taxied the plane across to the private hanger and shut the engines down.

"Give my love to Charlie. When she feels a bit better and can drive again, I'd like it if she could come down for the weekend. It'll do her good to have some sea air and relax a bit."

"I am sure she would love that. I'll get her to give you a ring," replied Daniel.

A car and driver were waiting for Suzi and she sped off into the sea fret, drifting in from the east coast. Daniel decided to call in on Anne Marie for breakfast and catch up on the news from the hospital.

"Do you still do good bacon and eggs?" he asked her on hands-free.

"Anything for you! I've got a surprise for you if you hurry up!" Anne Marie said intriguingly.

The motorway was blocked with some minor shunt, so Daniel had to make his way cross-country to Bedale via Northallerton. It was a murky autumn morning and the yellow leaves were falling from the trees and gathering on the road. He was glad to get to the gates of Anne Marie's house. He thought the owls looked cold on their lofty perches.

Anne Marie threw her arms around Daniel's neck and gave him a passionate kiss on the lips. It reminded him of times gone past.

"Well, nobody's looking!" smiled Anne Marie. "Two eggs?"

"And fried bread," he added. "Is Charlie OK? I couldn't ring her yesterday; I was stuck up in the hills on the Congo border."

"Well, that's our surprise!" said Charlie, as she appeared round the kitchen door, walking slowly on two crutches. Daniel was flabbergasted.

"Hello darling, what are you doing here? You never said you were coming out of hospital yet."

"I got bored and discharged myself! Give me kiss." Daniel obliged but was a bit confused having just kissed Anne Marie.

"So, are you well enough to come home?"

"Not really but I am here anyway! The doctors said if I was very, very careful, did nothing and was looked after 24/7 it would be OK."

"So, I am in charge of Charlie and you can only touch her when I say so," grinned Anne Marie. "Now come on or the bacon will burn; and tell us all about your exploits in Africa."

Daniel relayed the events of the last couple of days, which seemed like a week. He left out the interrogation bit as it seemed alien to a Yorkshire breakfast conversation.

"Do you think Didi is in South Africa?" asked Anne Marie excitedly.

"She might be, but I doubt it. I suspect she has been moved on somewhere else. America perhaps? Hopefully Max will be able to give us some more information in a couple of days. So, are we going home to the Mill tonight, Charlie?"

"No! She is staying here with me until she is completely better!" exclaimed Anne Marie firmly. "You can stay as well if you like, and then if you need to rush off somewhere, Charlie is not being moved around like a spare part."

"I would like to stay here for a while until I can look after myself," confirmed Charlie. "I can't even put my own trousers on yet. If that's OK with you darling."

"Of course. The dog and you are here, so I might as well stay as well!"

"That's settled then," said Anne Marie happily. "Earl Grey?"

"Yes please. Suzi sent her love by the way."

"To me?" asked Anne Marie, whose eyes lit up.

"No, she didn't mention you," laughed Daniel.

"I didn't like her anyway!" sulked Anne Marie.

"Yes, you do!" said Charlie. "There's a little flame there somewhere."

"There might be but she never comes to see me."

"Have you asked her?" enquired Charlie.

"No, I am afraid she'll say no."

"Well one of you needs to break the ice or we'll never make any progress," suggested Charlie, smiling.

"She's invited you to go down for the weekend Charlie when you are feeling better, confirmed Daniel.

"See, she likes Charlie better than me!"

"I'll put a good word in for you Annie after I have made love to her!"

"Yours is the burnt bacon!" said Anne Marie half joking.

* * *

The following morning was equally dark and miserable. A stark contrast to the heat of Africa. Daniel was up before daylight and left the ladies in bed. He loaded Abbey and Misty into the Range Rover and drove up to the Hall. He parked in the stable yard and Mac came out to greet him.

"So, how's things out in Africa? I understand you have been hunting poachers?" asked Mac.

"How did you… don't bother to answer that!" laughed Daniel.

"Are you coming in for a cup of tea? I've got the kettle on."

"Go on then. How's Annabelle getting on with the new baby?"

"Alright, I think? Tim looks a bit knackered! I was sorry to hear about your problems. Is Charlie OK?"

"She's staying with Anne Marie at the moment, so she is being spoilt and it's keeping her mind off the operation."

"Are you coping, OK? I know the women folk have to put up with these things but it affects us men too. Just look what it did to poor Tim. If you want to chat anytime you know where I am."

"Thanks Mac. It hasn't really sunk in yet. We'd never really given children any thought till it happened. It surprised us both I think. Anyway, it wasn't to be, so you can only look forwards in life sometimes. I just hope Charlie gets over it OK."

"She's a very special lady, Daniel; I am sure you'll get through it together. Now how are these puppies coming on?"

"I have a sneaking feeling they are being spoilt!" smiled Daniel.

"I have a sneaking feeling you might be right," confirmed Mac. "Look, whilst Annie and Charlie are focussed on Charlie's recovery, why don't you leave them with me for a couple of weeks and I will give them some lessons and get them back on track."

"That would be brilliant Mac, if you think you have got time."

"Well, the boss can't complain can she?!" he laughed. "Anyway, I was going to tell you that Sargent Pickles called in yesterday, to tell you what he had found out about that Indian man at Keighley and the sheep rustling. It appears that it was his younger son who was stealing the sheep. He's a bit thick, I think and got in with a wrong bunch of youths in Bradford. They were rounding up the sheep off the moor and taking them to the barn at the back of his house. A wagon then collected them the following day and they sold them to some rogue farmer in Wales. Funny people the Welsh – I think it's all the rain down there!"

"So, are they going to prosecute them?" asked Daniel.

"It's all a bit difficult really; the father is a councillor and gives a lot of money to various charities around Keighley. His mother does free care work at the hospice two days a week, and his first son is on the Rotary. It wouldn't look good if his other son was in court."

"What happened to British justice?" asked Daniel sceptically.

"Well sometimes you have to bend the rules a bit as I am sure you know Daniel," said Mac with a glint in his eye. "They have packed the son back off to India to work for his uncle in a leather workshop for a year. The father has sent Anne Marie a very generous cheque and also made a contribution to a red squirrel sanctuary above Hawes. His wife evidently met a very nice stranger in a park one day and thought it appropriate! These people are cleverer than you think Daniel. I suggest we let it rest and put it down to self-policing!"

"Annie will be surprised when she gets the cheque; she doesn't even know the sheep have gone!"

"Well, everybody is happy then," grinned Mac.

"I better go in and have a chat with Elizabeth and Edward about their daughter I suppose," said Daniel.

"Aye, they're a bit fed up with not having any grandchildren, but they'll have to get over it like the rest of us. Being rich doesn't make you immune to life!"

"Thanks for having the dogs and let me know how you get on." said Daniel, as he put his coat back on and ventured over to the Hall. Edward was in the kitchen having a cup of tea and a piece of toast.

"Now then Daniel, how did the trip to Africa go?"

Daniel repeated an in-law potted version.

"And how's Charlie getting on. I hear Annie has hijacked her. Elizabeth is a bit upset that she didn't want to come here, as she had got her bedroom all set up."

"I think she was worried about all the lifting and carrying that Elizabeth would have to do, because she is not allowed to do anything at the moment," Daniel fabricated quickly.

"Charlie has always been very considerate like that. I will explain it to Elizabeth and she will get over it."

"Mac has just been telling me all about the Indian rustlers. They seem to have sorted it all out between themselves."

"I never go south of the A59; it's a different world down there," said Edward, not in touch with the modern thinking on such remarks. "I could do with you coming up and having a look at the other new borehole, up at Annie's sheep sheds. We have got to sort out a few details of where to put the control systems."

"Of course, I could do with some fresh air after lunch. I'll go back to check Charlie is OK and pick you up at about half one. Is that OK?"

"Perfect. I've got the accounts lady coming this morning. Dreaded VAT time again!"

* * *

Max and Wam got up early and had some breakfast at the base camp in Virunga. They loaded up the pickup and made their way across the tracks to the Congolese border and headed south on the main NR2 road to Goma. The warehouse where Didi was taken, after her mother was killed, was down near Lake Kivu on the Avenue du Lac opposite the main hospital. The warehouse was easy to find, as all the roads had signs to the hospital. It was painted green, as the poacher had revealed, and was a fairly modern building with a large roller shutter door and some offices to the side, at the front. There were four cars in the car park and the usual security cameras dotted around the building, making a break-in slightly more difficult. They drove passed it slowly a couple of times and secretly took some photographs of the building.

"Let's go into the estate and see if we can get at the back of the building," suggested Max. So Wam drove along the main road into the estate and turned down a cul-de-sac ending next to the back of the green warehouse. There was a steel fence all around the building but another double gate for vehicles, which was locked with a chain and padlock. The yard was littered with old pallets and rubbish but no large piles of timber.

"They must have another yard somewhere, where all the timber is kept," said Max. "Probably down near the quayside so they can move it across the lake without too much attention from the authorities. Let's head down there and see what we can find."

Wam drove down to the lake side and along the Avenue du Port. There were endless small commercial boats being loaded with cargo of every description, from pallets with large white sacks of grain, to battered barrels containing cooking oil. Wam drove along the quayside, slowly passing warehouses, some modern and some from another age. The place was alive with workers fetching and carrying supplies, their bodies covered in sweat from the exertion in the heat of the morning. A bit further on they passed a small yard stacked with rough timber planks but Max felt it was too run down to be the yard they were looking for. The forklift was a rusty heap and the windows in the warehouse were long gone. The sign was written in the local dialect, but was barely discernible as most of the letters had long since peeled away with time. A bit further on was a stall selling drinks so they stopped to get some refreshment and ask the lady, dressed in a colourful yellow Liputa costume, if there were any timber yards along the lake.

"Mbote, two cokes please," asked Wam. "It's a fine day!"

"Yes sir. That will be 4000 francs," replied the woman smiling. "Do you want ice?"

"Yes please; love the dress," charmed Wam, in his best seductive voice. "Are you here every day?"

"Yes sir, my family have sold drinks here for ten years. It is only a small business but we are happy looking out over the lake and catching up on all the local gossip," she laughed. "Are you here on business?"

"I'm looking for some timber to build a boat house on the other side of the lake. I don't suppose you know any wood yards around here?"

"That depends on how much you want to spend. Is it a big expensive boat?"

"It's cool," said Wam. "Fifty foot long with four cabins," he lied. The lady was impressed.

"I would try Van Hoebeek's; it's about ten minutes along the quay. He's not cheap but he has really good stuff and sells it abroad as well, I think?"

"Thanks for your help. I'll give you a ride one day!" grinned Wam. The lady looked willing.

Wam drove along the quay, in the direction the lady had indicated, passed a plethora of colourful boats of every kind. Small traditional wooden boats back from a night's fishing, modern ferries pristine with white hulls carrying tourists to Idjwi Island to see the coffee, cassava and pineapple plantations, and rusting hulks of passenger barges littered with colourful plastic drums and sheeting. As the quay rounded a headland, an enormous timber yard came into view, with mountainous heaps of mahogany, iroko and sapele. Smaller piles of imported eucalyptus and palm trees were also scattered around.

Fishing on Lake Kivu

"What can you see?" asked Max.

"Piles of wood. Why? replied Wam. "What can you see?"

"I can see an enormous bonfire to act as a distraction, whilst we break in to the offices back at the warehouse!"

"Cool! I like it. The eucalyptus wood will get it going nicely. We'll need a timer and an incendiary device of some sort, to start the fire at exactly the right time."

"I wonder if the drones we're using up in Virunga can carry enough weight to do the job?" mused Max. "An aerial attack appeals to me! Let's ask Nzinga when we get back, if Fahd can organise something."

"When do you want to plan the break-in for?" asked Wam.

"Let's go for Saturday night, with a bit of luck they will all be out enjoying themselves, in the bars around town. I will ring Nzinga on the way back to base camp to organise everything and we will come down again on Saturday afternoon and go for it. The sooner the better I think."

"It will teach the bastard to pick a fight with gorillas," laughed Wam.

* * *

Daniel and Edward spent the afternoon measuring up where the controls should be for the new borehole at Anne Marie's sheep shed. It was freezing cold up on the tops and the few beech trees around the steading were fast losing their golden-brown leaves in the horizontal wind coming directly from Siberia.

"Are we done then?" asked Edward. "I think that's the best we can do for now. Can you have a word with the drilling company and see if we can get a better satellite link for the performance monitors? The BT cable up here is out of the arc and it's too far to run a broadband fibre cable."

"Will do; I will give them a ring tomorrow," confirmed Daniel. "I'll drop you off at the Hall and then I am off to Annie's for a hot shower. It's perishing up here."

"Time to get the thermals out!" joked Edward.

* * *

When Daniel got back to Anne Marie's house there was a hint of snowflakes in the air but nothing settling. He found Anne Marie in the kitchen with Jill making a beef casserole for supper.

"That smells good," said Daniel, leaning over Jill's shoulder.

"Want a taste?" she asked, offering him a steaming ladle.

"It's amazing. Secret Yorkshire recipe, I suppose?"

"Actually, it's a New England speciality, so there!" grinned Anne Marie.

"I knew that," Daniel lied. "Where is Charlie? Is she OK?"

"I put her in bed after lunch and said I would take her up a cup of tea about now. I have checked her a couple of times and she was fast asleep. It will do her good."

"If you make a pot of tea, I will take her a cup up," suggested Daniel.

"Coming up!" complied Jill.

Daniel climbed carefully up the stairs, carrying a tray with two cups of tea and a sliced Betty's tea loaf. He quietly pushed open the bedroom door with his foot and found Charlie still asleep. He placed the tray on the Ottoman blanket box at the foot of the bed and sat on the sofa overlooking the lake. The temperature was dropping quickly outside and a mysterious mist hung over the water. It slowly spilled out over the parkland until only the maple tops could be seen hovering above the shroud. A skein of Canada geese flew in a vee formation across the dale, heading for the warmer waters of Lightwater Valley. The leader occasionally turning away from the head of the vee, giving way to the following goose to take up the headwind. The characteristic call of the birds in flight, echoed through the frosting glass of the bedroom window. Charlie stirred under the duvet and opened one eye.

"Hello my darling. Sorry I didn't hear you come in. What time is it?"

Daniel lifted himself off the sofa and sat next to Charlie on the bed, kissing her on the forehead. "It's about half four. I have only been here a little while. Would you like a drink?"

"That would be nice. Let me just nip to the bathroom and clean my teeth. I think the antibiotics are leaving a nasty taste."

Charlie slowly lifted her legs out of bed and sat on the edge for a while, clearly in a lot of discomfort with all the stitches. Daniel helped her to stand up and passed her one of her crutches, taking her other arm and supporting her across the room.

"That feels better," smiled Charlie, shuffling out of the bathroom. Daniel leapt up and helped her back into bed.

"I think it will be while before Byerley gets another gallop up on the moor," said Daniel caringly.

"I will be fine. It will just take a while to get going again. How did you and daddy get on up at Anne Marie's sheep shed?"

"He has it all under control. I think he just wanted confirmation that he had made the right decision about the technical bits of the borehole control system. It's been quite a big project but it will make a massive difference this winter, not having to trail up and down to the river with the tractor and tanker every day."

"I thought you liked driving tractors and tankers, particularly those full of explosives!" laughed Charlie.

"That's different. That's work. Farming is just for fun! There is certainly no money in it!"

"That's true. We only do it because we love the landscape. Are we going to eat the Betty's cake or just look at it!" grinned Charlie. "So, have you heard from Max or Nzinga today? How are they getting on, planning the break-in at the warehouse?"

"Max is planning to bomb the wood yard from the air with an incendiary device under a drone, to create a diversion, whilst he and Wam break into the warehouse and rifle through the files."

"Sounds a bit over the top, even for Max." said Charlie thoughtfully.

"You are probably right, but it'll teach Mr Van Hoebeek not to mess with gorillas, and it'll hurt his pocket."

"When are they going in?"

"They are planning on Saturday night, in the hope that all the staff will be out on the town having a good time."

"Well let's hope they find some transport details that can lead us in the right direction. What about any data stored on their computers in the offices?" asked Charlie.

"That's a good thought, I will tell them to grab any hard drives and I will get Seb to hack into their cloud storage if they have any."

"How will he do that?" queried Charlie. "I thought these places were ultra-secure?"

"They are, unless you have a friend on the inside who builds them. Seb has lots of friends!"

* * *

Back in Virunga, Nzinga had made all the preparations for the attack on Saturday evening. Prince Fahd, her not-so-secret lover, had come up trumps again and arranged for his men to acquire some highly inflammable material from a local chemical works that he owned, something to do with nitro glycerine and quarries.

Nzinga, Max and Wam sat round the open fire on Friday evening finalising the plan for the following day.

"I think we should aim for ten minutes passed nine for the drones to set the wood yard alight," suggested Nzinga.

"If you give it ten minutes to get going and then break into the offices at nine-twenty. You should be OK for about fifteen minutes but the drones have infrared cameras so they can hover over the warehouse, after they have set the fire going, so we can warn you if anyone comes back to the offices."

"Do we know if there are any security men on site after dark?" asked Wam.

"Not that we have seen on their security cameras," replied Nzinga.

"How do you know what their cameras can see?" asked a mystified Wam.

"Something I learnt in Saudi when we rescued Rashieka. If you hack into the cameras, you can see what they see and also, you replay old footage to the warehouse owner, so all he can see is last week's recordings."

"I am glad you are on our side!" smiled Wam. "Are we coming back here afterwards?"

"No. I need all my software stuff back at Chyulu to analyse the hard drives, so I have asked Jahir to pick me up first, in the helicopter, and then we can rendezvous with you down at Goma and all go back to Chyulu together. He can fly you back to Virunga on Monday if that's OK with you."

"Yes, great, whatever."

* * *

Max and Wam arrived at the lake front in Goma just before seven on Saturday night. The sky was clear and the air filled with the joys of partygoers. They drove past the wood yard and, as they had hoped, it was deserted, lit only by the moonlight. So far – so good. They made their way back across town through the dimly lit streets to the warehouse. The lights were still on in the offices and two people could be seen working at their desks.

"Shit," exclaimed Wam. "Now what do we do?"

"Don't panic. We still have plenty of time before the air drop and we can always delay it if necessary. I will give Nzinga the heads up, so she knows there might be a problem."

Max parked a discrete distance away, across the road in the hospital car park. Wam opened up the backpack his wife had prepared and they ate the pork sandwiches and croissant she had made for them. Wam checked the Heckler & Koch handguns in the bag and handed one to Max.

"Hopefully we won't need these but it's best to be prepared," said Wam. "I've got the bolt-cutters for the gate padlock and the small angle grinder to take out the office door. And two lumps of plastic explosive if all else fails!"

"I hope you are better with that stuff than Anne Marie is," laughed Max.

"What was she doing with explosives? I didn't know she helped Daniel in the field?"

"Oops! Forget I said that," replied Max sheepishly. "I thought you knew about her exploits on the island."

"No, but you better tell me the full story now you have started. We have got two hours to fill!"

* * *

At nine o'clock, Max was just about to call the air drop off, when the lights went out in the offices and two girls came outside laughing and joking with each other, locked the doors and drove off into the night.

"That's lucky! God must be on our side," smiled Max. "OK let's drive round the back to the gates and wait for the fireworks."

At exactly ten past nine as planned, there was a muffled explosion down at the docks and huge fireball lit up the night sky. Police sirens screamed and the hordes of fun lovers spilled out of the restaurants and night clubs to watch the flaming spectacle.

"OK. Nzinga has text that the drones are overhead so let's go," whispered Max. Wam grabbed the bag with the bolt-cutters in and they crept up to the gates. The bolt-cutters made easy work of the simple padlock and they ran amongst the rubbish piles to the rear door of the warehouse. An automatic overhead light came on but Wam soon dispatched it with the pistol.

"Can you cut the lock with the angle grinder?" asked Max.

"The hinges will be easier," replied Wam and with two swift cuts the door fell open. They waited a few seconds to see if anyone had heard but the locals were more interested in the mahogany bonfire. They walked inside to a shambolic office with paperwork everywhere.

"Where the hell do we start. This could take hours!" exclaimed Wam.

"It looks like there are two main computers; you release them and put them in the pickup whilst I run through the desk over there. It looks like the boss's chair next to it."

Wam pulled out the cables and carried the boxes out to the car. Just as he got to the gates, two rough-looking men appeared from the shadows and challenged him.

"What the hell are you doing!" shouted the bigger guy in a bright yellow shirt. "Ring the boss," he ordered his diminutive sidekick.

"That's not a good idea," said Wam calmly. "Just walk away my friends. This is out of your league."

The yellow shirt pulled a flick knife and moved aggressively towards Wam. The little one egged him on.

"Don't do it!" warned Wam. They continued their approach aggressively.

Two shots rang out and they fell stone dead to the floor. Having killed them, Max put his gun calmly back in his belt.

"I had it under control," claimed Wam unrealistically.

"We haven't got time for long conversations with dross like them; put the boxes in the car Wam and come back inside to help me. I can't get the desk draw unlocked."

Wam made short work of the desk with his grinder. The desk top came off in one piece without touching the locks. Max grabbed some papers and they both scanned through the documents. Shipments of wood all around the world but mostly the US. Nothing to indicate anything else.

"Now what?" asked Wam.

"What's in the metal filing cabinet over there?"

"It's locked… it's not now!" smiled Wam having unzipped the front with his favourite weapon.

They each grabbed a hand full of files and flicked through them.

"Bingo!" said Max. "Shipments to Johannesburg. Looks like one every couple of weeks."

"How do you know it's for the baby gorillas?"

"You don't send timber by private jet!"

"Is there a delivery address?"

"There sure is. Right, let's get out of here."

"What about the two bodies?" asked Wam.

"Collateral damage. That's just between you and me. We wouldn't want to upset the ladies!"

"Wouldn't Nzinga have seen what happened on the drone camera?"

"Shit, I forgot about the spy in the sky!"

Max and Wam jumped into the car and with a squeal of tyres sped out of the estate and headed for the rendezvous with the helicopter at Gisenyi airport just over the border in Rwanda. When they arrived at the semi derelict airport, there was no security and the helicopter was already running and ready for take-off.

Nzinga slid open the helicopter door and Max and Wam jumped in with their bags and the computers.

"OK Jahir let's go," shouted Nzinga above the relentless thunder of the downdraft and they took off and headed for Chyulu.

* * *

Charlie, Daniel and Anne Marie were sitting in her kitchen having smoked haddock and dauphinoise potatoes with a gruyere sauce, when Daniel's mobile rang. It was Nzinga with an update from the helicopter. The connection was terrible so he took the phone, and his glass of grenache wine, into the study where there was usually a better reception.

"The line is awful Nzinga. I can hardly hear you."

"Missi……….. successf……. got address in Joburg…… and computers….will talk later."

"OK. Brilliant! Ring me tomorrow when you get back to Chyulu."

Daniel walked back into the kitchen and topped up his glass from the bottle on the dresser.

"Can we have a top-up too?" admonished Anne Marie with a grin. "What's happened?"

"Sounds like mission accomplished. They have found an address in Johannesburg. Nzinga is texting it across later. I will get Fahd to do a run down on the business at that address and get Seb to do a cloud search once Nzinga has fired up the computers they have acquired."

"Are they both safe?" asked Charlie.

"I assume so. I forgot to ask!" replied Daniel.

"Typical!" said Anne Marie. "Let's have a toast to Didi and her safe return."

They touched glasses and finished off the fish. Anne Marie made the coffee whilst Daniel fetched some locally made Wensleydale cheese and biscuits from the pantry.

"So, what happens next?" asked Charlie. "Are you going down to Johannesburg to find the traffickers?"

"Not unless I have too. I want to stay here with you. Max can take Bomani and Thulani with him. They will enjoy an expedition with the possibility of a fight at the end of it!"

"Do you think it will be dangerous?" asked Anne Marie.

"Could be. When you get closer to the end customer the financial numbers get substantially higher, and risks bigger, but the lads know how to look after themselves."

"Now Charlie, I think we should be getting you back into bed," suggested Anne Marie. "You shouldn't really be drinking whilst you are on antibiotics and painkillers."

"I am fine, stop fussing. The wine works better than the painkillers anyway,"

* * *

Daniel got up early as usual and left Charlie in bed, still asleep. He made himself a cup of tea and some toast and walked through to the study. There had been a light fall of snow on the moors above Leyburn overnight and the lake was covered in a thin layer of ice. The mallards were sitting on the edge trying to decide where today's meal was coming from. He looked through the messages on his phone and found the address in Johannesburg from Nzinga.

'*Woodside, Rudi Street, Bronkhorstspruit, Johannesburg. South Africa (near Petit Airfield).*'

Daniel decided to ring Max as they were three hours ahead at Chyulu.

"Hi Max. Well done for yesterday. Did it all go to plan?"

"More or less. A couple of self-defence jobs but no loss to humanity."

"How is Nzinga getting on with the computers. Any joy?"

"Not really. She got into them OK. The security was pathetic but there is no evidence that would hold up in a court. The only thing she has found is that the private jet landed at Petit and not OR Tambo International airport in Johannesburg. Why would a private jet risk landing at a derelict dump like Petit if they were legit?"

"Agreed. Have you had a look at this Woodside place on Google maps?"

"We have done better than that. Nzinga rang Fahd and he got some satellite images, from what we are not allowed to talk about. It's quite a smart ranch type house with a couple of barns that look like indoor stables. There is no visible security, like wire fencing etcetera, but there might be electronic stuff we cannot see."

"Did Fahd check the address out for company status?"

"Yes. It's owned by some offshore company based in Barbados with nebulous directors. Nzinga has sent the details to Seb in Cayman and he is working on it."

"What do you want to do then? I don't really want to leave Charlie again until I have to." said Daniel.

"That's fine. I was talking to Bomani earlier this morning and he is up for a trip down south, as long as I take him to a night club in downtown Joburg afterwards!"

"He's got a one-track mind! You better take Thulani as well, in case you hit real trouble. These guys will be well-paid and professional."

"OK. We will build up a plan to go on Tuesday and I will come back to you to confirm."

"Thanks Max. Don't take any risks. Speak later."

Daniel walked over to the window and scanned the lake for the mallards but they had been replaced by two otters playing on the bankside.

The larger one gingerly placed a paw on the ice but it would not take the weight and caved into the freezing cold water. The otter was not perturbed and dived straight in, protected by its thick dense fur coat. His mate soon followed and they shattered the ice into fragments as they frolicked in their freezing domain. 'I hope the Koi are asleep on the bottom,' thought Daniel, 'or it will be fish for breakfast.'

"I didn't know you liked otters?" came a voice from behind him.

"Hi Jill. I didn't hear you come down. They're amazing creatures aren't they? Don't seem to feel the cold."

"They have been here a couple of weeks. I think they are only passing through to the river Ure but they are fun to watch in the mornings."

"Does Anne Marie know they are there?"

"No. I think we should leave them to their own shadowy world. They deserve their quiet piece of the Dale."

"Any more news on our friendly Russian?"

"Not sure if he is friendly but he is still around, unfortunately. He is a persistent little Marxist. He was down at Ripon Farm Services last week asking questions about slurry tankers for pigs. They rumbled him straight away but he disappeared before they could work out what he was up to."

"How did you find out about it?"

"I made their service engineer a cup of tea last week, when he came up to give the big baler its annual service, and we were talking about foreign tourists and he just came out with it. Their boss thought he might be Ukrainian and not Russian from his accent because he had been out to Ukraine looking at Joskin tankers for importation. He thought it was all a bit odd but nothing more."

"Was it definitely the same guy?"

"I'll ask a couple of people I know in the offices at Ripon Farm and see if they saw him?"

"Saw who?" interrupted Anne Marie, who had just appeared at the door of the study in her dressing gown.

"Oh, just this Russian guy who keeps popping up all over the Dale asking questions."

"I'll go and put the bacon on for breakfast," said Jill making a discrete exit.

"I didn't know you had told Jill about him."

"I thought I should just brief her, as she is staying with you at the moment, so she knows what to keep an eye open for."

"Are you sure we can trust her?" whispered Anne Marie.

"I am sure we can," whispered Daniel back, not letting on the history between them. "Have you checked on Charlie yet?"

"It's a good job somebody cares for her," smiled Anne Marie. "Yes, she is fine. I have taken her a cup of tea and I am just going to help her have a shower."

"Don't get carried away!" smiled Daniel.

"What me with Charlie? Never," she lied.

* * *

After breakfast Daniel asked Charlie if she felt up to being driven to the Hall to see her mother and father.

"Snap! I was going suggest the same thing. I will give them a ring and see if they are around for lunch."

"No heroics mind you. Just the house. No horses or dogs."

"OK I promise," said Charlie with her fingers crossed behind her back. Her endless stoicism rekindled she thought.

* * *

As they turned into the familiar park gates of the Hall, Charlie turned pale, as her mind flashed back to the hospital and her loss of the twins. Tears filled her eyes and her inner strength evaporated in an instant. She froze. "Daniel please stop the car."

Daniel pulled slowly onto the verge and switched off the engine.

"Are you OK my love? What's wrong?"

Charlie said nothing, fell into Daniel's arms and sobbed uncontrollably, as the pain of her loss surfaced for the first time. It would haunt her for the rest of her life, erupting from nowhere when she least expected it. Daniel cradled her head and kissed her hair. He felt helpless but knew the pain Charlie was in, from the loss of his wife all those years ago. Charlie had helped his catharsis then. Now was his turn. Such is true love. They sat together for twenty minutes until Charlie had the strength to speak.

"I am sorry Daniel. It all just came flooding back. I thought I could control it and I can't. It frightened me. I was naked, my heart bleeding, and my soul ripped to shreds. I don't know what to do."

"I will always be here for you, my love. We will get through this together. It will take time. We will never forget them. They are part of our lives together and always will be. We will work together to build an inheritance for them that they will be proud of. They will look down, when we are gone, and say 'look how our mother and father made the world a better place for all the creatures on the planet and mankind itself.' We have a big job to do Charlie, and they will help us make it happen."

Charlie lifted her head and smiled at Daniel and he wiped away her tears.

"I love you my darling," she whispered. "Let's go and find mummy."

* * *

Max spent the afternoon at Chyulu formulating his plan for Johannesburg. He despatched Thulani down to Daniel's friend in Athi River to pick up some AK-47s and ammunition, for if things got ugly. He also borrowed Wam's plastic explosive and detonators in case he needed more firepower. Although it was over 2000 miles, he decided Jahir would take them in the helicopter. It would give them more flexibility at that end and also, if Didi was there, they could bring her back to Chyulu. In any case airlines were funny about AK-47s on a passenger plane!

"Seb has just rung me with some really interesting news," said Nzinga excitedly. "He has picked up some intel that Van Hoebeek, whose wood yard you reduced to ashes, has recently had telephone communications with a mobile somewhere in China. As far as Fahd can tell, he has no export arrangements with China and there are no previous communications with the Chinese. Maybe just a coincidence?"

"Well let's hope Didi has not got sent to China because we have no hope of retrieving her from there," suggested Max. "Has he found anything else out about the owners of the ranch house in Joburg?"

"No. It's all dark web stuff and bitcoin trading, which might link in with the Chinese. Most of the so-called bitcoin mining was done in China, until recently, when their government had the sense to shut it all down."

"I know. Most of the mining has now moved to Texas. God knows what the US government is doing letting that happen. It's just a criminal currency that gives thieves, poachers and drug dealers anonymity. It will all come crashing down one day."

"So, what do you think you will do when you get there?" asked Nzinga.

"I don't think we have much choice really. If we go around asking questions, we risk getting rumbled before we get a chance to break in. We will just have to lie low and observe what goes on for a couple of days and then go in guns blazing."

"Doesn't sound very sophisticated!" observed Nzinga, with a wry smile.

"Well unless Fahd or Seb come up with anything in the meantime, we have to make the best of it. I will ring Daniel later on and see if he has any other ideas."

* * *

Daniel was enjoying a quiet half hour to himself in Anne Marie's library with a glass of the malt whisky that he and Charlie had won at the Boxing Day flush two years before. Anne Marie was helping Charlie into bed and Gill was having the evening off and staying with her sister in Hawes. His phone rang.

"Hi Max. How are the plans going?"

"Well, they are not really. We know where we are going and why, but the how is proving a bit challenging. We can't get any intel on the place, about who or what's inside. It all looks innocuous from the satellite footage, but short of bursting through the front door, to find out, we are stuck. We can't blow our way in, in case Didi is inside and in a vulnerable situation."

"Mmm. OK you get yourselves down there and I will try and pull a few favours this end to try and help."

"Jahir is going to fly us down for obvious reasons, but it's long haul in a chopper."

"Still, it does give you options to get out quickly if you have to. Just remember though, Jahir is not up to combat like the other two, so look after him."

"Will do. We will set off tomorrow mid-morning and camp somewhere remote when we get there. I'll walk into town and hire a pickup so we are mobile."

"Sounds half a plan!" joked Daniel. "Take care."

* * *

Daniel rang his contact at Menwith Hill and explained the situation in Johannesburg. His friend offered to help in exchange for a little job he needed doing in Australia!

"Not next week I hope!" laughed Daniel, but agreed to take on the job.

"What job is that?" asked Anne Marie, sitting down next to Daniel on the sofa.

"Not sure yet. Something to do with the bloody Chinese again. I am going to have to learn Mandarin at this rate! Is Charlie OK?"

"Yes, she is asleep already. I love sitting and watching her sleep; she is so beautiful Daniel."

"I know. I am very lucky. She got very upset today about losing the babies. I think it is only just sinking in how nearly she died; and not being to be able to have children again."

"It's been a terrible few weeks for her Daniel, but we will get her through it together somehow."

"You're wonderful Annie. I don't know what I would do without you."

"Well, you are never going to find out! Right, I am off to do night stables. Aiden is off as well today. I will be back in ten minutes and we can finish off the malt together!"

After fifteen minutes, Anne Marie reappeared looking ashen-faced and dishevelled.

"Christ! What's happened Annie?" asked Daniel jumping to his feet.

"That bloody Russian was lurking in the hay bales. I went to fill Harry's hay net and he sat up from between the bales. He scared the living daylights out of me."

"Did he touch you?"

"No, he just scared me, Daniel. I didn't know what to do. He jumped down off the bales and ran out of the barn doors and up the field in the dark. I don't know where he went to after that. I'm shaking – I thought he was going to kill me."

"Come here, I will give you a hug. If he was going to kill you, I am afraid he would have done it straight away. It's all very strange. He clearly is not a Russian agent, unless he has gone completely off-piste."

"Do you want a drink?"

"No just keep cuddling me," smiled Anne Marie. "I'm enjoying it!"

"Good job Charlie is in bed or she might get the wrong idea!"

"Right idea, you mean."

"Enough of that. Malt whisky?"

"You better warn Aiden and Jenny that there is a vagrant about and to be careful going up to the stables at night. And don't you go up without Jill or me."

"So, what's all this with Jill then? She is clearly more than just a housekeeper with all your whispering and secret liaisons?"

"What secret liaisons?" asked Daniel trying to maintain the story.

"The ones up on the gallops in the mist."

"How do you know about that? You're getting more like Mac every day."

"Sexier though!" laughed Anne Marie. "Jenny saw you up there. She is into her betting and likes to watch the morning exercise, to spot the winners. She thought you might be having an affair with Jill!"

"I hope you squashed that rumour; I don't want Charlie getting upset?"

"Yes, don't worry. I said you were too old for all that stuff."

"Thanks!… Jill is an old friend and I asked her to look after you, living on your own. You can trust her completely."

"Another old flame, I suppose?"

"Shut up and go to bed."

"Yes master!"

* * *

Daniel was just about to go upstairs to bed when his mobile rang again. It was Menwith Hill.

"You know that job I said we wanted doing in Australia? Well, we think we might be able to kill two birds with one stone. We think your baby gorilla is in Australia?"

"How do you… don't bother answering that. Where exactly in Australia?"

"I am not authorised to tell you that yet."

"It's a big country you know!" jested Daniel. "Needle and haystack come to mind."

"It's very politically sensitive Daniel. Very. It could start World War III if you get it wrong. Just get yourself to Perth. We will book you into a safe house out of town. You can take one man with you that you trust completely. If anything goes wrong you are on your own."

"What's in it for me?"

"A baby gorilla called Didi. Don't be greedy. We might throw in a few quid if it goes well."

"When do we need to be in Perth?"

"By the weekend."

"But Charlie is not well at the moment. I really need a few weeks."

"Is she going to die?"

"No."

"Get a babysitter and get on the plane. Leeming Saturday morning. Six sharp. Bring your own H&K we will provide the rest."

"You're all heart!"

CHAPTER NINE

The Golden Pathway –
Lake Lefroy – Western Australia

Daniel went upstairs and crept into the bedroom. Charlie was in a deep sleep and did not stir. He took off his clothes and slid into bed next to her. The warmth of her naked body, next to his, made him smile and he put his arm around her shoulders. He knew that on Saturday he must leave her again and continue his restless search for Didi. Not just for one small baby gorilla but for the preservation of all her kin in Virunga.

* * *

"Now what's gone wrong? asked Charlie, knowing the look on Daniel's face, as he appeared round the bedroom door with a tray of toast and two cups of Betty's tea for breakfast.

"Well, it's good and bad news!"

"Tell me the good news first," smiled Charlie.

"We think we know where Didi is."

"That's amazing. Where?"

"That's the bad news. Australia!"

"Where in Australia? It's a big place."

"I don't know that till I get there."

"So how do you know she is definitely there?"

"Five Eyes."

"That makes me nervous. Why are they interested in an orphan gorilla?"

"Mutual target they think."

"Why can't they sort it out themselves?"

"Evidently, politically difficult."

"It's always politically difficult. They just don't like taking risks, so they can blame someone else if it all goes wrong."

"Something like that. You don't mind if I go do you? Annie will look after you whilst I am away."

"No, it's fine. She's better at it than you anyway!" grinned Charlie. "I suppose you have asked her if it's, OK?"

"Not exactly."

"That's a no then!"

"She will love having you around for a bit longer."

"Annie would love having me around forever!"

* * *

"Yes, yes, yes," cried Annie so the whole house could hear, when Daniel finally got round to asking her if it would be OK. "No need to rush back!"

"Thanks Annie you are a star."

"When are you going?"

"Early Saturday morning."

"How long will you be away for?"

"Not sure, yet. A while."

* * *

Later that morning Daniel rang Max.

"Hi Max. I've picked up a bit of intel that Didi might be in Australia. We need to get down there asap. Is that OK with you?"

"How long for?"

"About six months."

"Have you told the girls yet."

"Not exactly."

"That's a no then. Your impossible!"

"It's better if they get used to the idea slowly."

"Good luck with that one. I don't understand women. They terrify me. What about the Joburg mission?"

"I still want you to go down there and just blow the shit out of the place. If there is anybody in there, great. Just check the stables for wildlife before you press the button."

"Will do. Then what?"

"Get a plane to Perth on Sunday and I will send you a location to meet up."

"Do I need to bring anything with me?"

"Just your brains! This might be a tricky one."

"I suppose there is more to it than just a baby gorilla?"

"Could be."

* * *

The RAF Boeing Globemaster transport plane touched down at the Royal Australian Air Force Base Pearce, in Bullsbrook, north of Perth on Sunday afternoon. Daniel was glad to be on the ground again after the tedious long-haul.

"Thanks for the lift," Daniel shouted to the load master and impromptu chess partner, who had made the trip more bearable.

"Bit of a boil-over! Never beaten the flight deck before," replied his new Aussie mate. "Enjoy the sunshine!"

Daniel slung his much-travelled rucksack over his shoulder and crossed the tarmac towards the main building. Half way across the searing hot concrete an old Land Rover Defender pulled up next to him, driven by a very attractive young lady wearing a blue tracksuit and orange trainers.

"Looking for a young lady by any chance?" she smiled.

"That depends?" queried Daniel, hesitantly.

"This one's a bit hairy and cute!"

"Sounds my sort of girl," replied Daniel.

"Jump in. I know a quiet place we can get more acquainted."

Daniel climbed into the familiar sparse surroundings of the Defender cab and they sped across the airbase and headed for a small hanger on the edge of the airfield. The girl climbed aboard an ageing Pilatus PC-9 trainer and indicated Daniel to climb in behind her. She turned over the single prop and the engine burst into life with a cloud of not very environmentally friendly exhaust.

"Where exactly are we going to," shouted Daniel over the scream of the propeller.

"Widgiemooltha."

"Will this crate get us that far?" asked Daniel sarcastically.

"This is Australia. When it falls out of the sky, we will stop using it!"

"Very reassuring!"

"Sit back and enjoy the scenery. This is going to take a while. It's a big country you know."

Too big, thought Daniel. Maybe the Globemaster wasn't that bad after all. At least it had a toilet.

* * *

After what seemed like a million years the girl touched the plane down on a deserted saffron-coloured dirt track. It was a bumpy landing and the prop threw up clouds of dust, swirling high in air, until the whole aircraft was lost in a sandstorm.

"My name's Daniel by the way."

"Jondi. Pleased to meet you. Follow me."

Jondi lead Daniel along the deserted street, long since abandoned by the unsuccessful gold-prospectors of years gone by. It reminded Daniel of a set for one of those Spaghetti Westerns. If Clint Eastwood had come round the corner, cheroot dangling from his lips, he would not have been out of place. At the end of the street was a tumbled down hotel, but at least it had a roof. Jondi kicked open the front door, walked across the old bar, cluttered with empty bottles, and climbed the broken wooden stairs to the landlord's rooms. To Daniel's amazement the first room was clean and tidy with two beds, a table and two rustic chairs.

"This will be your base for the next few weeks. We might have to move you around occasionally but you should be reasonably safe here. The town is completely deserted but you are near enough to the highway to drive up to the mine quickly. There is a small solar generator out the back, with a diesel back-up. I will give you a code for the satellite phone on the table and you can contact me safely on it 24/7. Any questions so far?"

"My partner is flying into Perth tonight. What's the best way to get him here without alerting anybody?"

"We've organised Max a pickup at the airport. He can buy some supplies and drive over here. He should be here late Monday. It's a long drive but it will save a lot of questions trying to hire a vehicle locally."

"Armoury?"

"Two Heckler & Koch MP7s. Fitted suppressor and tritium-illuminated flip-up night sight. Nine hundred and fifty rounds a minute; effective range 200 metres. Fiocchi CPS black tip ammunition; defeats Kevlar body armour. You'll find them under the floor by the sink. I was told you have your own H&K handgun. Ammunition for the toy, same place."

"Cavalry?"

"None. You're on your own. We don't know you exist."

"Exit plan?"

"If you can get down to the coast at Esperance, we have a rubber dinghy there," she laughed.

"Thanks. What's the plan?"

"I have no idea. Not my security level. We will be in touch on Tuesday when Max gets here. There's a local tourist guide with the armoury. Have a fun evening."

Jondi lit up the old prop and disappeared in another mechanically induced sandstorm. Daniel sat down on a creaking chair and looked out, through the opaque glass window panes, covered in spider's webs and a century of nature claiming back the building. He enjoyed the isolation and the anticipation. He thought about Charlie and hoped Annie was looking after her well. He lifted the floorboard by the sink and checked the automatics. He picked up the tourist guide and flicked through the pages. Widgiemooltha was just off Route 94, the Great Eastern Highway from Perth to Kalgoorlie, where most of the working goldmines were. Lake Lefroy was to the north and Lake Cowan to the south. Both lakes were ephemeral salt lakes, usually covered with a thick layer of crystalline salt except when there were exceptionally heavy rainfalls. Daniel was just about to put the guide down when a small piece of plain note paper slipped from the back cover.

Target: Wangkatha Gold Mine – active, open pit and underground workings

Owner: Jack Kilpatrick – no known family – origin Perth

Links: Politicians/Investment banks/Educational establishments

External connections: Hong Kong/China

Location of residence: large estate – south bank of Lake Lefroy – heavily guarded

Wealth: Unknown – mostly off-shore. Assumed substantial

Crimes: no convictions – no active cases

Reason for target: secret

READ and BURN

Daniel pondered the contents in the failing light. He found some matches by the sink and struck one against the box. The flame flickered around the walls and flashed back from the window panes. He lit the bottom edge of the paper and it was soon consumed. He dropped the blackened remnants in the sink and it shattered to dust. Welcome to Australia he thought.

* * *

Later the following day, Max drove up to the hotel in a Ford Ranger pickup, covered in a thick layer of the ubiquitous red dust. It had seen better days.

"Welcome to Widgiemooltha!" said Daniel seriously.

"Is this all the Aussies can afford?" enquired Max with a smile.

"Apparently. It gets better inside. Slightly!"

They gathered up the supplies from the back of the truck and Daniel lead Max up the rickety stairs to the bedroom.

"Slight was an overstatement. Frugal would be more accurate," said Max walking around the room and inspecting the non-existent luxuries.

"So how did Joburg go?"

"Not quite as we expected. The stables were like a neonatal zoo; full of baby chimpanzees, evidently destined for South America, we found out later."

"What about the game dealers in the house?"

"There was some sort of party going on, so we waited till dark and set fire to the place with some of the incendiary devices left over from the wood yard."

"Did any of them escape?"

"Two girls ran out; hookers we thought, so we let them go. Three men attempted to dash out at the end, in flames. We thought it only right to put them out of their misery on humanitarian grounds."

"What happened to the chimps?"

"When Jahir had got us far enough away in the helicopter, I rang the local rangers and they rescued them. They knew about the place but were too scared to raid it themselves. Evidently the local police force was on a back-hander to ignore what was going on."

"Are the lads, OK?"

"Well, you know what their like; always up for a fight in a good cause. Jahir might need a bit of TLC but I'm sure Eshe will take care of that. What's the story here then? Do we know where Didi is?"

"Not far away, but it's complicated!"

"It's always bloody complicated when you're involved."

* * *

On Tuesday morning at nine-seventeen the phone on the table rang.

"Name of your escort yesterday?"

"Jondi."

"Head out to Route 94 and drive south for about twelve kilometres and you will see a track into Dordie Rocks Nature Reserve. Turn into the reserve and you will see an Avida Motorhome, with a slide out, parked on its own. Park 200 meters away from it. If there is no one around come over. Leave your guns in the pickup. If we have company, go for a walk for half an hour and keep coming back till it's clear."

"Understood," replied Daniel.

* * *

When Daniel and Max got to the reserve, the motorhome was parked on its own, near some rocks as advised. There was no one else around.

"Put your gun above the sun-visor, loaded and with the safety lock off," Daniel instructed Max. "If we need it, it will probably be too late, but at least it gives a chance."

"What about yours?" asked Max. "I thought these people were on our side?"

"They won't find it and nobody is on our side. The only person we can trust is each other."

The motorhome door was opened by an overweight, ruddy-faced yokel in shirt and shorts, featuring multicoloured dinosaurs. He looked more like an illywhacker than an agent of some sort.

"Come on in sports and have a beer," he offered.

"Bit early for us," replied Daniel suspiciously.

"Shame. I'm *Shane Warne* and this is my friend *Dundee*."

"You've put some weight on," said Daniel calmly.

"More into catching than bowling these days," he replied returning the recognition of understanding. "You've read the note?"

"I did but I have not briefed my colleague."

"Hi Max, excuse the frivolity but we need to be very careful around these parts. It's more like the wild west than West Yorkshire."

"It's pretty rough down there too!" clarified Max.

"So why are you so interested in Jack Kilpatrick?" asked Daniel.

"He owns the Wangkatha Gold Mine outright and also the large estate surrounding it. The gold is exported to various destinations but we know it all ends up in China. We think the Chinese finance the mine in some way. They are a very sophisticated operation and their software systems are impenetrable. This is not some local wealthy person acting on his own. He is an international player with Chinese government backing. They have been buying up huge tracts of Australian land and key infrastructure businesses. Our government now understands what he is about, but we have found it impossible to get any evidence that would stand up in our, or any other international court. We can't afford to upset the Chinese any more than we are doing with our trading restrictions. Equally one or two of his latest ventures are causing us enough concern to put a stop to it now."

"Any specifics?"

"They have infiltrated some of our top universities with student acolytes and they are starting to coerce large numbers of students into their communist thinking. If we let it run, in a few years' time these students will be running our institutions and even government departments which could be catastrophic for our democracy. The new AUKUS agreement between the US, UK and Australia is a recognition of the military and financial hegemony that China represents to the world."

"What exactly do you want us to do, that you can't?"

"We need you to infiltrate his organisation and find out as much as you can about his operation and then destroy it. We'll provide anything you need but it must not come back to us. Indeed, we don't exist, and after this meeting you will not see us again. You can talk to Jondi when you need to and she will relay anything back that you need to know."

"Do you want us to kill him?"

"We need you to frame him somehow, by implicating him in some illegal deal. Drugs, or something less obvious and more inventive would be better. It's better if he doesn't make it, but don't underestimate how hard that will be. He has the best security there is and is always surrounded by bodyguards."

"Any good news?" enquired Max.

"Your baby gorilla, Didi, I think you call her, is definitely there. If you can rescue her at the same time, then good luck."

"If you knew he was importing an illegal animal, why didn't you stop it on importation?"

"Because you wouldn't have come to rescue it and potentially solve our problem!"

"Thanks for the compliment!" smiled Daniel.

"You're very welcome," said Shane. "Nice to meet you both and I would have done the same with my handgun Daniel under the circumstances."

Daniel nodded in mutual respect.

Daniel and Max walked slowly back to the pickup, in the relentless burning heat from the late morning sun.

"What's Jondi like?" asked Max.

* * *

When they got back to the hotel, they grabbed a couple of warm beers from the fridge that didn't work, and sat at the table by the window to assemble a plan.

"I think that we should work separately on this one," suggested Daniel. "I am sure they will be suspicious if an American and Englishman turn up at the same time looking for work together."

"Agreed. I know nothing about mining so why don't you work on that end and I will try and get a job in security up at the house."

"That's good with me. We will need another vehicle so add that to Jondi's list."

"So, what's this Jondi like?" enquired Max again.

"I thought you were terrified of women," joked Daniel.

"I am, but I am hoping to meet a nice quiet submissive lady one day!"

"I think Jondi will be a bit out of your league then. She would eat you for breakfast!"

"Another dream shattered. What else do we want on the list?"

"We will both need new identities. Put Mr Daniel Day for me. I will need a passport, driving licence, work permit, some sort of mining qualification and an Aussie licence to handle explosives."

"OK. I will go with Max Jefferson. Passport. Driving licence. Work permit and a reference as a bodyguard from a couple of business people, in say Darwin, up in the Northern Territory. Hopefully they won't know too many people up there."

"OK. let's see if we can find any jobs going at Wangkatha?" said Daniel picking up the secure phone and starting a search."

"I'll go for a 'walkabout' –see, getting into the local dialect already – and reccy the lay of the land. Might find something useful?"

"Good luck with that," said Daniel. "Don't forget your gun."

Daniel pulled up the local newspaper, on the phone, called the *Kalgoorlie Miner*. Full of useful information like car crashes, minor robberies and planning permission arguments. There was a job section though, but nothing for the mine. However, there was a job going for a qualified technician at one of the largest companies supplying explosives and blasting technology to all the mines around Kalgoorlie. That appealed to Daniel's instincts and would get him on the inside of the mining industry, where he might find out a lot more about Wangkatha.

* * *

After two weeks, Jondi had come up trumps with all the items on the list, including a very old Holden Belmont HG Utility fitted with a five litre V8 engine.

"I'll have the Holden and you can keep *your* pickup!" joked Daniel.

"What do you mean *my* pickup. I drove it all the way here for *us* to use."

"Exactly! You're more used to it now, so we should stick with what we know! Anyway, I have an interview tomorrow with the explosives company, so I need to look respectable. They're running a training programme next week for their new wireless blasting system and one of their delegates got killed, two days ago, setting up a manual up-hole with ammonium nitrate and fuel oil. They were urgently looking for a qualified technician and they said I was perfect for the job."

"Sounds dangerous to me."

"Can't be any worse than Columbia!"

"That nearly killed you too. Charlie will not be pleased."

The mention of Charlie's name jolted Daniel into silence. He hadn't spoken to her since arriving in Australia and every day made it more and more difficult. He would give her a ring tomorrow.

* * *

The interview went well and his knowledge of handling explosives was as good as all the properly trained technicians on the course. It lasted three weeks, and Daniel learned a lot about remote firing techniques which would come in useful in future projects of his own. He also found out why he had blown himself up whilst disposing of the drug cartel in Columbia. A simple coding error on his laptop for the type of detonator he was using, initiated a premature ignition. He also found out that his new company might be doing some of the more complex blasting work at the Wangkatha mine. He needed to get closer to the technicians that did the work there.

"So how did today go?" asked Max, when Daniel got home from his first day of proper work.

"It was actually really interesting and I enjoyed setting up the new in-hole wireless primers. They work through hundreds of metres of rock without any wires. It will be really useful if we have to blow up any big buildings from a distance. A magical way to clinically destroy bankers that are financing poachers in Africa, or even mine owners in Australia!"

"What are the people like you've got to work with?"

"Just regular guys. Very well trained and professional. Got an invite to a barbie from one for Saturday. Could possibly find out more, in an informal situation."

"Good plan. What's he called?"

"Francesca."

"Have you rung Charlie yet?"

* * *

Max was getting very frustrated sitting around and not getting anywhere with his part of the plot to infiltrate the security guards at the big house. All the recruitment was done by a company in Perth and they were ultra-keen on following up references, which might cause an issue with Max's fictional ones.

"How's the reccy going of the outside perimeter for our eventual escape routes, if we get that far?" asked Daniel.

"You can't get anywhere near the house or even see the buildings. They are set in a bit of a hollow and surrounded by trees, which they have specially planted over the years. It's fenced all the way round to the shore line."

"Can you get any nearer on a windsurfer on the salt flats?"

"Possible. Never thought of that. I have seen a few lads out on the salt so I'll try and find out where they come from and join the club. Now, are you ready for tonight's culinary masterpiece? Chicken parmigiana – Again!"

* * *

The following day Max pulled up the *Kalgoorlie Miner* newspaper on the phone and searched through old editions for windsurfing clubs. Nothing. But after a bit more scrolling, he found articles about land-sailing which was evidently the right term around those parts. He finally fell on the Rockingham-based Sandgropers Land Yacht Club, who used to organise regular regattas out on the lake, which evidently had the perfect surface for high-speed racing. He found a telephone number for the club and decided to give them a ring that evening.

"Hi, my names Max. Is it possible to talk to someone about going land-sailing on Lake Lefroy?"

"Hi I'm Jenny the secretary of the club. Nice to hear from you. Do you live up in those parts?"

"Yea. Moved up here recently and I've seen the guys out on the salt and I thought it would be fun to give it a try and maybe meet up with a few folks for a beer."

"It's certainly good for that! The club tends to meet down at Lake Walyungup, south of Perth these days but I can put you in touch with a couple of guys in Kambalda that sail out on Lefroy regularly when the salt is good."

"That would be brill. If I get going and like it, I could come down to Rockingham and meet you all down there."

"Great. You need to ring Peter Petyarre. He has been sailing for years on the lake and knows it like the back of his hand. He works for one of the big gold mines and does it on his days off. I'll text you, his number."

"Thanks Jenny. You're a star. Hope to meet up one day and have that beer."

* * *

It was a beautiful cool evening when Daniel got back to the hotel and they decided to eat outside, on the part of the old veranda that had not succumbed to dry rot. They found two old bar seats, dusted them off, and dragged them out under the stars. The lack of light pollution around Widgiemooltha made the stars even brighter and the waning moon gave enough light for them to see the pavlova, which Max had acquired from a service station out on the main road. Max brought Daniel up to date with the progress he had made with the land-sailing contact.

"I'll give this guy, Pete, a ring later and see if we can arrange to meet up on the lake at the weekend. They sound a friendly bunch and he evidently works at one of the mines, so I might pick some more local intelligence."

"Sounds a plan. Well, I've had a stroke of luck today too, because I'm going to Wangkatha gold mine tomorrow with one of the trainers, to demonstrate the blast patterns we can do with the new wireless software. Historically, they have had problems at the mine with blasting, because of the variations in the rock strata needing different types of explosive charges. We can solve all that for them, which could give us some good business."

"You sound like a company executive already!" laughed Max.

They lounged back in the worn leather chairs and took in the enormity of the starlit sky. The silence was only punctuated by the distant howl of a dingo looking for a mate and the flutter of moth wings circling the light from the mobile phone.

Australian dingo

"Are you going to give her a ring or not?" asked Max after half an hour's silence.

"OK, OK stop nagging!" Daniel reluctantly agreed and walked across to the other side of the dusty road to ring Charlie's number. She replied instantly.

"Hi darling, how is going out there in marsupial heaven?"

"So far so good. How are you feeling? Is Annie looking after you properly?"

"I am feeling much better thank you. Walking without sticks now if I'm careful. I have got to go in for my check-up next Wednesday, so mummy is going to take me, to give Annie a break for a while. She has been brilliant. We couldn't ask for a better friend."

"Any sign of the Russian sneaking about again?"

"No sign. Jill is keeping a good lookout and goes up to the stables with Annie if she is on her own. So, all good."

"This might take a while out here but we are making some good progress. You will let me know if you want me to come home, won't you?"

"Yes, of course, but I am fine. Annie is looking after my every need!"

"I bet she is," laughed Daniel. "How's things up at the Hall? Are they managing without you, OK?"

"No problems. Tim is helping a bit more in the office to cover my jobs and Mac is picking up Tim's bits and pieces. I think they are all enjoying the extra responsibility. Mac's doing a good job with the puppies, mummy says and he has them out every morning up at the quarry getting them used to the guns."

"Sounds like they've got it all under control then?"

"I think so. Miss you loads. You take care out there, I want you back in one piece this time."

"I'll do my best! Give my love to Annie."

"Will do, and give mine to my favourite ski instructor!"

"Bye for now my darling. Please take care and don't do too much too soon."

* * *

Daniel felt a twinge of guilt having heard Charlie's voice. He always found it difficult talking to her on the phone. It wasn't that sort of relationship. He wandered back across the road and found Max fast asleep. He kicked his slumped leg and Max sat up in a start."

"Don't do that. I nearly had a heart attack!"

"It's alright for you windsurfing bums, some of us have to get up and go to work in the morning!"

"It's land-sailing actually and it may well be the key to getting Didi back, whilst you are playing at blowing things up," retorted Max. "I'll stay out here for a bit to see if any beautiful girls pass by."

"Good luck with that!"

* * *

Daniel was up at six and drove up the road to Kambalda in his Holden Utility, stopping at a servo on the way to get fuel for the thirsty V8 and a chicken sandwich, or chook sarnie as the attendant corrected him. He arrived at the factory gates, punctually at seven, showed his security pass to the rather large and frightening lady who operated the barrier and parked up. Francesca arrived at the same time and parked next to him in her new Land Rover Discovery.

"Good morning," said Daniel walking round her car. "Like the motor."

"Yea, I think it's cool. Only bought it last week."

"They're great machines, wish I could afford one."

"I'll let you drive it if you like after the barbie on Saturday," she smiled.

"That would be good. Never driven a Disco," he lied.

"Great it's a date then. We better go and fill the twin boom tanker ready for our visit to Wangkatha. We will also need to get special passes to get access to the site. They are very security conscious down there and we've to be impressive if we want to get the business. I've already been once and shown them the training video, you saw yesterday, so they know what to expect."

"I'll go and get the primers and codes from the store and load them into the auto-magazines," suggested Daniel.

"That's great thank you. Can you key in the codes into the laptop in the cab? It's got the site map saved in their file under Wang. Password Katha. Not allowed to write passwords down," laughed Francesca, not knowing Daniel's intentions.

"Will do."

Francesca drove the tanker along the service road, next to the southern bank of Lake Lefroy. The rays of the early morning sun were scattered by the salt crystals on the lake, creating a shimmering rainbow effect across its surface. The ochre dust from the road swirled behind the vehicle in cumulous-like clouds which slowly returned to the ground to await the next manmade storm. As they approached the huge steel gates that protected the mine entrance, Daniel's adrenaline lifted as he knew he was getting closer and closer to his target. They stopped at the gate and two heavily armed guards walked out to the tanker and asked for identifications and special site passes. Francesca passed down the documents from the cab and one of the guards took them into the metal cabin and made a phone call. After five minutes he returned and asked them for their dates of birth which he cross-checked with the passes. He seemed satisfied and waved them through.

"How far to the pit?" asked Daniel.

"A couple of kilometres up this track."

They climbed a slope away from the lake and up onto a ridge which opened out onto a huge plateau. The enormous crater of the mine with its stratified layers opened up below them. It reminded Daniel of looking into the volcanoes in Virunga, where Didi had come from.

They started to make the slow descent into the crater on the winding road clinging to the near vertical walls of the quarry. They occasionally had to pull over, into a passing place, cut into the rock, so one of the gigantic tipper trucks could climb past them with their loads of spoil.

"Not a drive for the faint-hearted," smiled Daniel.

"You get used to it. This is a good road down; you should see some of the rough tracks we have to deal with. One slip and your dead!"

"Very comforting. Do these roads ever give way completely?"

"We had one last year up at Kalgoorlie when the road gave way under one of the tippers. The driver was killed and they still haven't finished cutting a new road in. We tried to cut one in, half way down, but it got too dangerous, so we have been blowing out a new face all the way from top to bottom."

"Sounds expensive?"

"These owners have plenty of money and they pay most of the miners peanuts anyway. It's only the blasting crew that make decent money."

"Do you know much about the owners of this mine?" asked Daniel casually, looking out of the window.

"He's called Jack Kilpatrick. Australian guy, but there are lots of rumours about him. He's a nasty piece of work, and if you cross him, they say you're dead. He travels a lot; mainly to Hong Kong and China I'm told. He's in with all the movers and shakers in Perth so don't fall out with him."

"Have you ever met him?"

"No, he never comes down to the mine. His house is in a gulley further on, down near the lake. Bit of a paradise island in all this scrub. There has always been a huge natural spring down there so they can water all the trees and grasses, a bit like an oasis in the desert I guess."

When the road levelled out at the bottom of the mine, a man in a florescent yellow jacket directed them across the floor of the mine to the working face. They were met by the manager of the mine, who had discussed the blast plan with Francesca on her video demonstration visit. She jumped out of the cab and shook his hand and they engaged in cheerful conversation whilst Daniel set the pre-programmed blast plan up in the cab and linked into the GPS tracking systems. They were just about to start when a Mercedes G Wagon roared across the floor of the pit and came to an abrupt halt next to the tanker.

The manager tipped his helmet in reverence to the driver who climbed out and walked up to Francesca. He was at least six foot four and 120 kilos, with a drinker's complexion and a ginger beard.

"Kilpatrick, Miss. I understand you have a new box of tricks to show me?"

"Yes sir. Fully automated loading and firing remotely without wires. We can fire underground as well. Much more accurate than manual loading. Much safer for your staff and the information we have fed into the programme about your strata levels with optimise the explosive loads in each hole saving you a lot of wasted money."

"OK. Let me see what you have," he said in an intimidating gruff voice.

Francesca nodded to Daniel, who knew he was this close to killing Kilpatrick, and he may never get another chance. But he did not yet know where Didi was or what security there was around the house, so he contained his natural instincts and pressed the initiating button on the laptop. The tanker moved forwards on its own and at each borehole the feeder arms automatically located the holes and filled them with the ammonium nitrate and fuel oil mixture. The magazine then inserted the primer and programmed detonator. The tanker worked up and down the rows of holes quickly and efficiently with no manual intervention.

"Very impressive young lady. Shall we retreat for the firing?" said Kilpatrick in a lighter tone.

Daniel drove the tanker across the floor of the quarry to the manager's steel office container on the far side. He climbed out of the cab with his laptop and the four of them entered the hut. The manager sounded the blasting alarm to clear the workers from the quarry floor for safety.

Francesca checked the screen for errors but everything was clear to fire.

"Would you like to initiate the detonation?" Francesca smiled flirtatiously at Kilpatrick. Daniel could see the sweat on his brow and the dark staining down the shirt covering his gross torso.

"Yes please, young lady; that's very thoughtful and good business tactics!" he laughed, clearly enjoying the female company. He pressed the firing key and the ground shook, like an earthquake, as the solid rock was reduced to manageable piles of rubble.

"Are you happy with that!" asked Francesca.

"Looks good to me. We will know better when we get into the piles and see the size of the rocks lower down. So how much is this going to cost me, if we go ahead on a regular basis?"

"That depends on how often you want us to come and the number of firing holes per visit, but it will always save you money, because you will not need your own firing team; just the drillers."

"OK, we will give it a go for a month and see how we get on, but it must always be you and your mate. I don't want any strangers wandering around the site."

"That's brilliant, thank you sir! I will inform the company at my end and they will send you out a trial contract for a month." Francesca shook his sweaty palm and smiled, hiding her inner revulsion.

* * *

Daniel secured the delivery arms on the tanker and locked down the detonator magazines. Francesca said her goodbyes and climbed in next to him. As they ascended the sheer face of the quarry, Francesca turned to Daniel.

"What an obnoxious man. He made my skin creep."

"Not the sort of man you would invite to a barbie," laughed Daniel.

"That's for sure. Let's get out of this place and then we can stop for a drink at the servo out on the main road."

"Sounds a plan."

They pulled into the service station and Daniel went in and bought a couple of iced drinks and an iced bun each.

"So, Mr Day what is your plan?"

"Sorry, what plan?"

"Come on, you may fool everyone else, but I have been in this game too long to not recognise a fellow mercenary when I meet one.

"I'm not sure what you are talking about?" queried Daniel carefully.

"OK. forget I said anything. I'll get it out of you after the barbie."

Daniel looked her in the eye and then looked out of the window. What was she up to? Who was she and was she on his side? Or did she work for Kilpatrick. He needed to find out quickly, before his cover was blown.

CHAPTER TEN

Mysterious Mirage – Wangkatha Gold Mine

Max had arranged to meet Pete at Kambalda, on the western edge of Lake Lefroy at ten o'clock on Saturday morning for a trial run on the salt with the land sail. Pete arrived driving a brand-new Land Cruiser pulling a very smart double-axle trailer containing the brightly painted machine. Max was sitting in his pickup with the driver's door open and drinking a coke. He stood up and walked across to the Land Cruiser.

"Hi, I'm Max. Thank you for coming out to meet me."

"It's my pleasure mate. Can talk about sailing all day till the pub opens!"

"I know nothing about it, except I've seen a few on the lake and thought it looked fun to have a go. I didn't know there were two-seaters?" quizzed Max looking into the magnificent machine.

"Made it myself, so I can take friends out for a spin. I've got a class three that I use for racing, which runs well over one hundred kilometres per hour on a good day."

"It looks like this one is made out of fibreglass?"

"Mainly, but there is some Kevlar in there too to add strength without much extra weight. Give me a hand and we can launch it off the trailer."

Pete undid the ratchets on the wagon straps and fitted the ramps from under the trailer to the back. He slowly unwound the winch on the front of the trailer, whilst Max steadied the body down the ramp and onto the shore line. It was a lovely clear morning and the sun was glinting on the salt across the expanse of the lake. The breeze was coming from behind them so they could sail away and tack back. They lifted the seven-metre mast into position and locked it down. Pete fetched the carbon fibre seats from the back of his car and offered Max a helmet, knee-pads and gloves.

"We always wear these to be safe. If you catch a side wind it can flip the body over and the salt can be painful! Have you sailed a yacht on water before?"

"No," lied Max. "Bit of a landlubber myself. Like riding horses though."

"Snap! Do it for a living," replied Pete.

"I thought Jenny at the club said you worked at one of the mines?"

"I do. I run all the security at Wangkatha and spend most of my days riding round the estate keeping the place tight. It can get a bit rough sometimes; every bogan thinks he can break in and steal some gold and they only understand one thing."

Max felt his heart thump his chest but kept cool on the outside. He concentrated on the sailing and avoided the desperate urge to ask more questions. Pete set the sail and they glided slowly out over the salt.

"The important thing is to keep straight as you pick up speed. It's easy to get distracted and drift across the wind and turn over. OK, you take over and build up some speed."

The adrenaline was addictive and as they sailed up and down the lake, Max really started to enjoy himself.

"You're a natural mate! You could get good at this after a few trips," encouraged Pete.

"It's pretty sensitive as you get going faster but I love the speed and the silence. I'm really pleased I gave you a ring," grinned Max.

"OK, let's have break for a coffee and then you can have a go on your own."

Pete ran the yacht ashore next to the cars and they climbed out and leant on the bonnet of the Land Cruiser looking out across the lake. Pete got a flask and two mugs out of his car and they drank their coffees whilst discussing the different types of land-sailing and all the trophies Pete had won over the years.

"So, what are you doing in this part of the world? Bit off the beaten track for an American."

Max thought for a split second and took a risk.

"Long story. Caught two guys rustling horses one night on the ranch where I worked. I warned them off but they turned nasty and pulled a gun. They fired at my pickup but fortunately only grazed my head. I had no choice and shot them both dead. I buried them in the wood and left town."

"So why no police; I thought America was a civilised place?

"They were both black and I was white with no witnesses. I am not a prejudiced person but the chances of getting a fair trial in the southern states of the US, under those circumstances, is not good these days. The press would have made hay and I could have spent five years in prison, even if I was eventually found innocent."

"So, what are you going to do now?"

"Just drifting, I guess. Never been to Australia, so thought I would work my way across the country and then try New Zealand."

"It's a bit like the wild west round here too sometimes, so thanks for being so honest with me. Don't get to talk to folk from the rough end of life much. Are you going to have another sail on your own then?"

"That would be great if you don't mind," said Max casually. Hoping his story was not too extreme.

Max spent an hour sailing up and down the salt. He particularly enjoyed the challenge of tacking the craft into the wind and nearly flipped it twice when he was being a bit too ambitious with his turns. He sailed as close as he dared to the southern edge of the lake so he could get views of Wangkatha. It was a substantial property with a big, ranch-type house, complete with a wide veranda. The gardens were well-kept and verdant, with the regular watering from the spring. There were two other substantial buildings set back away from the main property and Max was certain that he heard the call of a chimpanzee, floating on the breeze. He tacked back towards Pete one final time, down the north side of the lake to make his reccy less obvious.

He sailed gently up to Pete who was enjoying a lie down next to the trailer.

"You're hooked then!" smiled Pete.

"You bet; it's amazing. Do you know anyone who would rent me one for a couple of weeks, while I am around these parts?"

"Sure. Dave who works with me has broken his leg, racing his Suzuki Hayabusa, so he won't be using his, for a while. How are you off for cash?"

"I have bit stashed but nowhere to keep the sail."

"No problem. He keeps it at my place anyway. I'll have a word and get back to you. Where are you staying?"

"I have a tent in the pickup. Used to sleeping outside."

"OK. I'm not working on Tuesday evening, so do you fancy coming over to my place to meet him and we can have beer."

"Sounds good to me. Where do I find you?"

"Just come to the main gate for the mine, ask for me and they will give me a ring. I will drive up and pick you up at the gate. They won't let you in without me being there. You would be amazed what people will do to get into a gold mine!" Pete laughed. "Turn up about six and I should be finished my last ride around by then."

"OK will do. Thanks for today. Haven't had that much fun in ages. See you Tuesday."

Max drove back to the hotel at Widgiemooltha, hardly believing his luck. He was dying to tell Daniel all about the day on the salt and his new mate, but Daniel had already left for the barbeque with Francesca. So, he had to make do with a lonely chuck sarnie and a tinny.

* * *

Daniel drove along the 94 in his Holden utility, wearing his best jeans and denim shirt, his arm resting on the open window. He needed to impress Francesca – but not too much! He took the Goldfields Highway spur road to Kambalda East and found Acacia Road on the outskirts of the housing estate as Francesca had directed. He drove down the road until he found her Discovery parked outside a simple wooden bungalow with a tin roof. He pulled onto the rough dirt driveway and parked next to it. He could see the smoke from the barbeque, as it drifted over the roof, bringing the aroma of burnt chicken. He walked down the side of the house to the ill-kempt grassy patch behind. No sign of Francesca, or anyone else come to that. He rescued the cremated chicken legs and sat down on the wooden stool next to a rusty metal table.

"Oh shit!" exclaimed Francesca running out of the backdoor, with her recently washed hair in a twisted towel on top of her head. "Is it edible?"

"Only if you like charcoal!" observed Daniel.

"Sorry. Bad day. Running late since breakfast and never caught up. Would you like a beer?"

"Cool. And you might want to…" Daniel gesticulated to her open shirt revealing rather more of her generous breasts than she probably wanted to, at this stage of the evening anyway.

"Sorry. Give me minute to shape-up. Help yourself to a beer from the fridge."

Daniel wandered into the chaotic kitchen, piled-high with yesterday's pans and empty beer cans. The fridge was empty, apart from the beer. Clearly this was a temporary abode. He opened a can of Foster's Lager and took a welcome swig of the cold nectar.

"Would you like one?" he shouted through the bathroom.

"Yes please, be out in a minute."

Daniel scanned the room and quietly opened the kitchen table drawer.

"You won't find anything in there."

"Sorry. Force of habit!" And he walked outside into the cooling evening air.

Francesca reappeared and Daniel could not hide his surprise at the transformation. Her bright copper-coloured hair fell in natural ringlet around her olive skin and her piercing green eyes were mesmerising. She was wearing tight Levi's and she had done a token button up on her shirt which hid nothing. Who cares about burnt chicken, he thought?

"Hi. Shall we start again?" she smiled lasciviously, using her eyes to perfection.

"Good idea! I thought there might be other folks coming?"

"They all cried off, so we are alone all evening," she lied.

"Saves the small talk, I suppose."

"Shall I go and get some more chicken from the mart?"

"Wasn't really hungry anyway."

"So, who are you working for?" she asked directly, throwing her head back and taking a slug of the amber stuff.

"Myself. How about you?" enquired Daniel.

"The same."

"How long have you been around?"

"Two years."

"Christ, it must be a big job?"

"Not really. Just not getting anywhere."

"Why don't you bale out?"

"Can't."

"Why not?"

"Gun at my head. Caught doing something marginal and seeking redemption."

"Government or criminal?"

"You ask a lot of questions. Government."

"Which one?"

"You know better than that."

"Sorry. Worth a try."

"I do do this for a living, you know. Anyway, what are you hunting?"

"Information."

"Target?"

"You know better than that!"

"Touché. Beer or bed?"

"Let's go with another beer for now. No offence meant."

"None taken."

Francesca fetched a couple more beers from the fridge and Daniel regrouped his plans.

"Let's see if we have any common ground or conflicts of interest. It would be a shame to kill you and then find you could have advanced my cause!" suggested Daniel.

"True. Let's compare skill bases."

"OK. You go first. It was my idea."

"Devious bastard!"

"Both true, but I will tell you my life history later," replied Daniel smiling.

"Well obviously I am cool on explosives, but more of a software analyst actually. How about you?"

"Vermin exterminator."

So far, so good, Daniel thought. Could they cooperate in some way? Did they have the same target? Would she be a liability? Or even worse, could *he* become a target for her puppeteers?

The evening sun was setting behind the trees, at the end of the garden, and throwing beams of crimson light through Francesca's scintillating ringlets. She took another swig of lager and Daniel's eyes struggled to avoid her cleavage. She was a very attractive woman in a hard sensuous way. Max would have heart-failure!

"So, how do we resolve the impasse," asked Daniel, "if we are going to help each other?"

"OK. Cards on the table, but we agree not to kill each other whatever happens. Professional honour and all that!"

"Agreed."

"I am trying to get into that creep Kilpatrick's systems. My masters are owed a lot of bitcoin money, like zillions, that went AWOL in a Chinese wallet that he was controlling. The wallet was moved off-shore to Taiwan and the Bitcoins just evaporated into thin air," relayed Francesca, obviously relieved to be sharing her dilemma with someone.

"They've got to have been stupid to put a single dollar into bitcoin, or any other virtual currency come to that. The whole thing is a con and even the Chinese have kicked the miners out of the country. They have all gone to Texas. No idea why the US is letting that happen."

"But a lot of syndicates have made huge wins as the prices have escalated in the last few years, helped by the odd big car manufacturer," joked Francesca.

"True but there is no security out there. The so-called blockchain is run by nebulous beings in the ether. It's not the currency of the people, as some gurus would have you believe."

"That might be true and I don't claim to understand it all but I need to track where Kilpatrick sent the money or I am dead."

"Where have you got to so far?"

"The nearest I have got is with you when we delivered the explosives. I figured that if I became a regular visitor,

I might be able to access their systems from the cabin at the mine face. I've tried hacking in from outside and it's useless. My masters have some of the best hackers in the world and they can't get in from outside either. So, what's your target?"

"Ditto!"

"So how far have you got?"

"When we delivered the explosives!"

"Great! so what's your angle?"

"Similar to yours. We might have a common goal if we work together; but I think that's enough soul-bearing for one night and I have some digging to do."

"The offer is still there," tempted Francesca, leaning forwards, exposing more of her breasts and looking Daniel straight in the eyes with her emerald weaponry.

"Work comes first!"

"I think it's going to be boring working with you."

"I doubt it," smiled Daniel, kissing her on the cheek and catching her breast with the back of his hand as he left her, frustrated and alone.

* * *

Daniel pulled-up outside the derelict hotel in Widgiemooltha to find Max having a relaxing evening under the stars.

"Did you know that Proxima Centauri is the nearest star to the sun?" asked Max.

"It's alright for some. I have been slaving away on top secret, dangerous work and you are stargazing!"

"Did you kiss her?"

"Of course not," replied Daniel disregarding the peck on the cheek and the fleeting caress.

"So, what's Francesca like?"

"Not your sort Max. You wouldn't like her."

"Not sure if I have a sort anymore," said Max sadly. "However, I have some amazing news, which will make your day seem trivial."

"Great. Let me get a beer and tell me all."

Max related the news from the salt lake and his contact with Pete from the mine. Daniel was genuinely shocked that Max had got an invitation inside the security fence by the man running it.

"It seems too easy Max. Are you sure it's not some sort of trap?"

"I took a risk, I grant you, but he seemed to swallow it, hook, line and sail. I'm going round for a beer on Tuesday night to meet his mate, who is one of the security men, and has a broken leg. I am planning to try and get a temporary job as a replacement until his leg is better. Could be good."

"Could be deadly Max. One wrong word and you're a goner. We better sure up your cv with Jondi, asap. Better give her a ring later."

"Did you learn anything interesting about Francesca?" asked Max.

"She says she is some sort of mercenary and has been trying to get inside the mine for two years."

"Two years! She can't be much good at it," joked Max. "What is she after?"

"To get into Kilpatrick's systems from the inside to try and track some stolen bitcoins. A lot actually. I am not sure we can trust her but I'll go with it for a couple of weeks and see how you get on first. If she is genuine and we can get her in, we might kill a bird with two stones."

"Sounds like a plan, even if it is muddled metaphor. Did you tell her about Didi?"

"No. I didn't want to complicate things yet, and anyway, if she is on the other side, we don't want to give them a bargaining tool."

"I'll go and ring Jondi. Are you sure I wouldn't like her?" mused Max.

* * *

Max arrived at the entrance gates to the mine on Tuesday evening, at the prearranged time. One of the security guards emerged from the metal cabin and walked up to the driver's door.

"Yes sir. Can I help you?"

"I am here to see Pete Petyarre."

"Have you got a pass?"

"No. He said if you gave him a ring he would come up and collect me."

"OK. Hang on a minute."

The guard retreated to the cabin and Max could see him make a call on a radio, through the dusty window. He put the radio down and gave Max the thumbs up, through the door. After ten minutes, Pete appeared in his Land Cruiser and the guard opened the gates.

"Hi Max, how's things? Just follow me in your pickup and we will drive down to my house by the lake; it's on the far side of the compound."

They bypassed the track up to the mine, that Daniel had taken with Francesca in the tanker, and dropped down to the lake side. The evening sun was getting lower in the clear blue sky and the rays were scattered across the salt in a mist of rainbows, obscuring the views. As they approached Kilpatrick's house, the verges became verdant and the trees magically grew in the alien environment. They turned up a hill that led them away from the lake, around the back of the house and then down into an adjacent valley, where the two large barns were. A small group of staff bungalows were located around a mown central lawn, complete with water fountain and a barbeque area under some trees. Pete lived in the largest bungalow, looking down over the lake and there were three land sails in a neat row on the grass by his garage. As Max got out of his car, a rough-looking guy hobbled out of the third bungalow, up on the right. His leg was in plaster up to the hip and he had two crutches to get around.

"Max, this is Dave. World famous for falling off motorbikes!"

"Very bloody funny," grumbled Dave, obviously frustrated with his situation.

"I'll fetch some beers if you two go and sit over there," said Pete, pointing at the wooden benches under the trees."

"So how did you break your leg? Pete said you fell off your Hayabusa."

"I suppose I was stupid, but I took my new bike down to Wanneroo raceway to give it a spin before the next club race and I took an adverse camber too fast and ended up in the barrier. Lucky I am still here I suppose."

"Easily done," consoled Max. "Is the bike, OK?"

"Think so; a few superficial scrapes but it's up at the workshops in Kalgoorlie being checked over this week."

Pete returned with some cans and they quickly downed the first round, quenching the thirst induced by the afternoon sun.

"Pete tells me you would like to hire my sail whilst I am out of commission?"

"Yea, if that works for you," replied Max enthusiastically. "I had a great time on Saturday with Pete and I thought I would hire one for a few weeks whilst I am around these parts."

"So where are you staying?"

"Just camping. I like being outdoors. Used to it, out on the ranch in the States."

"The thing is," enquired Dave hesitantly, "while I can't work and pay the rent, I am going to stay with my sister in Perth. But I don't want to lose my house here, so I need to let it to someone that Pete is happy with. The owner will not let it stand empty, the miserable bastard."

Max was shocked at Dave's attitude to Kilpatrick in front of Pete, but Pete showed no reaction to the derogatory comment.

"Looks out of my league I'm afraid," said Max, playing it cool and looking at the well-kept single storey.

"It's only $200 a week including water and electricity," replied Dave.

"Look, I am going up to the Kalgoorlie Boulder Racing Club tomorrow to try and get a job doing track maintenance till the season starts and then try and get a barrier attendants job later, loading horses into the gates. That pays better. They need people with experience handling horses and I've been with horses all my life. If that works out, I will come back to you."

"You didn't tell me he knew about horses, Pete. Why don't you let him have my job till I am fit to come back?" suggested Dave.

"You know what the boss is like about having strangers on the place. I think it's a good idea but I would have to get some references to make it official," mused Pete for a while. "I suppose it would solve a lot of problems though and Max knows how to look after himself. What do you think Max, can you come up with a reference?"

"Sounds a plan for a while, till I decide where to go next, I suppose," said Max thoughtfully. "I can get you a reference from the ranch owner in the States. He knows the circumstances of me leaving and was supportive in getting me out of town. Will that do?"

"What circumstances?" asked Dave inquisitively.

"Oh, just woman trouble," lied Max, smiling at Pete.

"OK Max, you come up with a reference, I'll get the suits to check it out, and you've got yourself a job!"

"And I'll throw in a free sail as well," laughed Dave. And they opened some more of the nectar.

"What's the wages like?" asked Max.

"For cash and off the books $750 a week. Twenty-four hours a day and no lunch. But you do get to sail on the lake for free," and all three of them downed another can, laughing.

"And what exactly is the job?"

"Keep all the bastards out and kill any that get inside the fence. Drag 'em into the bush and let the dingoes do the rest," said Pete calmly. He wasn't joking.

* * *

Max moved into Dave's single storey on Thursday afternoon, after Pete had cleared his references. Jondi had worked her magic and arranged for a suitable cv response from the US. She had also organised a mobile phone for Max to use, with special end to end encryption, so he could communicate with Daniel and herself in an emergency. Max scanned the place for bugs but couldn't find anything. The place was clean and tidy, simply furnished but adequate for a single guy. It was definitely better than the hotel at Widgiemooltha; it had a working fridge for the beer. Pete came over to check everything was OK and agreed to meet Max at the stable barn at seven o'clock on Friday morning to start work.

* * *

Pete dragged open the huge red doors of the stable barn to reveal four large boxes, a wash box and a pleasant tack room with seats and a table with yesterday's mugs. A stack of hay and straw were at the far end of the barn.

"So what breed are these?" asked Max, stroking the neck of a flashy chestnut with a large white blaze.

"We call 'em Walers. They are descended from horses shipped into New South Wales in the nineteenth century. Tough as nails, never go lame and not gun-shy. And no, you can't have him, he's mine! Yours is the black mare. The other two are youngsters I am bringing on, so you can help me with that in the evenings. We do everything there is to do with the horses; feed, muck out, bed up and exercise. The tack is in the cupboard. I like to clean mine every day and saddle soap it, but Dave just gave his a wipe over. Anyway, that's how I do it. You suit yourself."

"Where does the muck go?"

"Out the door, round the back and up the ramp into the trailer. The boss likes it for the gardener to put round all the

Australian Waler

trees and shrubs. He's a bit of a plant fanatic, so don't tread on his flowerbeds," laughed Pete. Max pulled the mare out of the box and tied her up outside. He looked her over and picked out her feet with his knife. Her coat was dull and her mane tangled with knots. He gave her a pat and filled the first barrow with the night's droppings and wet straw. As Max pushed the full barrow up the trailer ramp, he could see the second barn properly, for the first time. It had wire cages all along one side and closed sliding doors into the barn. All the cages were empty. He pushed the barrow back down the ramp and met Pete coming with his overflowing load.

"Are there more horses to muck out in the other barn?" asked Max casually.

"No, thank God. It's full of chimpanzees. The boss collects them for some reason. He hardly ever bothers to go and look at them. The girl that looks after them for him, lets them out into the runs occasionally but they live a bit of a dull life."

Max was desperate to look in the barn to see if Didi was in there but he had to restrain himself for a few more days. A chance would come.

"Come on then, let's tack up and I will give you a tour of the perimeter fence."

* * *

They set off down past Pete's place to the sandy beach that ran along the side of the lake and headed east. The sun was getting higher in the sky and intense heat was drifting towards them from off the salt.

"Don't people try and get in off the lake with no fence?" asked Max.

"No, it's quite slushy all along this side of the lake because of the spring up the hill. Some have tried but vehicles and horses just sink without trace. We find the odd body floating when the rains do occasionally flood the lake but nobody has made it in so far. In any case all the locals know we will shoot trespassers."

They rode for about ten kilometres along the edge of the lake until they reached the four-metre high, green wire fence that ran out about fifty metres into the lake. The fence was topped with razor-barb, that would shred a man's flesh if he tried to climb over it. They turned along a narrow track inside the fence and picked their way carefully between the jagged boulders that littered the ground.

"I see why you need the horses now; a jeep wouldn't handle this," observed Max.

"Yea. They were going to clear a road all round the perimeter before I got here but I managed to persuade them it was a bad idea. It would have made it too easy to get to the mine if anyone did breach the fence. Anyway, I like riding round the estate. Good way to make a living!"

"Do you see much wildlife on your ride around fence each day?" asked Max.

"Not much. It's pretty desolate round here and there's not much water about. You see the odd euro, but they are mainly nocturnal, and the occasional dingo."

"What's a euro?"

"It's the local name for a wallaroo; a kind of kangaroo but stockier. I think they are mostly young males; never seen a female with a joey in its pouch."

"Can you eat them?"

"Only if you are dying from hunger!" laughed Pete, pushing his horse on down into a gully. "We'll stop here for drink and a bite to eat."

They let the horses drink from a clear puddle of water under the bank, which was the only source of water on the fence line. Pete opened his saddle bag and offered Max a sandwich.

"Thanks," said Max, "I didn't realise we would need any food. The estate is much bigger than I thought."

"We're not half way yet. The fence swings out round the mine workings and then covers a large area further on where the boss hopes to open up a titanium mine next year. It then runs back to main gate, which is the only way into the property, so it's pretty easy to keep secure."

When they had finished lunch Pete pulled a leather gun slip from behind the saddle and withdrew an automatic machine gun and threw it across to Max who caught it professionally.

"Seen one of those before?" asked Pete seriously.

"SIG MCX Low visibility assault weapon, range 500 metres, thirty-round STANAG box magazine. We call 'em Black Mambas in the States."

"You know your guns then, but do you know how to use it?" Pete handed Max the magazine and pointed out a small tree about 300 metres away down the gulley. Can you hit that?"

Max inserted the magazine into the gun, checked the safety and stood square on to the tree. Within ten seconds he had shot off the four branches on either side of the tree and splintered the six-inch trunk, so the whole tree crashed to the ground.

"You'll do," smiled Pete. "I'll give you Dave's gun tomorrow for your saddle bag. We always keep them covered near the gates so visitors don't know all our security secrets. Right, we better get going."

When they got back to the barn at about three, they hosed the horses off and gave them some hay from the stack. Pete made up the feeds for later, whilst Max skipped out the other two youngsters.

"Right, I'm off out tonight, so if you can feed up and skip out at bedtime, it will save me getting changed when I get back."

"No problem. I'll sort them out," replied Max.

Although he desperately wanted to get into the barn to see if Didi was there, he restrained his enthusiasm and sat on his porch after dinner, looking across the lake. The sun was setting in the west and, as the rays turned from amber to red, the whole lake disappeared in a scarlet mist above the salt. The few clouds that were in the sky, reflected the sun's rays and blinded his vision. It was a magical moment that he had never experienced before. For a brief moment, he thought he could see someone moving along the sandy beach, almost floating above the ground in the vermilion haze. He stood up from his chair and took a couple of steps forwards to try and get a clearer view, but he could see no one. Then, as the mist became more translucent for a brief moment, he saw a beautiful, tall slim girl with naturally blonde wavy hair cascading down her back, dancing elegantly in front of his eyes. But the deep crimson mist closed around her again and she was gone. Was he dreaming? Was it a mirage? Who was she, in this remote, arid and deadly world?

CHAPTER ELEVEN

Seascapes of Love – Anderby Creek – Lincolnshire – England

It was April in Wensleydale and Spring had arrived with enthusiasm; a flush of birdsong, vibrant colours and new life in the trees, hedgerows and paddocks. The Swaledale ewes were busy tending their snow-white mule lambs in the lush green fields and the bright ginger Limousin calves were constantly pestering their mothers for more milk.

Swaledale ewes

The rooks were busy in their nests, high up in the sycamore trees around Haggs Gill and the red squirrels at Charlie's reserve were busy gathering last winter's hidden nuts for their new arrivals, hidden in a hole in an oak tree. Charlie had not seen Daniel for over six months but they had managed tentative phone calls every couple of weeks. She understood his desperate need to get Didi back and make the perpetrators of the poaching trade pay for their hideous actions. She had made a full recovery from her hysterectomy, physically at least, but occasionally drifted into thoughtful days when she struggled with what had happened to her. A long hack up on Masham moor with Byerley or a busy day tagging and tailing lambs with George, the shepherd, relieved the negative thoughts. She had loved being looked after by Anne Marie and the two had grown very close but she had moved back to the Mill so she could feel closer to Daniel again in her own house. One morning she was working in her studio and an email unexpectedly popped up in her inbox from Suzi, the typhoon pilot.

Hi Charlie,

I heard about your operation and I am so terribly sorry about your loss. I hope you are recovering satisfactorily and that Annie is looking after you well! It seems an age since I last saw you but I did not want to impose on your grief and recovery. Hopefully you are now well on the way to being able to travel again? I am on holiday in a couple of weeks' time and I was wondering if you would like to come down to my house on the Creek for a few days. The beaches are still fairly free of tourists and the sea and

*the dunes look amazing in the morning sunlight.
I thought we could walk a bit and you could take
some seascapes with your amazing camera? Please
say yes. As you know, I work in a man's world and
am starved of intelligent female company!*

Love Suzi.

*P.S I could drive up and fetch you, if you are not up
to driving yet.*

Charlie felt the genuine compassion behind the words 'loss and grief' and thought a few days away with someone different, who understood her hidden pain, would be good for her. Annie and her mother could not have been any kinder or understanding, throughout the whole ordeal, but Suzi's offer of a few days away seemed to have arrived at just the right time for her to move forwards. In any case, it was an opportunity to get the Canon out again and get some different landscapes for her files.

Hi Suzi,

*It was lovely to hear from you and I would love
to come down to see you. I could do with a few
days away and some intelligent female company!
I am fully up and running again, so driving down
to Lincolnshire is no problem and I will bring my
camera! Can you send me a date that suits you for
me to turn up and I will sort everything this end?*

Love Charlie xx

A reply came back straight away.

Hi Charlie,

That's fab! Can't wait to see you. My holiday runs from the eighteenth to the twenty third of April, so why don't you come down on the afternoon of the eighteenth and we can have a quiet evening together and then venture out along the beach early the following morning? Please stay as long as you like – it will be fun!

Love Suzi xx

When Charlie told Anne Marie where she was going, she was insanely jealous in a light-hearted way.

"Can I come?" asked Anne Marie.

"Suzi only invited me," replied Charlie smiling.

"That's not fair. You already have Daniel and me."

"She did kiss me passionately once," teased Charlie.

"When? You didn't tell me that. Now I'm really jealous. What was the kiss like?"

"Sensual!"

"You're winding me up! She never kissed you properly?"

"Certainly did, and it was very nice too."

"Where did she kiss you?"

"On the lips!"

"I know that, but where were you both on your own?"

"On my sofa in the Mill when she came up for your party."

"So how long did it last?"

"At least half an hour! She stroked my thigh too!"

"Stop! Stop! Or I'll have an orgasm thinking about it!"

"All right calm down. I'm only teasing you! She did try to kiss me though. She thought I had invited her to stay, to start a relationship and I guess it was my fault for being too friendly."

"I like it when you are too friendly!"

"So do I," smiled Charlie, softly squeezing Anne Marie's hand.

"So go on then what happened?"

"Suzi was very distressed that she had misread things and wanted to leave, but I persuaded her to stay and come to the party. She opened up about her past and how she had been badly treated in the forces, because she was gay. But I will let her tell you all about that one day."

"Do you think she likes me?" asked Anne Marie eagerly.

"She did, but I am not sure now. She did make a small positive comment about how kind you were, so I think there is still hope for you."

"When are you going? I can't wait to see what she says. I really like her Charlie. Not as much as you, but Daniel is ruining all that."

"Ruining is harsh."

"Sorry! Complicating then."

"That's more generous. I will do a bit of fishing for you when I am down there and send you a report."

"At least daily!"

"You're keen then," teased Charlie again.

"As much as I have ever been. Apart from with you."

"You don't need to keep saying that. I know how much you love me and how wonderful you have been, looking after me whilst I have been poorly, but we need to find you another partner that you can love and spoil and have fun together."

"Sounds exciting. Please make it work for me Charlie?"

"I will do my best."

* * *

Charlie drove down to Lincoln in one of estate's Range Rovers. She wanted to go in the Ferrari but the clutch was heavy and her tummy muscles were still a bit tender for a repetitive clutch workout. She took the Horncastle Road out of Lincoln, then up to Alford and along the sea road to the small village of Ainderby Creek itself. Suzi's house was at the far end of Sandy Lane which runs parallel to the North Sea. It was a grey afternoon and a sea fret was being blown in off the sea which hid the waves, that she could hear hitting the dunes below. It seemed a wild place, living so near the powerful sea eroding the natural landscape.

Charlie pulled up on the short drive of the ultramodern, multifenestrated house, which looked out over the sea. Suzi rushed out and kissed Charlie on the cheek, looked a bit horrified and said sorry, worried she had made the mill mistake again. Charlie told her not to be ridiculous and they grabbed the bags and rushed inside to get out of the wind and rain.

"Sorry about the weather! It will get better I promise," smiled Suzi. "I am so pleased to see you. Did you have an awful trip?"

"No, it was fine. A bit blustery in places but the good old Range Rover sailed majestically through it all as usual. You have a fabulous house. I bet the views are amazing if it ever stops raining." And they both burst out laughing.

"Would you like a cup of tea? I've made some salmon sandwiches if that's OK."

"Sounds wonderful."

"Earl Grey?"

"Thank you for remembering!"

Charlie followed Suzi into the immaculate kitchen. "Who owns the house?"

"It belongs to an architect in Lincoln. He won several awards when he first built it ten years ago. It was on one of those television programmes about designing unusual houses. Unfortunately, his wife died, before it was finished, so he never moved in and I have rented it for the last five years. I absolutely adore being here after all the stress of flying the typhoons and chasing the Russians away. It's peaceful, in a rugged sort of way. I love lying in my soft warm bed at night, listening to the waves crashing on the beach. It makes me feel safe."

"I think it's a wonderful house Suzi, I can't wait to see the panoramic views of the sea tomorrow."

They took the tea through to the sitting room, on a tray, and sat on the sofa together. Suzi lit the modern gas fire. "Sorry we don't have a proper fire but I am not here often enough to use a wood burner."

"If you say sorry again, I am going home!"

"Sorry! I'm just nervous of being close to you. I know that might seem odd to you, because I kill people for a living, but you are the only person I have ever opened up to about my past and I am terrified I will say or do the wrong thing."

"Look, just relax. I was hoping you were going to look after me!" smiled Charlie. "Tell me how your family are getting on. Has your father still got all his pigs?"

"Oh, he's got even more now! He's signed a new contract with one of the big supermarkets to supply his organic pork and it's a big commitment. Having pigs farrowing outside in little huts, in the fresh air, sounds wonderful when it's nice and sunny, but when it's pouring with rain and freezing cold, half of them die and he hasn't got enough to meet the contract."

"And how are your brothers getting on?"

"Oh, that's quite funny. My brother who is an artist has a big commission, to paint a concept mural, whatever that is, so he is rolling in money at the moment. Mind you, it will not last long; he has no idea how to manage money and it will all be gone before you can say Toulouse-Lautrec."

"How about your other brother, the hedge fund manager?"

"I suppose relatively, he is ridiculously rich, but he got stung investing in some cryptocurrency thing and he feels really stupid for having got involved. One of his colleagues had made a huge amount of money out of it last year and I think Paul just felt he had to have a go before he got left out. A bit of a tulip bulb moment I think!"

"Always been a bit of a bricks and mortar person myself. If I can't touch it, I don't buy it," laughed Charlie.

"I thought we might go down to the pub for a meal this evening. The forecast is for the rain to ease off soon, so we shouldn't get blown off the dunes! It's just a little local place but the couple that own it do really good seafood, fresh from the fishing boats every day."

"Sounds wonderful. Shall I take my bag up to my room and get changed then?"

"Of course," said Suzi, grabbing Charlie's bag before she could get there.

"I can still carry a bag," smiled Charlie.

"I know, but you did say you were expecting me to look after you! Just mind the stairs. There's no handrail and they are these modern floating things so a bit minimal."

Suzi showed Charlie into an immaculate bedroom with a double bed covered in a magenta-coloured duvet. Suzi had folded three pure white Egyptian towels on the bed. There was a large picture window with linen curtains, cocooning the room from the sea. And soft wall lights mellowed the fabrics. Suzi carefully put Charlie's bag on a strategically placed chair and opened the bathroom door to reveal a chrome and glass haven, a bit like Anne Marie's, but in miniature.

"It's lovely, thank you Suzi. I will feel very safe in here."

"I hope I have remembered everything. Sorry I haven't had a visitor before."

Charlie frowned at Suzi.

"Sorry, I said sorry again!"

"I'll forgive you this time!" grinned Charlie. "Is jumper and jeans OK for the pub?"

"Of course, whatever you feel comfortable in. I will do the same."

Charlie grabbed a quick shower and lay on the luxurious duvet for half an hour to rest for a while after the drive. She felt really well but was taking the doctor's advice to take things easy, until she was one hundred percent again. She looked at her phone but still no messages from Daniel. She just hoped he was OK and making good progress in planning the release of Didi. She pulled on her denims and her favourite Ryeland sweater, leaving her hair free on her shoulders in unbrushed ringlets. Suzi was waiting for her on the sofa, in front of the fire.

"Am I allowed to say you look amazing?" asked Suzi, standing up. "I love your hair like that."

"You can compliment me as much as you want," laughed Charlie, "as long as you don't kiss me again!"

"Spoilsport," joked Suzi, half seriously, handing Charlie her coat.

"Come on let's go! You can hold my arm, on medical grounds, so I don't fall over."

Suzi linked her arm through Charlie's and they walked down the lane in the moonlight. The waves were still rumbling up the beach, at the bottom of the dunes, but the wind had died down and it was a pleasant short walk to the Creek Tavern in the village. The old oak beams in the ceilings were covered in horse brasses from years gone by, reflecting the flames from the real fire crackling in the smoke-tinged fireplace. They took off their coats and sat at a table near the fire and Jeannie, the landlord's wife came over and gave them a real Yorkshire welcome.

"Now then Suzi. Have you shot down any of those bloody Russians this week?"

"Only six this week," joked Suzi. "Can we have a bottle of my favourite wine please?"

"Of course, my darling, and who's this elegant young lady?"

"This is Charlie, an old friend of my family," Suzi lied.

"Bottle of Jacob's Creek coming up."

"I thought you were meant to keep your job secret?" whispered Charlie.

"You can't keep secrets long in this village. They're better at finding things out than the KGB! Sorry about the family friend thing. They'd have us married by next week if they knew the truth!"

They had planned to get up early the following morning, as the forecast was good, and walk along the beach so Charlie could get some seascape shots. Suzi brought a mug of tea, with toast and marmalade up to Charlie's bedroom and pulled the curtains open to reveal a stunning sunrise on the horizon. Charlie leapt out of bed and grabbed her camera. Suzi opened the balcony door and Charlie went outside and captured the crimson landscape painted by the sun.

"That's an amazing sunrise Suzi and the view is just fantastic. You are so lucky to wake up to this in the mornings."

Charlie came back inside and sat on the bed with Suzi, to eat breakfast.

"Did you sleep OK?" asked Suzi.

"Like a log thank you. The duvet is so soft and luxurious. Where did you get it from?"

"I bought it in Norway a couple of years ago when we were up there on exercises. It's real eider-duck down and as light as a feather – literally!"

"I will have to get one when I get home. I love it. So, what's the plan for today then?"

"I've made up a crab pâté salad for lunch and a flask of coffee so we can walk as far as you would like and just have a break when we feel like it."

"Sounds perfect. Give me ten minutes and I will be down and we can set off."

Charlie fetched her Billingham camera bag from the Range Rover and checked that her camera was fully charged. She fitted her wide-angle lens to the Canon R5 and put her favourite 20–70mm lens in her pocket in case she needed it. They set off over the dunes and down onto the beach. As Suzi had predicted, it was deserted apart from the odd villager taking their dog for an early morning constitutional. The cumulous clouds in the sky were still tinged with pink from the sun's rays and the North Sea unusually calm, with gentle waves rolling in onto the golden sands.

"I'll just go down to the water's edge and try and get a shot across the waves as they roll in. With a bit of luck, they will catch the colours from the clouds."

"Don't get your feet wet!"

"I'll try not to," smiled Charlie, as she ventured down to the limit of the incoming tide.

Suzi sat down on a small dune and watched Charlie set up her camera, as Daniel had done by the lake in Chocorua. She tried not to think of the ill-fated kiss at Charlie's barn but couldn't help wishing things had turned out differently for them. She tried to focus on a future with Anne Marie but the more she admired Charlie, busy dodging the incoming tide, the more difficult it became. After ten minutes Charlie walked up the beach to Suzi and sat next to her.

"Did you get the shot you wanted?" asked Suzi.

"I hope so. What do you think?" Charlie brought up the images on the screen of the camera and Suzi leant over her shoulder and admired the pictures.

"You are clever Charlie. I have been trying to get that image for years, and just failed miserably!"

"I don't suppose I could get decent pictures of Russian jets at 30,000 feet either," replied Charlie turning her head towards Suzi and smiling. For a fleeting moment their eyes met, before Suzi made herself look away before she ruined her possible future with Anne Marie. They walked on a bit further and Charlie noticed a pile of shells thrown up by the previous evening's tide. The shapes and colours were kaleidoscopic which fascinated Charlie, so she quickly swopped lenses and captured some lovely shots of the sunlight glinting on the shells.

"I thought you only took landscapes?"

"I do most of the time but sometimes companies, putting together visitor guides, like a close-up shot to give the brochures an 'arty feel'. Little photos like this can add a natural flavour, which customers really react to."

They walked as far as the outskirts of Chapel St Leonards, a caravan haven, and decided to walk back to a quieter patch of dunes to eat. Suzi laid out a tartan rug and arranged the salad neatly on a white, square plate.

"Do you like balsamic vinegar on the salad?"

"Perfect. You've gone to a lot of trouble Suzi. It's really kind of you."

"Oh, I always have salad on the beach for lunch," smiled Suzi.

As the sun reached higher into the sky, the temperature lifted in their sheltered spot and they relaxed with their coffees and talked about landscapes, love and life.

"Did you say Daniel had been away for a while?"

"Yes, I suppose it's nearly six months now. It's a secret, but I know I can trust you; he is in Australia and thinks he has found the baby gorilla we call Didi. He is trying to get it out of a private collection owned by a wealthy owner of a gold mine. It's very complicated so it's taking a long time to sort it out."

"Well, I hope he gets it sorted soon and back home to look after you."

"I have been very lucky having Annie as a friend. She insisted that I stay at her place when I came out of hospital and she has been brilliant at looking after me, in Daniel's absence."

"How is Annie? I was hoping she might call after the party but I expect she has lots of friends and a very busy life."

"Did you like Annie then?" asked Charlie directly.

"Well… er… quite a lot actually, but please don't say anything. I don't want her to feel uncomfortable with that."

"Why didn't you give her a ring then?"

"I just felt she was out of my league. She is incredibly beautiful and very intelligent. I didn't want to make a fool of myself in front of her."

"But you are incredibly beautiful and intelligent, Suzi. Why do you think it would be problem?"

"Now I'm blushing," smiled Suzi, "I guess I am frightened that she will not like me and I will get hurt again. I suppose that's why I live on my own; I am not very good at taking risks with my personal life. Look what happened when I tried to kiss you!"

"Don't be silly. I was very flattered. You nearly changed my life for ever!"

"Do you honestly think Annie might be interested in seeing me again?"

"I have a sneaking feeling that she might be very receptive to the idea but let's wait and see. She is a wonderful person but is very careful who she lets get close to her. She is fabulously wealthy and she always worries that people can't see past the money."

"I can't stop thinking about her and how wonderful she was at the party. I've tried to stop myself thinking about her but she keeps coming back into my head to haunt me!" laughed Suzi.

"I tell you what. When I get home, she is bound to ask how we got on and I will do a bit of fishing for you."

"That would be great if you don't mind. I am really excited now. I want to kiss you... Sorry only joking. I know she loves you Charlie but I also know you love Daniel, and I guess losing the babies has brought you two even closer together."

"It has, in a strange sort of way. He looked after me so well when I was poorly in hospital and we have grown together dealing with the loss but he has been away for six months and we have only spoken on the phone. I love him very much but feel lonely and empty some days, which was why I was so pleased when you rang and invited me down. A tear trickled down Charlie's cheek as the loss of the twins came flooding back. Suzi put her arm around Charlie's shoulder and held her tightly.

They sat for a while in silence, with the waves rushing up the beach as the tide turned. The gulls hovered effortlessly above the rising swell as the westerly breeze aided their flight. A small fleet of fishing boats headed north towards Grimsby with their catch for the tables of starred restaurants across the moors and dales. Suzi slowly packed away the picnic and they walked back, arm in arm, to the warmth of the cocoon.

Charlie stayed for a few more days and their relationship grew ever closer. Their mutual history of abuse and their battle to rebuild their lives gave them a common bond which would last throughout their lives.

* * *

Charlie had only just walked through the kitchen door back at the barn when her mobile rang.

"Are you back safely? You promised to ring me. Did she mention me? What did she say?"

"Slow down Annie, I have only just walked through the door. You better come round for supper!"

"On my way. I'll bring a casserole. You raid the cellar!"

* * *

Anne Marie swept through the kitchen door, threw her arms around Charlie and kissed her passionately on the lips. Charlie couldn't help feeling a touch of happiness at being next to Annie again.

"Er I think you are getting carried away again!" smiled Charlie.

"You know you like it and, in any case, no one can see us and I am so excited that you are back."

"Will you stop kissing me if Suzi says yes?" inquired Charlie grinning.

"Probably not because I will always love you the most, but let's cross that bridge when we get there. So, what did she say?"

"Glass of red?"

"Stop teasing me. What did you find out?"

"She definitely still fancies me!"

Annie tickled Charlie in fun but Charlie winced as her tummy was still sensitive.

"Oh God, I'm sorry Charlie, I forgot about your tummy. I will behave now."

"Good! Warm the casserole in the oven and I will light the fire. Then I will tell you what actually happened."

They sank into the old sofa in front of the roaring fire with flames licking up the chimney. They each had a tray on their laps with a bowl full of Annie's beef casserole and dumplings. Charlie raised her glass and toasted being back at home with her best friend. "Cheers!"

"So come on, what did she say about me?" enquired an excited Anne Marie grinning like a teenager. "Seriously, this time."

"I had a lovely time and she made me really welcome. She had made a huge effort to make my room nice for me and to cook me delicious meals. We had some wonderful gentle walks along the beach and I managed to get some fantastic photographs of the seascapes."

"Yes, yes, but what did she say about me!"

"Calm down and pass me the wine, I'm coming to that."

"I think she is a beautiful, intelligent lady and she fancies you like mad but is worried that she isn't good enough for you."

"Rubbish. Why didn't she ring me after my party?"

"Why didn't you ring her after the party?"

"Touché!"

"I think that you are both too worried about getting involved and it not working, when it has the potential to be a sensuous, long-term relationship."

"Is she worried I am too old?"

"You're only forty, for God's sake and in your prime."

"How old is Suzi – about twenty-five?"

"I honestly don't know but I would say early thirties. She is very beautiful and has a fantastic figure."

"Have you seen her naked?"

"Nearly!" joked Charlie and toasted Annie with a smile.

"I can't just invite her up to stay with me, it will be too obvious. I would feel embarrassed that she would think, I just wanted to make love to her."

"Well, you do, don't you!"

"Desperately, but that's not the point!"

Why don't I invite her up to the Mill, in a couple of weeks, for the weekend and you can come over for a meal."

"I am nervous already," grinned Anne Marie.

"That's a good sign."

* * *

Monday morning. Email.

Hi Suzi,

I just wanted to thank you for inviting me down to stay with you. I had a wonderful time and I really enjoyed being with you. Your house is lovely and so different to all the old houses up here. Our walks together were very relaxing and I can't remember having enjoyed anyone else's company so much for a long time. I will be editing the photos that we took together over the next couple of weeks and I wondered if you would like to come up one weekend to see the finished article. We could maybe invite Annie around for supper one night and see how you two get on in neutral territory. I would love to see you again so please say yes.

Love Charlie xx

There was no immediate reply so Charlie decided to go up to the Hall and see her mother for a cup of coffee and a chat. Charlie pulled up in the stable yard where Mac was just setting off with her dog for a training session. Charlie made much of the puppy, to Mac's disapproval.

"You'll undo all the good training I've put in over the last few weeks," he smiled.

"Oh, go on, I've seen you giving Molly a quiet cuddle when you thought no one was looking!"

"Only when my boss stresses me!" he laughed.

"Are mum and dad at home?"

"Your mums in the kitchen, but I saw your dad leave early this morning. Off to some meeting, I think. He looked all dressed up with his best suit on."

"Is Sally OK?"

"Yes, fine thank you. She's off into Harrogate, meeting some friends at Bettys for lunch. No doubt she'll come back with some oriental recipe for me to suffer tonight."

"She's the best cook in the world Mac. You are a very lucky man."

"I suppose so," he muttered reluctantly.

Elizabeth was busy over the Aga as usual, creating a new culinary masterpiece with some herbs from the garden.

"Hello darling. Did you have a nice time with Suzi?"

"Yes, it was a lovely, few days and it was nice to go somewhere new and see the sea. She was a wonderful hostess and made me very welcome."

"Did you get some good photographs of the sea?"

"I did, and one very special one when the sky was all pink and reflecting on the waves. I will bring a copy over tomorrow for you to see. Where has daddy gone by the way? Mac said he was all dressed up."

"Not sure actually. He was being very secretive. I suppose all will be revealed in due course."

Charlie put the kettle on and made the coffee whilst her mother finished the dish she was making. Charlie's phone pinged.

Hi Charlie,

That's a lovely idea and thank you for the invitation, can't wait to see your photographs. The first weekend in May is my down time, on the flying rota, so I could come up on Saturday morning and be with you for lunch if that's OK with you. It would be great to meet Annie again if she can spare the time.

Love Suzi xx

Charlie forwarded Suzi's email to Anne Marie and got an immediate reply.

Will have to consult my busy schedule but I might be able to squeeze it in!!! Love Annie xxxxxx

CHAPTER TWELVE

Stranger in the Dale –
Masham – North Yorkshire

Edward's mysterious lunch was with his friend John, who was Lieutenant Colonel at Catterick garrison, amongst other things which he kept confidential. He was of course Charlie's god father and was also responsible for her reunion with Daniel at Chocorua after his 'death'. John had rung Edward the previous evening and invited him for lunch at Swinton Castle, the magnificent, 20,000-acre estate on the outskirts of Masham. They sat down in Samuel's award-winning restaurant, surrounded by sumptuous décor and attentive, friendly staff. They ordered a bottle of Louis Jadot Gevrey-Chambertin 1er Cru Lavaux, one of Edward's favourite burgundies from 2015, to go with the Estate venison, celeriac puree and poached pear main course.

"So, what have I done to deserve lunch at Swinton, paid for by HM Treasury?" asked Edward.

"It's a long story," replied John, tasting the wine and giving a nod of approval to the sommelier. "You will remember that a while ago, you mentioned there was a Russian gentleman poking about in the Dale and asking strange questions about tractors and slurry tankers."

"I do; and he seemed to be looking for someone in particular. Why? Is he still around?"

"Well, he is actually – and staying here at Swinton. He will be joining us for lunch shortly."

"It can't be the same person. The one that Anne Marie saw was a vagrant type and snooping about barns at night. Daniel thought he was too old to be a Russian agent."

"Firstly, he is not Russian and secondly he is not an agent for anyone. He is actually Ukrainian and a friend of a chap called Dimitri, who Daniel knew."

"That's interesting because when he was in Ripon Farm Services, the local John Deere tractor dealer, he was asking all sorts of odd questions. The owner thought he was possibly Ukrainian. So well done him!"

"We took an interest because we don't like Russians randomly turning up and asking questions near to the army base. However, it turns out, he just dressed down so no one would recognise him, and he has been coming back here every night and living in luxury, as a bona fide visitor to the UK."

"So, what's he up to then?"

"I will let him explain. We think he is looking for Daniel, but he didn't know his name or where he lived. He only has limited information to go on, so was fishing in the dark really. He is obviously a very clever chap and well off. He has passed all the clearances, down at the River House, so we can talk openly with him. As Daniel is away, I thought it best if you and I tried to get the bottom of what he wants. I didn't want to trouble Charlie with it at this stage, with all her recent problems."

"Well, that's very considerate of you John but she is doing really well now and seems to be coping well with the loss of the babies. However, I think you are right. We need to understand what he wants and if there is any danger in his presence."

"Ah, here he comes now. Just take it slowly and we will see what we can find out."

"Marko?" asked John politely, shaking his hand.

"Marko Kharchenko sir; very pleased to make your acquaintance."

"This is my colleague Edward, who might be able to help you find the person you are looking for?"

"Very pleased to meet you, Edward; I certainly need your help. I am fed up with being a beggar!" Marko smiled.

"Can I get you a glass of wine," asked John, offering to pour a glass of the burgundy.

"No thank you. I don't drink alcohol. I think you say teetotal? I will have a glass of still water please."

"Of course. Please help yourself from the jug. We've ordered the venison; is that ok for you?"

"Yes, thank you. I have been staying here for several weeks so I know the menu well!" he laughed. "Thank you for inviting me for lunch and taking an interest in my quest. I thought your security team might catch up with me eventually. I am just pleased you didn't shoot me, like the Russians would have done."

"You don't like the Russians then?" asked Edward.

"Does anybody?" queried Marko, raising his lip in disdain. "Most Ukrainians have terrible family memories of the evil the Russians perpetrated on our grandparents during the famine in the 1930s, when they stole all their food and left them to starve to death in the winter blizzards. Millions of people died because of Stalin's greed and aggression."

"I think we all agree on that," concurred Edward. "So, tell us a bit about yourself Marko; what line of business are you in?"

"I have been involved in banking and finance all my life, but about ten years ago I started my own investment business involved in managing cryptocurrency transactions."

"Mention bitcoin and my mind goes blank," laughed Edward.

"You, and most people I think," confirmed Marko. "I suppose it's like the South Sea bubble in the 1700s. People invest in things they think will make large amounts of money forever, but that is never the case of course. Things inflate in value and then ultimately collapse to a normal commercial level. The way to make money is to have the software to facilitate the transactions for investors and take a percentage. That's what the Dutch did during the tulip bubble and the best traders came out of it successfully when all the investors went bust."

"You are obviously making a good living out of it," observed John. "So why are you in England and trying to find someone, dressed in a disguise?"

"It's complicated, as are a lot of things in life. This is very confidential and I am trusting you two gentlemen with my life."

"You have our word as English gentlemen that this conversation will go no further than this table and if we can help you with any legal endeavour we will do so," confirmed John.

"Thank you, gentlemen. Here we go – as they say! I live in northern Ukraine at Dvorichna and had a very old friend called Dimitri who was killed by the Russians, on the night of the big explosion at their secret base just over the border. I am not sure how he was involved in the explosion but it was very successful for my country and Dimitri has now become a folk hero in my part of the world. He was a real character and quite a secretive person. I do not know how he made all his money but he used to give me piles of cash to put in his cryptocurrency wallet for safe keeping. He did not trust the banks and anyway I am not sure how much of it was legitimate. But let's not go there! He left an e-mail for me before he died saying that if he was killed, he wanted the money to go towards a conservation project in Kenya that his friend ran. All he said was that his friend was called Daniel and that he lived in Yorkshire. Normally I could have tracked this Daniel down easily but he seems to be under the radar and have no NI number, no address and doesn't seem to pay any tax!"

Edward smiled at John.

"You know who this Daniel is then? I have had to be very careful because I did not know if he was a government agent of some sort, or a murderous criminal. I didn't want to get arrested or my head blown off!"

"We might be able to help you," said Edward thoughtfully, "but tell us some more about the money first, and where it actually is."

"I do not know exactly how much there is, but it is in bitcoins and he has been buying them pretty much from the start, so it will be a substantial amount by now. It's in a cold wallet, so it is safe from fraud, but I can't get the money out without the password. All I know is, that it is something to do with a ballerina that dances elegantly like a cat seeking its prey. Evidently, Daniel will know what that means. Do you know him and where I can get in touch with him?"

"I think I might be able to help you but he is out of the country at the moment on business. If I can get in touch with him and get the password, how do we know that you will not just take the money and disappear?"

"I am insulted sir, by your inference, But I will forgive you, as this is a bit of a strange situation and I understand your caution."

"No offence intended," replied Edward. "Just naturally cautious. Let's eat lunch and then decide on a way forwards."

After the meal they retired to the classical sitting room, overlooking the lake, for coffee. Edward and John had a quick word on their own in the gents and decided that Marko was probably genuine but they would not give him the password, without Daniel being present to control the situation.

"Marko, we do know Daniel," confirmed John, "and we will help you to get the money for the conservation project that Daniel runs. He is not a criminal or a secret agent. Just a very private and successful business man like yourself. Edward will speak to him and explain the situation and find out what he wants to do. How long are you planning to be in England?"

"I am only doing this because it was the last wish of my dear friend Dimitri. I am not taking anything out for myself. I will cooperate with whatever plans you make. I have to go to Texas tomorrow but I will leave you my contact number and hopefully we can carry out Dimitri's final wishes to help the animals in Africa."

"You are very kind," said Edward, "and we respect all your efforts to try and find Daniel. I am sure he will be extremely grateful.

They finished their coffees and said their farewells, not realising how this stranger in the Dale would have a life-changing influence on Daniel's plans.

* * *

In the next two weeks Anne Marie was either on the phone to Charlie or in Charlie's kitchen, talking about Suzi and planning her weekend visit.

"Where shall I take her on Sunday? What shall we cook for her on Saturday night? Should I wear my tight jeans or buy a new sexy dress?" mused Anne Marie.

"I should remind you; she is coming to see me. You are incidental!" joked Charlie. "I think you will ruin it all, if you carry on this way. Just relax. Remember she is scared of you!"

"Rubbish! I am worried she might seduce you before I get a chance."

"If Daniel doesn't hurry up and come back soon, I might let her," laughed Charlie.

"So, are you starting to feel a bit more romantic again?" asked Anne Marie sensitively.

"If you mean do I feel like making love again then surprisingly I do. I thought it would take longer but the doctor has given me some hormone tablets to replace the ovarian ones and they seem to be doing the job. I just need Daniel back to try them out properly!"

"I could give you a test run!"

"You don't want to use up all your energy before Saturday do you," teased Charlie. "You are getting on a bit, and she is much younger than you remember!"

"Bitch!"

"In your dreams! Now shall we have an English or exotic meal on Saturday night?" asked Charlie defusing the inuendo. "I have no idea what she likes."

"I have a great idea," suggested Anne Marie. "Why don't we book a table at The Devonshire Arms and then she can choose what she likes from a menu and we don't have to worry. I stayed there when I first bought my house and the food was amazing. It's a really super place and they were very helpful and friendly. I will ring them in the morning and book a table."

"That sounds like a good plan and we can both dress up and you can seduce her with your body!"

"As long as you wear something old and drab. I don't want any competition."

"I might do that… or I might wear the blue velvet dress that Daniel bought me in France."

"Don't you dare!"

* * *

Charlie got up early on the Saturday morning of Suzi's visit and threw open her bedroom window. It was a fabulous spring day and the heat from the sun was already working its magic, as the bees moved from bloom to bloom on the apple trees by the mill race. The lemon-yellow aquilegias and tall spires of violet delphiniums filled the cottage garden with a haze of insects, seeking sweet nourishment in return for fertilising the plants desire. A lone otter, its fur glistening in the sunlight, slipped silently into the rill and disappeared for its daily siesta.

Otter

Charlie pulled on her jeans and one of her favourite white Orvis shirts and went downstairs to take Abbey out for a walk along the shadowed lane that ran from the mill, up towards the moor. The still air was full of perfume from the host of wild flowers that grew below the moss-covered stone walls and the blackbirds were busy scratching through the undergrowth for worms to feed to their broods. Abbey's extra training with Mac, whilst Charlie was ill, had paid dividends and she was now instantly responsive to the whistle and a pleasure to spend some time with, along the peaceful lanes. Charlie had just turned around, to head back towards the mill for breakfast, when her father pulled up in his enormous new John Deere tractor.

"I think we will have to get the lane made wider for your tractor, Daddy!"

"I think you might be right! How are you feeling my darling?"

"I am feeling so much better now it's spring. It's impossible not to feel optimistic on this sort of day."

"My favourite time of year too. I was hoping I might catch you for a quiet chat. It's about this stranger, who has been snooping about the Dale. Well, John and I had lunch with him yesterday up at the Castle and it turns out he is an old friend of someone called Dimitri, who I think Daniel knew well?"

"He was a very good friend of Daniel's and unfortunately, he got shot by the Russians when he was doing a job for him. He was a lovely man and always very courteous to me." added Charlie.

"I didn't realise you knew Dimitri. That makes things a bit easier."

"I thought he was some sort of vagrant or spy?"

"Far from it. He is very wealthy and has access to an inheritance from Dimitri, for Daniel's conservation work in Kenya."

"So why was he lurking about in the dark?"

"It's a long story but he didn't know who Daniel was, and if he was dangerous."

"He's certainly that," laughed Charlie.

"Next time you speak to Daniel on the phone can you explain what's happened and ask him what he wants us to do. The chap is called Marko and he needs some sort of password to open the account where the inheritance is."

"It all sounds very exciting. Do we know how much money there might be?"

"Marko didn't know exactly because it's all in something called a cold wallet, but it's saved as bitcoins and he evidently has been banking them for years so it could work out to be quite a lot. That's if we can get them out, and Daniel knows this cryptic password. And, of course, it depends on whether we can trust this Marko chap. He seems genuine enough but you can never tell with these foreigners."

"Daddy, you can't say that sort of thing anymore."

"Why? Are the blackbirds bothered," Edward joked. "Sorry, birds of colour!"

"You're impossible!"

"That's what your mother says too, but she seems to have stuck around!"

Charlie smiled and gave her father a hug and a kiss. "Love you Daddy; tell Mummy I am having dinner at The Devonshire Arms with Annie and Suzi tonight."

"Will do… and let me know what Daniel thinks about this Marko chap."

* * *

When Charlie got back to the mill and had finished breakfast, she thought she would have a quick soak in the bath and decide what to wear in the evening for the meal. It didn't take long to pick the blue velvet dress just for fun and to tease Anne Marie.

She had not been down in the kitchen long, when Abbey barked, as a car pulled up on the drive and parked next to Charlie's Ferrari. Charlie opened the kitchen door.

"Hi Suzi, did you have a good trip up?"

"Yes, fab thank you. Love your hair, Charlie!" Suzi gave Charlie a kiss on each cheek with a big grin.

"Love yours too. When did you have it cut?"

"I saw a picture of this fabulous model last week, with a very short silver blonde bob and I thought it might suit me. Do you think Annie will like it?"

"I am sure she will love it. You look fabulous!"

"Is that your Ferrari?"

"Daniel bought it for me as a present. I thought we could go out in it, to the hotel tonight."

"Sounds amazing, but I didn't bring a dress. I thought we were staying in?"

"Don't worry, I have a few nice dresses you can chose from. Come on in and have a coffee. Mummy has made us a Victoria sponge cake to keep us going till tonight! Actually, shall we sit in the garden? It such a lovely day to be inside."

"That's a good idea and you can tell me all about Annie. Is she coming over this afternoon?" asked Suzi eagerly.

"Slice of cake?" teased Charlie.

"Oh, please tell me. Since you invited me up, I can't stop thinking about her. She must be slightly interested or you wouldn't have invited me."

At that point Charlie's mobile went. It was Anne Marie, so Charlie stood up and wandered over to the rill.

"Has Suzi arrived yet?" whispered Anne Marie.

"Yes."

"Well, has she mentioned me?"

"No." Charlie fibbed.

"Is she still coming tonight?"

"Possibly… Yes of course she is coming, but take it slowly or you will frighten her off with your usual enthusiasm."

"What is she wearing?"

"A shirt slashed to the waist and jeans ripped up to her thighs."

"Your joking!"

"Yes! Stop fantasising and go and get ready. She looks fabulous by the way." And Charlie cut her off, much to Anne Marie's frustration. Charlie wandered back across to Suzi, who was feeding some sponge to Abbey."

"Sorry, is she not meant to have cake."

"There's that word again,"

"Sorry."

"Aghh!… Right, you kill people for a living, yes"

"Well, a few."

"So, you are perfectly capable of being a little distant from reality. Just take it slowly and enjoy being with Annie but don't worry about rushing things. You need to get to know each other properly, if you want the relationship to go anywhere. I love you both dearly and I don't want either of you to get hurt. I think you are made for each other, if you give it time."

"OK I will try. Kick me under the table if I do anything wrong."

"Let's go and find you a nice dress and some shinpads! And then I will show you my seascapes from the Creek."

* * *

Charlie had arranged with Anne Marie to meet at The Devonshire Arms at seven o'clock for dinner and not go in the same vehicle, in case things didn't go as planned. When Charlie and Suzi arrived at the luxurious, privately-owned country house, they were guided to park the Ferrari in the premier parking at the magnificent entrance. It was a beautiful, warm spring evening and the design of the immaculate gardens reminded Charlie of Versailles, with parterres, fountains and generous planting. The surrounding landscaped parklands, made the setting perfect for a very special romantic liaison. Anne Marie was sitting under the shade of a stretched awning, sipping her flute of Louis Roederer Cristal. She was wearing a fuchsia pink, Zuhair Murad designed jumpsuit with wide palazzo trousers and scalloped sleeves. She looked sophisticated, stunning and a million dollars. Suzi gasped when she saw Anne Marie and grabbed Charlie's arm, as she slipped out of the Ferrari.

"She will never go for me; she's in the super-rich league."

"Take a deep breath," whispered Charlie, "wait till she sees your dress!"

Charlie had leant Suzi her azure blue-velvet, sensual number that Daniel had bought for her at Caralys's in Nice, and in which she had seduced him many times. The pink silk lining, highlighting the lowcut neck line, was pulse-racing whatever your proclivity. Anne Marie turned and saw Suzi holding Charlie's arm and her heart beat a thousand times in that second. She knew instantly that this incredibly beautiful young lady, wearing Charlie's silk dress caressing her sensuous body, had to become her dream lover. She walked across to meet them, with double faire la bise each. Suzi's perfume was hypnotic.

"Well, you two look amazingly beautiful. I adore your dress Suzi: I am sure I have seen it somewhere before Charlie?" smiled Anne Marie.

"Well, you said 'I' couldn't wear it!" laughed Charlie. Suzi looked confused.

"Come and sit down and have a drink in the sun before we go into dinner. What would you like to drink Suzi?"

Charlie noticed she had already been demoted to second place and she smiled to herself at the good omen.

Suzi scanned the extensive wine list. "Can I have a glass of the Amarone della Valpolicella please," obviously familiar with the Italian wine. Anne Marie was quietly impressed.

"Can I have the same please," chipped-in Charlie, momentarily distracting Anne Marie from taking in Suzi's green sultry eyes.

The cheerful waiter took the order and disappeared to get the drinks.

"So, what have you two been up to all day?" asked Anne Marie.

Charlie wanted to say 'making mad passionate love in my bed' but resisted the temptation to tease Anne Marie.

"We have had a lovely afternoon sitting in the sun and looking at Charlie's fantastic photographs of the seascapes around the Creek at my home. She created amazing pictures in half an hour, that I have been trying to get for years."

"It's just luck you know. She takes millions of pictures and just shows you the good ones!"

"Well, I think she is a wonderful photographer and very highly skilled," replied Suzi, taking Anne Marie's comment seriously.

"Just ignore her Suzi; she is winding you up,"

"Sorry, I didn't realise!"

Charlie winked at Suzi so Anne Marie could not see. Suzi smiled but was not too sure what was going on.

They finished their drinks and the waiter showed them through to the Michelin-starred Shaun Rankin restaurant. Anne Marie took the lead and Charlie followed, linking arms with Suzi to give her some confidence.

"You are doing fine. Just relax; she fancies you like mad," whispered Charlie into her ear.

"Do you think so? I still prefer you!"

"Give Annie a bit more time. She can be a bit overwhelming at first. She will soften to you with time."

"What are you two whispering about?" asked Anne Marie turning around suddenly.

"We were just saying how lovely you looked in that jumpsuit Annie," fibbed Charlie, again.

The waiter took them their circular table, softly lit by a crystal chandelier and overlooking the pool in the gardens. The classical décor, with white Roman pillars, Wedgewood green walls and gold-framed oil paintings created the perfect setting for the start of a love affair. Charlie hoped.

Anne Marie tried not to look directly at Suzi, although the low neckline of Suzi's dress was hard to avoid. Suzi tried to evade direct eye contact with Anne Marie but wasn't averse to discretely straightening her back occasionally to emphasize her décolletage. Charlie was enjoying the simmering passion.

"Shall we look at the menu and order some more drinks," suggested Charlie.

"When I stayed here last time the langoustines in elderflower were superb," said Anne Marie. "What do you fancy Suzi?"

"I think I will go for the venison loin with blackcurrants and celeriac."

"Good choice," concurred Charlie. "I will go with the venison too. Shall we have some champagne to celebrate?"

"What are we celebrating?" enquired Anne Marie.

"Who needs men!" laughed Charlie.

"That deserves the best in the house!" smiled Anne Marie, looking directly at Suzi. Suzi returned the smile and blushed slightly.

Anne Marie ordered a bottle of Krug Vintage, much to the pleasure of the sommelier.

As the champagne relaxed the evening, the conversation became more animated and the laughter softened Suzi's self-consciousness. They relived their adventure in Agatti, when the three of them rescued Rashieka, Prince Khalid's wife, from the Ecuadorian kidnappers. Anne Marie's self-deprecating story of how she nearly blew them all up with the explosives, made Suzi giggle and she put her hand on Anne Marie's forearm as they enjoyed the memory together. Charlie noticed a tiny movement of Anne Marie's arm towards Suzi, accepting the first physical contact with a smile.

"And when the Discovery was blown into the swimming pool, I thought we had definitely blown our chances of success," joked Charlie.

"You were brilliant Suzi, the way you despatched the kidnappers," said Anne Marie looking straight at Suzi. "Without you the whole thing would have been a disaster. You were so cool; it was very attractive!"

"I thought Charlie's cleavage distraction was inspired," said Suzi, obviously still impressed with the vision herself.

"I'll never forget that kidnapper's face when you bent over and sprayed him with the pepper."

"I sometimes think our cleavages are our best weapon against men!" suggested Charlie.

"Oh, I can think of other attributes that can work just as well!" proposed Anne Marie; and they all dissolved in stitches of laughter.

The moment was interrupted by the waiter serving the first course. "The langoustines for you mademoiselle and the venison for you, and for you," he said, as he placed the plates with flamboyant style. "Is there anything else I can get for you?"

"Another bottle of the Krug, please," ordered Anne Marie.

"I think we will need a taxi to get home. The Ferrari will need a room for the night!" grinned Charlie.

"I don't normally drink this much," said Suzi, taking another sip from her glass. "But it's the best champagne I have ever had, thank you Annie."

"I am pleased you like the vintage my darling. It's my favourite too," said Anne Marie, placing her hand delicately on Suzi's forearm, this time. Suzi did not recoil and seemed to enjoy the touch. Their eyes met for a split second, and Charlie knew her plan was going well so far.

"Have you spoken to Daniel lately?" asked Anne Marie, ensuring Suzi got the message that Charlie was spoken for. Charlie immediately knew the game Anne Marie was playing.

"I have no idea where he is, or when he is coming back," lied Charlie. "I do get lonely on my own," she smiled at Suzi.

"Good job I'm staying with you tonight to keep you company then," grinned Suzi and holding Charlie's hand. The dynamics were changing and Suzi was starting to enjoy the interplay.

The main course was consumed in a flash of laughter and inuendo. And another bottle of Krug. They ordered the Lanark Blue and Columbian cappuccinos whilst they planned what to do the next day.

"Would you like to come over to my place for lunch and we can go for a walk down by the river and get some fresh air?"

"That sounds a great idea Annie," agreed Charlie. "We can take the dogs."

"It's ages since we did that together. I seem to remember you fell in the river last time and I had to rescue you," said Anne Marie, scoring another point.

"I enjoyed the hot bath afterwards!" Charlie remembered, fighting back.

Suzi was even more confused, but was enjoying the evening so much she didn't care. The Dales were so much more fun than flying typhoons.

* * *

Charlie was fast asleep when her mobile rang. She sleepily grabbed it off her bedside table. It was Daniel.

"Good morning my darling; did you have a nice meal with Annie and Suzi at The Devonshire?"

"How did you know… don't bother answering that! How are you getting on out there?"

"Slowly, but M has made real progress and is in, on the inside. We have a plan at this end but need an exit strategy for Didi and her mates. Can you contact Nzinga and ask her if we could borrow one of Fahd's 747s to airlift them, and us, out and back to Nairobi. She will need to set up a liaison with the orphanage, to take care of them temporarily until we get our new facilities built."

"What new facilities?"

"I will explain when I see you. I will need you, Annie and Suzi to fly out here separately to help with the release."

"Sounds dangerous!"

"You know I wouldn't put you in any danger my darling. I just need some brains on the ground to organise things with Five Eyes."

"OK but we can shoot, you know."

"And blow yourselves up, if I remember correctly!"

"Need to make love to you soon."

"Are you feeling OK now?"

"Fully recovered and need your touch."

"Can't wait. Did your father tell you about Marko?"

"Yes, but how did you know all about that… I know, don't ask."

"I could probably use his skills out here. Can you ask John to fly him out here for me?"

"Of course, but will he want to come?"

"Tell him there is a couple of million dollars in it for him, if our plan works."

"That might help!"

"Right. Better go now before someone tracks this phone. Love to Annie and Suzi."

"Bye my darl–" The line went dead.

Charlie pulled on her dressing gown, opened the curtains to a glorious day, and went down to the kitchen to let Abbey out and make some tea for Suzi, who was still fast asleep after all the Krug. Charlie walked back upstairs with the tray and quietly pushed open Suzi's bedroom door. She was lying naked on the bed, the duvet long gone onto the carpet. Charlie stopped in her tracks, stunned by Suzi's fabulous body. Her high, elegant cheek bones and soft complexion were in contrast to her silver cropped bob. Her long, slim and sensuous body was immaculate and her legs seemed to go on for ever. Charlie was mesmerised. Suzi slowly opened her eyes and looked across at Charlie.

"Do you think Annie will like my body?"

"Let's put it this way. I've just shot Daniel!" smiled Charlie.

CHAPTER THIRTEEN

Landscape of Lies

Daniel and Francesca were on one of their routine visits to Wangkatha mine and stopped at the main gate for the usual security checks. The security guard came out of the cabin to look at the paperwork and passes. It was Max. This left Daniel in the surreal situation that his fellow infiltrator was now authorising his entrance credentials. Not only that, but he couldn't say anything, because although Francesca seemed to be on his side, he could not be sure and could not risk breaking Max's fortuitous cover. Max looked up at Francesca, who was driving the tanker full of explosives.

"Good afternoon mademoiselle, you are too beautiful to be driving this dangerous stuff around!" flirted Max, not anticipating the reply.

"And you're too handsome to be stuck in that hut all day!"

"It's a date then," suggested Max jokingly.

"You're on. I'll give you my number on the way out and you can come over for a barbie." offered Francesca.

"Great. Can't wait."

Daniel sat motionless in his seat, staring at the sky in disbelief. This could get very complicated he thought. As they drove down the precarious track into the mine, he tried to defuse the situation.

"Don't you think it's a bit risky getting into bed with one of the security guards?" Daniel suggested.

"I thought I'd leave that till the second night," laughed Francesca, shaking her red hair back provocatively. "Anyway, he's rather cute and you're way too serious to be fun."

"No joking apart, don't you think it might mess up the years of work you have put into this? You are this close, to getting into their systems and you could ruin it all, with one wrong word or gesture."

"But it could work out perfectly, because he must log into the systems to check our passes and if I can extract his passwords out of him, then I can maybe dig into the central databases."

"His access will surely only allow him into a very limited part of the software so you've no hope of getting any further."

"You underestimate my systems skills, Daniel. I'm not as dumb as I look!"

They arrived at the bottom of the mine and were directed along a lateral shaft that went underground. They travelled for about a thousand metres and reached the blasting site.

"Did they say why they wanted this tunnel widened out?" asked Daniel. "There are no gold seams down here, are there?"

"I wouldn't have thought so. They're probably looking for titanium or some other metal perhaps?"

"It's a bit odd," said Daniel. "When we have set up the auto ANFO injector and they have all retreated, I will have a quick look around, whilst you lock the tanker booms down."

"OK. Good plan."

After the injections were all in place, Daniel walked along the shaft with the torch from the tool box. After about fifty metres he came to a pair of big steel doors blocking off the tunnel. The doors were relatively new and ran on tracks, so were obviously controlled by motors from the other side. Daniel returned to the tanker and climbed back into the cab.

"Do you know where we are? asked Daniel. "The tunnel seemed fairly straight, so I reckon we must be nearly under the main house where Kilpatrick lives."

Francesca checked the GPS linked to the injection software.

"You're right. We are about fifty metres from the house and about 200 metres down."

"Interesting," mused Daniel. "I wonder what the tunnel is used for?"

"I could interrogate the guard on the gate!"

"I thought we decided that was not a good idea?"

"You thought it was not a good idea. I thought it was a great idea and he is very young and muscular. Just my type!"

On the way out, Francesca gave Max her phone number and confirmed the invite for Saturday night.

Daniel was conflicted. Should he put Max off or should he let him go? He could use it to test Francesca's loyalty to the rescue. On the other hand, Francesca's raunchy approach might scare Max to death!

Daniel decided to invite Max back to the derelict hotel in Widgiemooltha, on Wednesday evening, to compare notes and start to work out a plan. Max arrived at seven sharp in the rusty old pickup and parked next to Daniel's Holden. Daniel was sitting outside on one of the old leather chairs they had dragged from the bar at the start of the mission, drinking a tin of lager.

"Steak and chips?" said Max with a smile.

"You'll be lucky. It's a chuck sandwich again," replied Daniel.

"No. I've got us steak and chips in the hot box in the pickup. I thought you might need a decent meal, living in this dump."

"It's all right for some living in a luxury single storey by the lake."

"It's hard work chatting up all these beautiful wagon drivers on the gate. Very stressful. Your face was a picture!"

"What were you doing on the gate? I thought you were a stockman on the fence line?"

"Oh, both the normal gate men were off sick so I got lumbered with the job. Boring as hell."

"But it could be very useful for our plan," suggested Daniel. "We could easily make them sick again."

"That's true. The thing that has surprised me is how few guards there are on the place. We were led to believe it was like Fort Knox, but apart from a few Chinese guys who live in the other houses it all seems pretty relaxed."

"So, what's the camera security like?"

"The house and surrounding grounds are covered in them and the main entrance is covered. But it all seems strangely devoid of normal security."

"It's all a bit odd. I will ring Jondi later and see if her colleagues at Pine Gap have any recent intel on the mine security. How are you getting on with Pete, your land-sailing friend?"

"At face value, he seems to trust me completely, but I have no idea how loyal he is to Kilpatrick. I think it's too soon to ask him probing questions without creating suspicion."

"I am sure you are right, but be very careful Max, he is the sort of guy that would kill you and ask questions later. Life is pretty valueless out here."

"Thanks. I'll get the steak!"

They drank two more beers and ate their way through the tepid steak and cold chips. But the thought was there.

"Have you been able to confirm that Didi is actually in the barn?"

"No, not yet. Pete thinks there are about ten chimpanzees in there but he wouldn't know a baby chimp from a gorilla, so it could be a mixture."

"It would be helpful if we knew how many we are rescuing! I have asked Nzinga if she can borrow one of Fahd's jets to take them back to Nairobi but we will need to know numbers, to fit the plane out with the right number of travel compartments."

"How will we get them back to the airport at Perth?"

"Another request for Jondi, I think? I have asked Charlie to ask Annie and Suzi to fly out with Nzinga, when we are ready, so we have plenty of support on the ground. If we pull it off, we don't want to be hanging around to be shot by disgruntled Chinese warlords."

"Is Charlie well enough to travel all the way out here?" asked Max, knowing how Daniel was less attentive than he should be.

"Yes, she is fine. Seems to be back to normal," said Daniel, not realising the complexities to come. "Now, I need to brief you about Marko and Dimitri's will."

"Whose Marko and what will?"

Daniel explained the whole saga and how Marko had the expert knowledge in mainstream banking and cryptocurrency systems.

"I have offered him £2 million to come out to Australia to try and crack how the Chinese are funding their aspirations in Australia and solve all the problems that Shane and Dundee from Five Eyes told us about."

"And where are we going to get £2 million from?"

"I am sure the Australian government has no idea exactly how much currency the Chinese have invested over here, or anyone else come to that. It's all smoke and mirrors with a bit of dark web thrown in. If the odd few million goes astray no one will know."

"Does that mean there is some for us too?" asked Max hopefully.

"Well, plenty for the new gorilla conservation project I've got planned, anyway!"

"What new gorilla project?"

"Nzinga and Fahd will tell you all about it when they come to help us get Didi out."

"So, this will, that Marko purports to know about, did you have any idea it existed?"

"No. I was a bit suspicious that something was going on in Dimitri's head when he kept talking about his cat, but I couldn't work out why. You saw his place; I had no idea that he had any money, except when he was shot by the Russian border guard, it was obvious something financial was going on. I have no idea whether it was legal or not, but as long as it hurts the Russians who cares."

"Do you think we can trust this Marko chap? We could get him inside Kilpatrick's computer systems so he can locate the currency, and he could then move it somewhere else and we wouldn't have a clue?"

"That's where Seb in Cayman and Francesca come in, I hope. I have got Seb to check all our dark-web friends to see if he can come up with anything. It's up to you to get as much out of Francesca as you can. If you think we can trust her, we will get her out of trouble with her South African masters in return for her checking what Marko is doing."

Will that be enough?"

"Well, I wouldn't know a blockchain from a concrete block so we are going to have to trust someone."

"So, I can go to the barbie at Francesca's on Saturday? It should be fun meeting a few local girls."

"I have a sneaking suspicion you will be the only guest and you will be lucky to come away with your virginity intact!"

* * *

For the next few days Max was back on fence duty, riding the boundaries of the estate in the heat of the day. On Thursday evening, his boss, Pete was away land-sailing with some mates somewhere near the coast, so Max decided to go for a quiet ride on one of the younger horses, along the beach next to the Salt Lake. The evening air was cool and refreshing, after the tropical daytime temperature, and he was enjoying the exuberance of the youngster under the saddle.

He was just rounding the headland, out of sight of the main house, when he saw the girl again, who he thought was mirage last time. Only this time it was real and the young lady walked slowly towards him. Her naturally blonde wavy hair cascaded down her back. Her softly tanned pale skin was perfection, with beautiful high cheekbones and gentle blue eyes. Her slender body moved elegantly under the gossamer thin silk beach dress, as she strode barefoot across the golden sand. The breeze drifting off the ephemeral salt lake, filled the air with the scent of eucalyptus. It flurried her diaphanous dress. Her long elegant thighs flashing, tantalisingly, between the high slit. Elegant long gold earrings caressed her shoulders. A threaded gold choker, tight around her neck, had four slender chains disappearing mysteriously down between her diminutive breasts. She looked directly into Max's eyes and smiled.

"This is a private estate," said Max formally, stuck for a good opening line.

"I'm a very private person," she said softly and instantly vanished into the lakeside flora.

Max sat on his horse totally entranced. Who was she and what was she doing in this godforsaken place?

* * *

When Pete and Max were tacking up the horses the following morning, in preparation for the daily routine, Max risked asking about the girl.

"I was riding my youngster along the beach last night and I came across a young lady walking towards the house. I assumed she was a guest of Kilpatrick's?"

"Long blonde hair and thin as stick?"

"Yes, that's her. Who is she?" asked Max casually as he tightened up his girth.

"She's Kilpatrick's whore. She's been here a few months and goes up to his house every evening. Sorry, I should have told you about her. She's not allowed talk to anyone except the Chinese girl who looks after the monkeys."

"She's very pretty," ventured Max.

"Don't go there, mate. If he catches you with her, he'll blow your balls off!"

* * *

Max drove up to Kambalda East in his pickup on Saturday night and found Acacia Road where Francesca lived. Daniel had briefed him what to expect and he was the only guest for the bar-b-q as Daniel had predicted. What he didn't expect was Francesca dressed very smartly in a long green skirt and white shirt with kimono sleeves. She had braided her hair and looked very sophisticated.

"Hi Max, glad you could come; would you like a lager from the fridge?"

Max was a taken aback by how lovely she looked and was a bit lost for words.

"Er… Yes please."

"Just help yourself and bring me one please, whilst I turn the steaks."

Max went into the tidy kitchen, with not a dirty pan in sight; not at all what Daniel had indicated. It made Max uneasy but he got a couple of cans from the fridge and walked back outside.

"Take a seat Max. Do you like corn on the cob?"

"That would be great thank you."

Francesca forked the steaks onto plates and added the sweetcorn. "Mustard on the table. Tuck in."

"Which part of the States are you from Max?"

"Worked all over really. Drifted from job to job," he lied.

"So how long have you worked up at the mine?"

"Only a few weeks. I was just passing through and looking for some temporary work and the security guy offered me a job. How long have you been doing the explosive thing? Looks dangerous?"

"A couple of years around here. It's not that dangerous if you know what you are doing."

"And your partner in the wagon; who's he?"

"He's called Daniel, not been with us long. Nice enough guy but not very interesting to talk to. Keeps himself to himself. A bit boring actually."

Max smiled to himself.

"So, are you married? Any kids?" quizzed Francesca.

"No. Never settled down really. Women scare me," joked Max.

"Do I scare you?" grinned Francesca, looking straight at Max.

"Not so far!" laughed Max.

The steak was delicious and beautifully cooked, as was the sweetcorn.

"So, what do you actually do in security?"

"Mostly ride the fences and look after the horses. Pretty easy job really. I like being outside in the fresh air."

"I loved riding when I was younger," said Francesca. "Did some show jumping with my dad in Joburg. Was actually quite good at it and won a few prizes at local gymkhanas. We'll have to rustle up a couple of horses sometime and go for a ride together, or is that too much of a busman's holiday!"

"Sounds good to me. Spent my life on a horse. Always enjoyed riding with friends. Used to ride thoroughbreds out for a trainer back in the States."

Exercise at dawn

Francesca fetched a couple more cans from the fridge and they watched the sun turn crimson as it sank below the surrounding houses. The conversation flowed freely and Max was beginning to enjoy Francesca's company. She was clearly intelligent and she seemed honest and open about herself and her family.

"Have you got any brothers or sisters?" asked Max, genuinely interested.

"I had a brother, but unfortunately he got killed by a lion they were loading at my father's game reserve. It somehow got loose when they were transferring it to a transport crate and it was understandably upset by the procedure. Robert had done it a hundred times before, but I guess these things happen so quickly."

"I am really sorry. That must have been awful for you," consoled Max.

"It was a few years ago now and you just have to get on with your life. We can't get him back now. My father blamed himself, but he was away at an auction for captive bred southern white rhinos, for his reserve. Fortunately, no one else was injured and they managed to tranquilise the lion and get it back into the crate."

Max thought he had found some common ground and took a risk.

"Did you know that Kilpatrick has a collection of young gorillas and chimps up at the mine. He keeps them in small cages in a barn on the far side of the house."

"I know. I have heard them calling after the detonations down in the mine. I guess they are scared of the noise of the explosions. It's terrible to keep them in this alien environment; the poor things must be frightened to death," said Francesca emotionally. "God knows where he got them from."

"I wish I could help set them free but they would die out here very quickly." Max floated the idea to see her response.

"Maybe we could do it together one day," smiled Francesca. "We could take them back home to Africa; I am sure my father would help."

"Sounds a nice dream Francesca, Maybe, one day we could make it happen."

"We could write a book about it and call it *In to Africa*!"

"I know a good photographer who would do the pictures," Max suggested half joking. "So how did you get into the explosives business?"

"Well, there wasn't enough work for me on the game reserve and my father knew a few people in the mining industry. I looked into it and it seemed a lucrative career so I went to the University of Pretoria and did an honours degree in mining engineering. We did a module on the use of explosives and I found all the modern technology really interesting, so I did my certificate in blasting engineering. I then got a job with a big mining company near Joburg."

"Beautiful and clever," flirted Max. "So how did you end up out here?"

"Long story but I saw this job advertised and thought the experience would help my cv," she lied.

"You've certainly led an interesting life. Well, I suppose I had better get off. I've got an early start in the morning," said Max reluctantly.

"Thank you for coming over Max. I have really enjoyed your company. Hopefully we can get that ride out together soon."

"I would really like that," said Max. "You've got my number and if you can find some horses, you can give me a ring."

Francesca walked back round the house with Max to his pickup, and he hovered by the door but she didn't attempt to kiss him. He climbed in and put his arm on the open window rest. Francesca touched his arm lightly with her hand.

"Bye Max. Hope to see you soon."

Max drove down the Avenue and back out onto the main road. He had really enjoyed the evening and the time had flown by. He thought Francesca was fun and very attractive. He wished he had kissed her then, but he knew he was playing with fire. He liked the touch.

* * *

Max arrived back at the derelict hotel in Widgiemooltha to debrief Daniel on Francesca.

"She thinks your boring!" related Max gleefully.

"Did she invite you into bed?"

"No, that would have been crude on a first date," suggested Max.

"A first date eh?! I thought you were meant to be working?"

"I was – sort of," said Max defensively.

"So go on then, what did you find out?"

Max described how beautiful she was and how sophisticated she looked in her long green skirt. He related her family history and how they had the wildlife reserve in South Africa, including southern white rhinos. Daniel started to show some interest.

"I will get Nzinga to check her story out with our contacts in Joburg. If it's true then maybe we can use her as part of our plan?"

"She seemed genuine enough to me," said Max. "I know you said she was here because some big company was blackmailing her to find something out from Kilpatrick's systems, but apart from that, her story all seemed to stack up."

"Have you arranged to see her again?"

"She says she is going to take me riding."

"I bet she is!" said Daniel cynically.

"So, what do we do next?" asked Max.

"We need to understand why there is so little security at the mine and also what's behind those big steel doors under Kilpatrick's house. None of it makes any sense at the moment. Can you keep a check on the comings and goings next time you are on gate duty? There must be more to it? And also try and find out a bit more about the Chinese living on site. Where do they work? In the house or down in the mine. Also, how many of them are there?"

"OK. I will see if I can get anything out of the whore, I saw on the beach the other evening. I can't believe she thinks Kilpatrick is Mr Universe. She might be open to giving me some information? Most prostitutes aren't that clever or they would be doing something more worthwhile with their lives. Shame really, she is very pretty!"

"I thought you loved Francesca?" laughed Daniel.

"You've got two ladies," contested Max, referring to Charlie and Annie.

"That's different, one of them is gay. Although I'm not always sure which one!" replied Daniel grinning.

* * *

The following Thursday was Pete's day off again, so Max decided to try and find out more information from the Chinese girl who looked after the apes in the barn adjacent to the stables. He mucked out the horses very slowly, with only a few shovelfuls in each barrow-load so he had an excuse for frequent trips to the muckheap. On the fourth load he caught the girl coming out of her barn with a barrow full of muck.

"Hi there. How are you doing?" enquired Max with a big smile.

"I no speak much English."

"I no speak any Chinese," laughed Max, trying to break the ice. "Do you like the monkeys?"

"They not monkeys. Called apes."

"Ah what sort," asked Max, playing dumb.

"Six mountain gorillas, very rare, three lowland gorillas and one chimpanzee. Mr Kilpatrick very famous conservation. Helping breed in captivity."

"Really. Does he like the apes? Does he look at them often?"

"No, he very busy man. I look after."

"Could I see them sometime?"

"You come now quick. He is away until Saturday."

"Great thank you. What is your name?"

"Quinyang."

Max followed Quinyang through the big sliding door into the barn. There were twelve cages with metal grills down one side of the barn and straw bales against the opposite wall for bedding up. Max was horrified by the conditions. The apes were on bare concrete floors with only a small pile of straw in one corner of each cage for bedding. There were no branches to climb on, or any other psychologically stimulating objects for them to play with. They were in very poor condition and obviously not being fed the right sort of food.

"When do they go outside into the runs, so they can get some exercise?"

"I have stopped letting out. Not come back in."

Max walked up the row of cages looking at each animal but got no response from the despondent captives. It was very depressing and he was concerned some of the younger ones might die before they could rescue them. He knew one of them was Didi but could not tell which one she was.

"You like my little charges, yes?"

"Thank you for showing them to me Quinyang. Do you live with your husband in the single storey?"

"Yes, the one top of row. Best house. He computer champion," she said proudly.

"Does he work at the mine?"

"No, he work in big house for Mr Kilpatrick. He head computer man."

"Ah very clever man," said Max. "You are very lucky lady. Thank you for showing me around, Quinyang. I had better get back to work."

Max went back to finish mucking out all the horses and then he tacked his own horse up to ride around the fence line, but he could not get the images of the poor gorillas out of his head. He decided to go back to see Daniel later that evening to tell him the bad news.

* * *

"God it's horrific Daniel. Their coats are heavily soiled and their hair is falling out from malnutrition. The Chinese lady looking after them is totally ignorant of what they need and thinks Kilpatrick is some sort of conservationist who is going to run a breeding programme. I have no idea what is he thinking or why he would want to collect wild animals at all?"

"A lot of these wealthy people just like to collect wild animals. It's some sort of competitive dominance thing. His Chinese masters probably collect giant pandas and he is trying to impress them with the gorillas. He wants shooting; in fact remind me to do that before we leave."

"If I don't get there first!" said Max angrily.

"I wonder what's going on in that house. It's not that big. Do you think there is some sort of underground complex behind those steel doors in the tunnel?" pondered Daniel.

"But there are no large numbers of people coming and going either into the house or even the mine come to that. In fact, there are very few vehicles fetching ore from the mine, relative to its size. None of it is logical. Do you think the mine is just a front for something else?"

"Mm, could be. You will just have to keep on digging Max. Have you seen the whore again to see if she knows anything?

"No. I have kept an eye out for her in the evenings but no luck so far. How about Francesca, has she revealed anything else?"

"That could be taken two ways! Not really. Seb sent me a message to say that her father does have a game ranch near Joburg and that the rest of her story she told you stacks up; so, I think we can trust her for now, but only on a need-to-know basis. So, no pillow talk next time you meet her for your horse ride."

"Chance would be fine thing. She has never rung me back," said Max sadly.

"She will tomorrow."

"How do you know?"

"She asked me if I knew where she could find some horses for hire," smiled Daniel.

"And did you?"

"No, but Jondi did!"

"Is that strictly Five Eyes stuff?"

"Sex is their most effective weapon!" grinned Daniel.

* * *

The following day, Max was sitting outside his house having a can of lager after his long ride around the fence line when is phone rang.

"Hi, it's Francesca. How are you doing?"

"Good thank you. Just having a beer in the sun. How about you?"

"Lying in the garden improving my tan," she said seductively.

"I need another cold beer now!" joked Max and she laughed at the other end of the phone.

"I've found us a pair of horses to hack out. How are you fixed for Saturday about four? We could have a bar-b-q after if you like?"

"That sounds great. Shall I pick you up at home?"

"Brill. See you then."

Max leant back in his chair and smiled to himself. He had found a woman he liked and was going on a date. Sort of. He shut his eyes and thought about Francesca's hand on his arm. His body stirred.

His dream was broken by a tap on his kitchen window behind his head. He looked round but could see no one, and settled down in his chair again. Then the tap, tap came again. He turned and saw a face inside the window partially hidden by the drab curtain. He got up from the chair, looked around and walked back into the house. It was the young girl from the beach looking frightened.

"Hello, how did you get in," asked Max softly, taken aback by her vulnerability.

"Sorry should I go? I needed to talk to someone. Can you help me?

"Of course, I will try. But I understood you were a friend of Mr Kilpatrick's. I was told not to speak to you or he would be very angry."

"He has told Pete to tell everyone that, so I cannot talk to anybody and I am very alone and lonely. I am frightened of him and worried he will kill me if I try and leave."

"Well, he's away at the moment so you are safe. Would you like a drink… Sorry, what's your name?"

"Mia. Just water please, but no one must see me."

"I have seen you dancing on the beach. You are a very beautiful dancer but how did you end up here?"

"I was a ballet dancer at the Sydney Opera House."

"What ballet were you in?

"I was working on *Anna Karenina*, Tolstoy's great tragedy. I was only in the corps de ballet, that's the extras."

"Yes, I know what the corps de ballet is. I have been to the Met in New York a hundred times."

"What is your favourite ballet?" asked Mia, relaxing a bit at their common interest.

"*La Bayadère*. The Kingdom of the Shades is magical."

"And your favourite ballerina?"

"Of all time? Alina Cojocaru; she is just amazingly beautiful and so elegant. I adore young slim elegant dancers," Max smiled and Mia got the message. "How did you end up here, in the middle of nowhere?"

"I was not earning enough money to send home for my sick father, who is dying of lung cancer, so I took a part time job as a dancer in a Sydney nightclub. I hated it. It seemed such an insult to all the sacrifices and hard years of physical training to become a ballerina. But there are limited ways for a young girl to make money fast, in a big city, and some of my fellow ballerinas secretly do it all the time. Sometimes in life you just have to focus on where your train is going and not look out of the window at the passing dross."

"When did your father become ill?" asked Max.

"He worked all his life in a coalmine, south of Sydney, owned by some Chinese conglomerate. They didn't care about health and safety and the coaldust got onto his lungs, so he had to retire early, and he has not got long left. He spends his days sitting on his veranda, with his old kelpie sat at his feet. I am just trying to earn enough so he can die peacefully at home, with his dog at his side."

"Is your mother not around anymore?"

"No, the bitch ran off with a young American lieutenant when I was four years old. My dad brought me up and we are very close. He has been my idol. I love him so much; but life is cruel sometimes. He deserved so much more out of his life."

"But how did you end up with Kilpatrick?"

"After several performances I noticed this obviously wealthy older man leaning against the wall at the entrance to the club. You get used to the voyeuristic eyes of the hormonal young guys desperate for sex, but he was different. It was more obsessive. He only came in to see me dance and as soon as I had finished each session he disappeared. He never bought a drink; just tipped the bouncers excessively and disappeared. After about a week he came up to me after my dance and put a $1000 note in my garter and asked to speak to me later. He offered me ten times what I was earning at the Opera House.

"I didn't know what to do. Was he a criminal, would he rape me and kill me or was he just a lonely old, but wealthy man?"

"So, you accepted the job and came here?"

"Yes, but I accepted it for the sake of my dad, and I cried every day for a week."

"So, are you a prisoner here?"

"No, it's a golden gaol really. I can have whatever I want but I am trapped by the money."

"Does he force himself on you?"

"No, it's a bit weird. All I have to do is dance for him every night at seven o'clock. For fifteen minutes. But it is very lonely. Nobody is allowed to speak to me or they lose their jobs. I have a nice lodge and I really enjoy watching all the monkeys he has in his collection. It's one of the biggest in the world you know. He is highly respected as a conservationist, so at least I am helping that in an obscure way."

"Let's talk about that some other time," replied Max, not wanting to cause an upset, now he had made a potentially valuable contact. Mia did not respond to the comment and Max was not sure if he could trust her.

"I must go. I have stayed too long already," Mia said nervously.

"Look we are friends now, and I will try and help you, but you must just carry on as normal until we can work out a plan to get you away from here safely. Next time Kilpatrick is away, you come and see me again."

"Thank you, Max. Please save me from this hell?"

"It will be fine. Just trust me."

Mia threw her arms around Max and kissed him passionately. Suddenly Max had two ladies vying for his affections and he was starting to enjoy it.

* * *

When Max arrived at Francesca's house on Saturday afternoon, she was sitting in her Discovery looking at her phone.

"Hi," said Max. "Am I late?"

"No, you're bang on time; just looking up directions."

"Where are we going?"

"My partner, Daniel, found this place up near Coolgardie which is meant to have some really good trekking horses that we can ride up to Kangaroo Hill Timber Reserve. I've packed a picnic so we can stop and have something to eat before we ride back. Does that sound OK to you?"

"Great. You are very well organised."

"I try to please," smiled Francesca. "Jump in; or we will be late."

When they arrived at the yard to get the horses, they were a bit surprised to find it was a private stud farm and not a livery yard. The place was immaculate and the yard manager was extremely polite and well spoken.

"Good morning, are you Francesca?" he asked.

"Yes, but I am not sure we are at the right place. We have come to hire two horses to ride out for the afternoon."

"Yes, this is it!" he smiled. "The boss said to let you ride his two best horses."

"That's very kind of him," said Max. "Do you let many horses out for hacking?"

"Never!" he smiled. "You must have some rich friends. There's nothing to pay, my boss was just pleased to help."

The groom led out two beautiful chestnut thoroughbreds with white socks. Their coats shone in the afternoon sunlight and the pristine brass buckles on the bridles reflected the rays. Francesca mounted the first horse and it was immediately clear to Max that she was an experienced rider. She leant down and tightened the girth and made herself comfortable in the saddle. Max had not noticed her cream-coloured jodhpurs in the car but they clung tightly to her slim legs and the touch of Francesca's hand on his arm came flooding back.

"Are you going to get on that horse or spend all afternoon looking at my arse!"

"Sorry, yes," stuttered Max, slightly embarrassed. "It is a nice arse though!" he risked.

"Thank you, kind sir! Shall we give it a work out."

They trotted up the lane towards the reserve and when they were happy the horses were worked-in, they cantered up the forest track for a while. After ten minutes Francesca eased her horse back into a walk and they walked quietly along through the dappled sunlight filtering through the eucalyptus trees. It was a warm afternoon and the horses were sweating a bit behind the saddles so they dismounted and found a shady spot to give them a break. Francesca untied her bag from behind the saddle and they sat down on the grass next to a fallen tree.

"That was fun; it's ages since I've been on a horse," said Francesca as she laid out a relative feast of a picnic.

"They're good sorts aren't they. I wonder who the owner is?"

"I don't know; it was Daniel's suggestion. He does have his uses!"

"You don't fancy him then?" enquired Max, hoping for a negative response. He didn't expect the reply he got.

"No, he is much too old for me. I like handsome young men who can ride!"

Max was a bit taken aback. He had spent all his life being rejected by prissy and avaricious American blondes who wanted bankers and yachts. This was new territory for him but he liked the feeling Francesca was giving him. She might be working for Kilpatrick and eventually kill him, but at least he would die happy.

Francesca opened the sandwich box, took out a bread roll, leant forward and passed it to Max. Her white cotton blouse was taut across her breasts and the material tugged at the small ivory buttons. Max dropped the roll, put his hand firmly behind her neck, amidst her copper ringlets and pulled her towards him.

Francesca kicked the picnic to one side and sat squarely on his lap. She leant her hands each side of him, with the log behind his back and kissed him with a passion that he had never felt from a woman before. She moved her hips hard against him and the gentle touch at the car window, grew into a racing desire to have her. He fumbled with the buttons on her shirt, so she sat upright and ripped them adrift herself.

"Kiss me," she demanded, pulling her gossamer bra below her lavish breasts, firm with longing for his reaction. Max did as instructed, and kissed her slowly at first and as she reacted, he increased the tempo, teasing her nipples with his tongue.

"You are wonderful Max; I adore that. More. Harder."

Max complied and moved his hips against her.

"I want you now Max! Stop messing about and get your jeans off, before I rip them off!"

Max stood up and followed her wishes, as she peeled off her jodhpurs and sat down on him, hard. She screamed with elation and they instantly climaxed together. They both burst out laughing.

"You are amazing Max. Can we do it again?"

Max hoped he could, but Francesca made sure he did. Twice. Submissive women were now off his agenda for ever.

CHAPTER FOURTEEN

The Magnificent Seven

"So, when are you inviting Suzi up again?" asked Charlie tentatively, as she walked along the bank of the River Ure with Anne Marie, on a sunny afternoon with Abbey and Misty.

"That's an interesting question," replied Anne Marie cautiously. "I thought that last time she came up, we got on really well; we had a lovely evening at The Devonshire with you and she looked amazing. She is so beautiful. But she didn't even try to kiss me, when I left her at your place, and I desperately wanted her to."

"So why didn't you kiss her?"

"You said not to rush things and I am not sure she really wants to start a relationship?"

Charlie threw a stick in the river and both dogs leapt into the water, in a race to retrieve it. Misty won.

"Don't you think you're being a bit overcautious?"

"I guess I am just confused Charlie. You know I love you more than anybody and it's difficult to risk losing that, for someone who might string me along because I am old and rich."

"That's ridiculous. You are not old. You are a very beautiful and sensuous woman and, in any case, whatever happens, it will not affect our relationship."

Anne Marie linked her arm in with Charlie's and gave it a squeeze. They walked for a while in silence, enjoying being together and watching the dogs playing on the bank.

"How is Daniel getting on in Australia?"

"He said last night that they are finally making some progress and he wants us to fly out to Australia, when they launch the rescue. He asked if Suzi could come too to provide some back-up. That would be a good opportunity for you and Suzi to be together without any pressure for either of you."

"That sounds a good plan. When are we going?"

"I'm not sure yet. Soon I think; Daniel is keeping me posted, most night's now, so we'll know soon."

"Are you two, OK?" asked Anne Marie. "You have not been together for ages."

"I am sure we are," replied Charlie confidently, "but can I tell you a secret; you mustn't tell Daniel or anyone else come to that."

"You know you can tell me anything Charlie, what's the matter?"

"I can't stop thinking about losing the twins and I know it's stupid but it has made me want my own baby even more. I keep telling people that Daniel and I have all the children at Daniel's orphanage in Tsavo, but that is increasingly just becoming a cover for a deep feeling of loss and uselessness. I can keep it suppressed for a few days and then it just comes boiling back to the surface and I find myself crying alone, cuddling a cushion on the sofa."

Anne Marie took Charlie in her arms and held her tight. Charlie burst into tears and sobbed on Annie's shoulder. After a few minutes Charlie lifted her head, with tears running down her cheeks.

"I am sorry; I know it's stupid."

"Don't be ridiculous. I am sure it's a natural reaction to the horrific problems you've had and I am annoyed at Daniel for not being here to give you more support."

"He is busy rescuing Didi and destroying the horrible people that kill the mothers so cruelly. I accept he will always be passionate about conservation, as I am, and until now it has all worked fine. It's just that with everything that has happened, my brain is doing strange things to me."

Anne Marie wiped away Charlie's tears softly, with her handkerchief, and they sat down on some stones from a tumbled down dry-stone wall. Abbey and Misty ran up and sat loyally at their mistress's feet.

"I could buy you a baby from Indonesia or somewhere. I saw a programme all about it on the television," suggested Anne Marie thoughtfully. It made Charlie smile.

"Can you get them from Amazon?"

"Probably, if you are a member of Prime!" grinned Anne Marie. "At least the suggestion cheered you up a bit. But seriously we have to be practical here. You haven't got any ovaries so you can't do this on your own."

"I know the options are limited because I spoke to Mummy's brother who is a gynaecologist in Harley Street and he ran through them with me. Basically, we could adopt a baby, although that might be very difficult with Daniel's background! We could foster a child or perhaps find a surrogate mother who would carry a baby for us; but that's very complicated in the UK and can cause all sorts of issues going forwards. You can actually buy fertilised eggs, that have been frozen in some countries, but I can see that being a nightmare. So, I think I will just have to get used to the situation and put my energy into my photography and running the estate."

"Well, we have got a trip to Australia to look forward to and hopefully we'll get Didi back to Africa."

"And I have got to get you and Suzi into bed, before you are both too old to enjoy it!" teased Charlie.

* * *

Daniel picked up the secure phone from the table in the derelict hotel and rang Jondi at Pine Gap.

"Hi Jondi. Is it OK to talk?"

"Yes of course. What's up?"

Daniel relayed what they had found out to date, and the roles that Marko, Francesca and Mia could play in the attack.

"Can you check up on this Marko character? We have researched him and he looks OK but I would like your views. He will be critical to help solve the problems your colleagues outlined."

"Will do. We still don't understand the lack of security you have found. All our intelligence is, that the place was very well guarded."

"I presume they don't have a fibre line out to the mine?" asked Daniel.

"No. It only gets as far as Coolgardie, after that, you are down to mobile phone or satellite connections."

"I can't believe they are working off mobiles, and in any case, you would know about it?"

"They have a satellite dish," admitted Jondi calmly.

"Why the fuck didn't you tell me and where is it?" asked Daniel crossly.

"Calm down," said Jondi. "We have our reasons."

"I thought this was meant to be a joint venture?" argued Daniel sternly.

"It is – just not an equal one."

"We're risking our lives out here for you. What else haven't you told us?"

"Have you seen any diesel generators at the mine or around the house?" queried Jondi purposefully. "Any overhead power lines? Any solar panels or wind turbines?"

"No, no, and no?"

"How do you think they power everything then?"

"Hamsters in wheels!" suggested Daniel angrily.

"Nuclear power."

"What! Now you tell me. I could have blown the whole place up and Pine Gap would not have been pleased."

"Don't worry we wouldn't have let you do that."

"How would you have known?… I know, you know fucking everything."

"Your language is not suitable for an English gentleman sir!"

"Sorry Jondi, just frustrated. OK give me the full works now please; if you want me to stay around."

"The satellite dish is cleverly disguised in the roof of the monkey house. We missed it for a year and it was only one night when there was a heavy dew that we saw the disc in the roof line. It's about two metres across and you would only see it from a plane under those conditions. Otherwise, it's invisible."

"Where did Kilpatrick get a nuclear reactor. I thought they were enormous?"

"We think it's a nuclear engine out of a small Chinese submarine. Properly managed it's a good way to generate enormous power from a small space without anyone knowing."

"I presume it's in that lateral tunnel with the steel doors?"

"Correct. They need to widen the passage to get a second one in, which was why you and your lady friend were asked to widen the tunnel. They needed it done very accurately, so they had to have your remote blasting system or it could have taken the other reactor with it."

"Thanks for the warning!"

"You're welcome!"

"In any case she's now Max's lady friend," corrected Daniel, lightening the mood.

"I hope he's got a good hormone level!"

"So, what's your take on what is going on at the mine?" asked Daniel. "Seb thinks it's something to do with the dark web and cryptocurrencies, that the Chinese are using to finance their infiltration of your universities and critical infrastructures."

"I think Seb maybe right," confirmed Jondi. "Who is Seb, by the way?"

"I thought you knew everything!" retorted Daniel with a hint of sarcasm.

"If we knew everything, we wouldn't need you, would we?"

"Equal partners then and no more secrets?" said Daniel.

"Agreed. What else do you need from me?"

"When we are finished at the mine, I need a Chinook helicopter to take my team and ten apes to the air force base north of Perth. I want full clearance for a Saudi Arabian transport plane to land, take us on board and leave with no paperwork. We don't exist."

Chinook helicopter

"Will Prince Fahd be on board?"

"All right smartarse, can we get on with the plan!"

"Language!"

"Sorry again. We will need a full radiation team on standby in case one of Kilpatrick's team decides to press the nuclear option."

"We will have a decontamination unit set up and ready, a few miles away from the mine, that we can draft in at a moment's notice. God forbid we need it," exclaimed Jondi.

"You better have an SAS team inside the fence, in case we are eliminated by something we don't know about. I will need a direct line to them during the operation," requested Daniel. "I will also need a secure bank account that we can transfer all the money to, if we can find it. There will only probably be a split second available to extract the money, transfer it to you and cut the communication lines to the Chinese acolytes, whoever they are."

"All will be done sir, as you request. Just try not to syphon off too much money for your friends, human and otherwise."

"What me. Never gave it a moment's thought… but now you've suggested it Jondi!"

* * *

After speaking to Jondi, Daniel made a call to Charlie who was in the bath.

"Hi darling, how are things at your end?"

"Wet, warm and bubbly!" replied Charlie, smiling to herself.

"I think I'll come home now. I am missing Mozart."

"How are you getting on? Do you have a date yet?"

"We are planning on the week after next, but we have to be sure Kilpatrick is in residence in case we need to extract any information from him, like passwords etcetera. We will also need Quinyang's husband to be around, as he is the computer guru running the systems. Max is going to find out what their diaries look like and then we will finalise a date and time. Have you briefed Annie and Suzi?"

"I have told Annie and she is up for it but I was waiting to speak to Suzi till the plans were more advanced," said Charlie, not mentioning the potential lover's complications.

"Can you send her a text today, because she will need to give the base some notice if she wants time off?"

"Will do. What about Nzinga and Fahd?"

"I spoke to Nzinga yesterday and she has got Fahd all organised with his jet. She has had the transport crates built for the gorillas and Fahd is going to fly to Nairobi and pick her, and the crates, up at the airport. Those two are super stars. I am so pleased Nzinga has found happiness with Fahd. They are a great couple."

"Please be careful my darling," said Charlie. "We are getting to the dangerous bit now and I am worried we don't know enough about what resources the Chinese might have at the mine."

"Don't worry; it will be fine. Max and I will spend the next week getting as much detail as we can about the site and I have organised some back-up with Pine Gap."

"I know, but you know what they are like. The slightest hint of things going the wrong way and you will be on your own."

"These are Australians not the British. I am sure they will come to the rescue if we need them."

"I hope you are right! OK I will get in touch with Suzi later and see if she can make it."

"Great. I will ring you every day with an update. Can't wait to get home and join you in the bath with Mozart!"

* * *

Later that evening, Max came over to the hotel to run through the plan with Daniel.

"So, who have we got on the team and who are the enemy?" mused Daniel over a can of lager.

"Well, I don't think we can trust Pete, although he would probably be ambivalent about the whole thing, it's just too big a risk. I wouldn't want to take him out, but I will neutralise him somehow. I don't think we can trust any of the Chinese. I have no idea how fanatical they are but I think they are all collateral damage. Obviously, we will need Quinyang's husband to help decode the systems and I suggest we use Quinyang as a lever."

"What about the other guards on the gate?" asked Daniel.

"I will get rid of them one way or another. Having talked to them, I think a few dollars and a free night off will do the job. What we don't know is, who else is hidden down in the mine or if any of the mining staff could be a problem. If we attack after seven, hopefully the last shift will have finished and they will all be long gone till the morning."

"Good so far then," said Daniel thoughtfully. "And what about your two ladies?"

"They are not *my* two ladies! Francesca is wonderful and I would trust her with my life. Mia is a frightened mouse and wants out, to look after her dad, so we can count on her up to a point, but if she is challenged in any way she will melt."

"Great. I hope you are right about Francesca because we need her in on the plan and fully behind it. If your analysis is wrong you might not have a life! Why don't you invite her out, for the evening next Saturday, and bring her over here for a chat? Don't give her any details in advance, but we are going to have to take a risk and let her in on the plan. Remember she doesn't know we are on the same side, so don't let on till you get here and we will see what her reaction is."

"That should be fun!" said Max.

"The trip back to her place could be. You'll either have to make love to her or kill her! Are we sure there are no secret tunnels into the mine? Old mine workings or air shafts that could be being used by Chinese to get into the space under the house? We don't want to get down there and find a whole bloody army of kung fu experts."

"I haven't seen any evidence of another entrance and I ride around the place every day. The only option would be if a tunnel went all the way under the lake and came up on the north side. I'll take a drive around the lake one evening just to check. I know there are no Chinese-owned mines on the other side, so they can't be linked together."

"So, what's the plan for Mia then?" asked Daniel.

"If we offer her enough money to look after her dying father, I'm sure she will help. He's failing fast, because the Chinese owners of the mine where he worked didn't care about the men getting lung damage from the coal dust. She'll enjoy getting her revenge. She has to go up to Kilpatrick's at about seven every night to dance for him. Don't ask – it's all a bit weird; but if she puts on a particularly erotic show for him, it will keep him out of the way, till we get established and secure on site."

"OK sounds good. What about getting Charlie's team in, to rescue Didi and her mates, whilst we are taking care of the computer stuff?" asked Daniel.

"When the guards have gone, I'll unlock the main gates to the mine and leave them open. They can drive straight in, on our signal, and bypass the house so hopefully keep out of trouble. If all goes well, the Chinook can take us all out together and we can leave Jondi and her lot, to clear up the mess."

"Have we forgotten anything?" asked Daniel thoughtfully.

"Well, we've got a week to refine the details. I will come round again on Friday night, before I bring Francesca on Saturday, to compare notes. I assume you have sorted Marko?"

"Yes, he will get here a couple of days before we go in and we will need him to meet Francesca, so they have a plan for trying to get into the software and find the money. He is doing some homework with Seb, in advance, to see what they can find out."

"Piece of cake then!" said Max, hopefully.

* * *

Charlie made herself a cup of coffee and sat down on the sofa with a pile of proofs that she might use in the book about Africa, that Anne Marie had suggested. She wasn't sure it would ever happen, but was toying with the possibilities. She was just about to ring Suzi about the Australian project when her phone rang.

"Hi Charlie, how are you getting on? It seems ages since I saw you."

"That's spooky, I was literally just going to ring you."

"Has Daniel found someone else and dumped you?"

"No!"

"Shame," Charlie could tell Suzi was joking. A bit.

"Why were you going to ring me?" asked Charlie.

"I haven't heard from Annie since I came up, and I thought we had had a really fun time. I wondered if she had mentioned me?"

"I think she was hoping you would ring her. She really likes you Suzi but is worried she is a bit older than you and doesn't want to push you into something that you both might regret."

"That's rubbish; she is amazingly beautiful and anyway I prefer ladies her age. I can't tolerate younger girls who just want to be in bed all the time. I want somebody who is intelligent and interesting to be with and who I can have fun with, doing things together."

"Well, I might have a plan to get you two together again shortly, if you can get the time off."

"That's not a problem at the moment because my Typhoon is having its TAS 1600 service so I am just filling in time on the ground for a few weeks."

"Sorry to be ignorant, but what's a TAS service?" asked Charlie.

"Oh sorry, just like a car service. Every 1600 flying hours, our planes have to be stripped down and a major maintenance programme carried out. So, what's your plan, it sounds exciting? I am desperate to see Annie again."

"Well, Daniel knows where Didi is in Australia. He wants us three to fly out there and help extract Didi and nine other apes from an illegal private collection. Only it's a bit more complicated than that because Pine Gap is involved."

"Sounds interesting. As long as Five Eyes are happy with it, I'm in! When are we going?"

"We're not exactly sure but probably next week. The plan is that you and Annie can fly us to Nairobi in Annie's jet and then we will hitch a lift with Nzinga, and you know who, to Australia."

"Wow. I will book a couple of weeks off, and you let me know where you want me, and when."

"Great. I will let Annie know you are coming and wind her up for you."

"Thank you, Charlie. You are wonderful; can't wait."

* * *

Daniel and Max had their agreed update at the hotel on Friday night and everything was going to plan. They briefed each other on their recent findings but there was nothing to derail the strategy so far. The planned meeting with Francesca was arranged, and Max was to pick her up at seven from home and bring her to the hotel in Widgiemooltha. She still did not realise that Daniel and Max were on the same side.

Max pulled up on the grass outside Francesca's house and climbed out of his ancient pickup. She waved to him out of the front window to come in through the back door.

"Hi, are you ready?" called Max through the bedroom door.

"Nearly. Help yourself to a beer. Just doing my hair. Where are we going?"

"It's a surprise."

"What do you want me to wear?"

"Just casual will be fine. Something sexy underneath would be good," he joked.

"That's already done. Hope you can stay later."

She reappeared with her red hair braided neatly, in the French style. She was wearing tight black leather trousers, a white crop top and leather jacket.

"Will this do?" she grinned, doing a model's twirl.

"Fab!" said Max, "You look very desirable!"

"That's the general idea," and she put her arms around Max's neck and kissed him lasciviously.

"I think we better go, before my response explodes!"

"It will be fun waiting, you'll see. Shall we go in mine?"

"Good plan."

"You can drive," she said, throwing Max the keys, and they set off.

"So go on, where are you taking me to on this mysterious trip?"

"Not far."

Francesca leant over, slid her hand into the front of his jeans and squeezed. Max, distracted, drove off the side of the road, screamed to a holt in a cloud of dust and nearly hit a eucalyptus tree.

"Where?" she demanded, not letting go.

"Widgiemooltha!"

"That's more like it," she said removing her hand, grinning with satisfaction, "but that's a derelict dump. There's nothing there."

"That's the point. Just control your inquisitive desires, we are nearly there."

Max pulled up outside the old hotel, took Francesca's hand and walked into the bar. Daniel was sitting on a tall stool drinking a lager."

"Drink Francesca?" laughed Daniel.

"You bastards. I knew there was something going on. Your face at the gates to the mine was a picture, when Max came out of the security hut. What are you two playing at then. I hope you are not cocking up my plans."

"Are your plans going anywhere?" asked Daniel cynically.

"Slowly," Francesca replied defensively.

"As a snail," observed Daniel. "Do you want in, on our plan, or do you want to flounder around on your own for another ten years?

Francesca looked straight at Max. "Only if I can partner with Max!"

"Whatever, as long as you two concentrate on the job in hand, when things get serious." instructed Daniel. "You can do what you like afterwards."

"OK. I'm in. How are we playing it?"

Daniel outlined the working plan, and briefed her about the gorilla youngsters for the first time.

"The miserable bastard! I'll kill him before I leave."

"You're third in the queue," said Max seriously.

"We will need your expertise on the computer systems after we get into them," briefed Daniel. "You won't be on your own. We have an expert on blockchain technology coming to help. Let's call him M for now. He should be here on Tuesday, so I want you two to meet me here at 5 pm so you can work out how we get into their systems; how we locate the cold wallets where ever they are, including yours in Taiwan, and how we hack into the Chinese corruption funds here in Australia."

"Will we be able to transfer all the missing South African money back to my masters, so I can get them off my back," asked Francesca nervously.

"Hopefully yes, but you better come up front and tell us what you did that was so wrong, that they have a gun to your head?" enquired Daniel.

"Long story," said Francesca hesitantly.

"Try the short version," requested Max.

"Basically, I borrowed a few dollars off the company to help my dad out, who was having a cashflow crisis at the time. They had millions sitting there, doing nothing, and I only needed it for a month, until a big transfer that was due to dad, turned up."

"So, if you are so hot on computer stuff, how did they catch you?" asked Daniel.

"It was just a simple error by my dad's bank. When the dollars arrived by auto-transfer for his account, a stupid bank clerk rang the mine's accounts department and asked if they could send it in rands instead. The bank actually has a standing instruction to turn all incoming currency into rands, because we get all sorts of currencies turn up from visitors to the reserve, but this clerk didn't read the instruction and ruined my plan."

"Did they throw you out for theft?" asked Max.

"No, they let dad keep the money in return for me coming out here and trying to get some of their stolen bitcoins back from Taiwan. They don't play around these mining guys; if I don't get their bitcoins back, I will end up in a block of concrete at the end of a disused mineshaft, a mile underground."

"Charming!" observed Max. "We'll find it, don't worry."

"See Daniel. Max and I are a great team."

"Well, let's hope so. Do you know how to shoot?" asked Daniel.

"We always had guns in the house, because of the wildlife on the reserve and also some militant natives were not averse to slashing you to bits with a machete."

"Have you got a weapon here in Australia?"

"Always carry a Walther P99 but I can fire anything with a trigger and a full magazine."

"Have you ever killed anyone before?"

"No comment."

"Good enough," said Daniel respectfully. "Any questions Francesca?"

"What's Kilpatrick's firepower like?"

"Difficult to say," replied Max. "Pete carries a SIG MCX low visibility assault weapon and he kindly gave me one too! We call them Black Mambas in the States and they are pretty lethal. I think we can assume that Kilpatrick will have at least one in the house, and we have no idea what any of the Chinese guys have, but I have never seen them with a weapon."

"What about the gorillas, do we attack the house first and then rescue the gorillas afterwards, if we are still alive?"

"All that's taken care of," said Daniel. "We have another team following us in, who will rescue them."

"Who are they? Do they know what they are doing? Gorillas can be a bit dangerous you know!"

"Don't worry, they are part of my African team and deal with them all the time."

"I didn't know you had an African team?" queried a surprised Francesca.

"See, not as boring as you thought," smiled Daniel enigmatically. "I'll tell you more, on the plane back to Africa, if we are successful. That's assuming you want to go back?"

"Can Max come too?" asked Francesca, looking at Max who winked at her.

"Yes, he is coming too," sighed Daniel jokingly. "This could get boring!"

* * *

Although it was only a short drive back to Francesca's house, the hormones boiled over in the Discovery before they got there. She undid the strategically placed zips on her leather jacket and trousers, causing Max to nearly demolish

303

another eucalyptus. Before the dust settled, she was astride his lap and tearing at his shirt. He buried his face into her breasts and she grabbed the roof handles. Max didn't get home on Saturday night.

* * *

Sunday morning was a cool day with a wind blowing across Lake Lefroy. Max met up with Pete at the stables to do the routine mucking out.

"Shame we are working today. It would be a good day to be out on the salt," suggested Max, subtly.

"Good idea Max. Why don't we both ride the fence line in opposite direct directions and get back early afternoon. We can then take the sails out for a couple of hours. Kilpatrick is away this week, so nothing much is happening at the mine."

Max was taken aback by the news on Kilpatrick, because it could wreck all the carefully coordinated plans for Saturday. He decided to ask about his return later, so as not to alert Pete.

Max found a dingo tangled up in the fence, about halfway round, and rang Pete to see what to do with it. Pete was more interested in getting back for sailing and told Max to shoot it and leave the carcase till tomorrow, when hopefully most of it would be inside some other carnivore.

Pete and Max took both land sails down to the lake and had an enjoyable early evening, speeding up and down the full length of the salt, in the strong breeze. Max had a close shave, nearly turning over his craft, when he took a tack too early on a return run, but survived with a rush of adrenalin.

"That was nearly curtains," laughed Pete, when Max returned to the shore line near the trailer.

"I think I was a bit ambitious there," agreed Max. "It's difficult to accurately predict when to go for it."

"Just comes with experience. Fancy a beer?"

"Great idea." And they sat down on the sandy shore to contemplate the world.

After a few mundanities, Max got round to asking about Kilpatrick.

"So is the boss off on his holidays somewhere?"

"What him, holidays? You must be joking. He only knows work and money. That's all he cares about, apart from his whore."

"Bit of a sad life really?" proposed Max.

"He's a miserable sod, but very rich I suppose. He's flown out to Guangzhou to bring a couple of his Chinese mates back, to look at some new equipment for the mine. We will have to tighten up security whilst they are here."

"When are they due to arrive?" ventured Max.

"He told me to expect them Friday and they are staying for a couple of days, I think. Don't worry, they won't bother us, they will spend all the time in the basement playing computer games. They've got hundreds of computers down there."

"Ah well, each to their own I suppose," replied Max casually, knowing the new intelligence would make life much more difficult on Saturday; but at least all the key players were now in the right place.

* * *

When Max got back to his house, he briefed Daniel about the new intelligence and that Saturday was now live. Daniel, in turn, briefed Jondi to prepare her side of the operation for seven on Saturday evening. He then sent a text to Marko

Hi M, I hope things are good with you. Your planned holiday is now all organised and I have your tickets to the main event on Saturday. The music will be fab! I have arranged for a lady to pick you up at the arranged place on Tuesday. She has red hair and will be carrying a board with your friend's name on it. She will bring you to my hotel and we can discuss the arias for the opera. Looking forward to seeing you and going over old times. Best wishes D

Daniel then rang Charlie, who was in the bath again.

"You are the cleanest person I know!" joked Daniel.

"It's the only place I feel close to you at the moment; anyway, are we on for this week, because Annie is desperate to see Suzi again?"

"But is Suzi desperate to see Annie?" asked Daniel.

"I think so, but they are dancing round each other like butterflies. I am not sure what will happen, when they finally get to kiss each other."

"A bit like Nzinga and Fahd then, but they managed it in the end."

"Talking of which, I have got some great news Daniel, but you can't tell anyone ever."

"OK, sounds exciting, has Mac cuddled a badger?"

"Stop it! This is really exciting. When I rang Fahd to confirm the plan to rescue Didi, he told me that Prince Khalid's wife, Rashieka is pregnant."

"That's not only exciting it's a bloody miracle! I am so pleased for them. Is everything OK, when is the baby due?"

"In a couple of months. Mummy's brother evidently flew out there and helped them sort out the problem. Not sure how, but he's now the richest gynaecologist in the world!"

"That's wonderful, hopefully we can go out and see them after the baby is born. Now, can you organise everything your end, to get everyone to Nairobi for Wednesday and then get to Perth for Thursday? Fahd will have to stay with the plane, because we can't risk the Saudis getting tangled up in a battle with the Chinese. So, we will have you, Annie, Suzi and Nzinga to rescue Didi and friends, and then Max, Francesca and me to take on Kilpatrick. The Magnificent Seven!"

"OK will do. Can't wait to hug you. Seems an eternity," said Charlie, with a tear in her eye.

"I think everything is in place and we are good to go," confirmed Daniel, insensitive to the baby conversation. "See you soon!"

Charlie retreated to the sofa and hugged the cushion.

CHAPTER FIFTEEN

Breaking the Blockchain

On Friday evening, as the light was failing, two black limousines purred up the drive and stopped outside Kilpatrick's grand house. The chauffeurs hauled their huge frames out of the plush interiors and opened the rear doors so their masters could alight. A further two bodyguards climbed out of their respective passenger doors and took guard at the front of the vehicles. Kilpatrick was in the leading car and he was followed out by a very small Chinese man, dressed in an obviously very expensive suit. Two other younger Chinese men got out of the second vehicle and were equally smartly dressed. The two bodyguards scanned around the surrounding terrain but failed to see Max hidden in the trees above the house. When they had all disappeared inside, Max made his way back through the undergrowth to his house, to update Daniel on the phone.

When he arrived in his kitchen, Mia was hiding behind the door into the bedroom looking terrified. Her hands were shaking and her face pale with fear.

"Did you see the big cars arrive?" she mumbled, her voice trembling.

"I did; who are they?"

"They are Kilpatrick's bosses from China. I hate them. They are really nasty people. Be careful, they don't kill you!"

"It's OK Mia, calm down, you are safe with me. I will get you a drink and you can tell me all about them." Max poured out two Cokes and they sat opposite each other at the kitchen table. "Do you have to dance for them tonight?"

"No, but tomorrow they will want me to, and last time they were here, one of the young men attacked me and the others just laughed. Even though I was screaming for my life, he pushed me backwards onto a chair and tried to rape me in front of the others."

"Did he hurt you?"

"A bit, but Kilpatrick pulled him off and said, '*She's only mine young man – have some respect*'. The father nodded to the boy and then he let me go; I managed to run off, with all of them laughing at me. I was terrified."

"That's awful Mia, but I thought you said Kilpatrick never touched you?"

"He doesn't; I think he is impotent, but he is a revolting fat slob and even having him look at me, makes me want to throw up."

"Mia, I want you to listen to me carefully. I have a plan to get you out of here for good, tomorrow night. When it is over, I will give you enough money to look after your father properly, but you have to trust me first, because I want you to be very brave."

"I will do anything to get out of this hellhole, Max. I will sleep with you tonight if you want. I am very good in bed," she lied innocently, her virginity still intact.

"That won't be necessary," Max assured her. "Believe me, I hate him more than you, for other reasons, but I

309

need you to be very brave and dance for them one more time. I will be there all the while and I will kill them if they touch you. I need you to keep them occupied for as long as possible, so I can get what I want out of the house."

"What are you looking for, maybe I could help?"

"I just want you to concentrate on keeping them occupied, I will do the rest."

"But what if they see you first and kill you. What will they do to me then? I won't have any clothes on to hide a gun, and they will beat me mercilessly until I tell them what is going on."

"Don't worry, Mia I will take care of everything else; you just give the most sensual performance of your life. It will be the last time you will have to dance like this and then you can go back to being the best ballerina in the world."

"I will do my best Max, because I trust you. Please don't let me down like the rest of the pathetic men in this world."

Max took Mia in his arms and held her slender form next to him. He wanted to protect her and he adored her submissive character.

* * *

When Mia had left, Max rang Daniel to update him on the situation at the mine.

"They're back, but there's a major problem. There are three Chinese men who appear to be Kilpatrick's overlords and four hefty bodyguards. I didn't see any weapons but I'm sure they will be armed, so we might have a fight on our hands."

"That's not a problem Max; that's really good news. We would never have got to them in China. At last, we've got a chance to get rid of the whole bloody lot of them in one go. We better draft Suzi into our team and leave Charlie, Annie and Nzinga to get the gorillas and chimp out."

"I think we should do our bit first and neutralise the Chinese before we let the girls come on site. If we get overrun, we can't risk them getting trapped by the heavies," said Max, concerned about the girls handling the bodyguards.

"That shouldn't be a problem; we can delay the Chinook if we need to," confirmed Daniel. "We are good this end, Marko and Francesca have built a plan to access their servers through TOR which is something to do with the dark web but don't ask me any more than that!"

"It's The Onion Router, TOR is The Onion Router!" replied Max knowledgeably.

"OK, you can hack into it then!"

"I only know what it's called; I didn't say I could drive it!" laughed Max. "And where are the others?"

"All staying nearby and being looked after by Jondi. No idea where. Bit frustrating, but we are taking every precaution. They will be ready for our signal, any time after seven, and can be on site within ten minutes."

"OK, when Kilpatrick calls for Mia, I will send you a signal to approach the big house with Suzi. We will have to deal with the bodyguards first, but it will depend where they are. If there are any outside the house, you can take them out and I will deal with the two inside. Hopefully the three bosses will not be armed in the evening but let's see. If we can keep the older guy alive as a bartering chip that might help. I assume the two younger ones will know something about the systems, so we should try and keep them alive as well. We will need Quinyang's husband to help us and hopefully he will already be down stairs playing on the computers."

* * *

Saturday morning was weirdly normal. Max helped Pete muck out the horses and Max waved to Quinyang when they just happened to approach the muckheap at the same time.

"If you ride the fence line today, Max," instructed Pete, "I will stay and keep an eye on things here. I don't like having these Chinese around and I don't trust the heavies not to cause trouble. Last time they were here, they were trying to shoot birds down on the beach with machine guns. They're brainless idiots."

"What do we need to do security-wise tonight?" asked Max, pretending to be conscientious.

"I would just keep out of the way, unless there is any trouble; in which case I'll give you a ring," suggested Pete. "They'll not be going anywhere this evening. I will lock the main gate at five, when the last shift leaves, and just sit under the tree and have a beer."

"What about Quinyang's husband and the other Chinese on site, will they be invited to the party, or do we have to worry about them?"

"No, they will all be in Kilpatrick's house working; they seem to work round the clock when the bosses are here. I have no idea what they do. None of them speak any English so they just get on with it."

"Right, I'm off round the fence line," said Max, swinging himself into the saddle. "I'll see you later. Nice day for a quiet ride."

* * *

Daniel lifted up the floorboard by the kitchen sink, in the old hotel at Widgiemooltha, and extracted the two Heckler & Koch MP7s, fitted with suppressors and night sights. He loaded the ammunition into a rucksack, and secured his own handgun in the belt behind his back. Jondi was supplying Charlie, Annie and Suzi with suitable weapons. Nzinga had her hands full with the equipment to anaesthetise the apes and restrain them, in the undignified transfer to the Chinook. Francesca had her own gun and her job was to protect Marko until they got him safely in front of the main computer, in the basement of the main house.

Daniel had arranged for Jondi to drop Suzi off, in some eucalyptus scrubland at the side of Lake Lefroy on the way up to the mine. He would rendezvous with her there and wait for Max's signal to go up to the house, under cover, whilst Mia was doing her distraction dance.

The daylight was fading as Daniel drove the Holden off the road and into the bushes. Jondi and Suzi were already there in the Defender that Jondi had picked him up in at the airport.

"Do you only own one car?" said Daniel, giving Suzi a hug and looking at Jondi smiling.

"I love my little Land Rover, so you leave it alone."

"Are your SAS friends nearby, we might need some cavalry?"

"They'll be around if you get stuck, but we would rather you did it all, so we are not involved. I will be here if you need me. Suzi's got my number as well."

"OK. Suzi and I will move up closer to the house. The gate is opened as planned. Don't let Charlie's team in until we give the signal."

"Will do, good luck Daniel. We have a drone up, so I will keep an eye on things from above and warn you if we see any danger."

"Thanks Jondi – see you on the other side."

* * *

Max had invited Pete for a lager at his house at six-thirty and they sat at the kitchen table talking about sailing, Chinese films and dead dingoes. After about half way through the second can, which Max had spiked with drugs, Pete collapsed on the floor shaking, with saliva dripping from his mouth. Max checked he was breathing all right and moved him into recovery position for safety. He gave him a further IV injection of vecuronium to keep him sedated for a few hours. Max hoped he would be OK, because without him, this rescue would not have happened.

After a few minutes, there was a tap on the kitchen window and Mia's face appeared against the glass. Max let her in.

"God, what happened to him!" exclaimed Mia, seeing Pete collapsed on the floor.

"He's just having a rest for the evening. He will be fine tomorrow apart from a bad headache," assured Max. "What time have you got to be at the house?"

"In about ten minutes, they said," her voice trembled. "I'm really scared Max; are you sure this is going to work?"

"It will be fine. Just think of your dad and concentrate on your last dance tonight. I will follow you across to the house, but hidden in the bushes. I can get a good sighting of you dancing on the terrace, where they have been eating. If anything goes wrong, I'll come in and rescue you."

"I love you Max, you're my hero!" Mia pulled him down with his shirt buttons and kissed him on the cheek and disappeared into the moonlight.

Max signalled Daniel and Suzi. *'We are go.'*

Max tracked Mia down the stone pathway to the big house, keeping a discrete distance behind her and hidden from view. She climbed the steps up to the terrace and stood alone in front of Kilpatrick, who was already half-inebriated and laughing loudly with his fellow guests. The two young Chinese sat forward in their chairs in anticipation, ogling her body, scantily clad in a diaphanous dress clinging to her slender form.

"What's the music tonight for my honourable guests, Mia?" asked Kilpatrick as he lifted his vast bulk from the chair and walked across to her. He put his enormous sweaty hand under her fragile chin and lifted it, bending her neck roughly backwards.

"It better be good tonight," he said intimidatingly. "My friends are very important people in China."

Mia handed him a memory stick, and he turned and put it into the audio. The first soft chords of Ravel's *Boléro*, with its universal sensual intimacy, drifted off the moonlit terrace and swirled into the night air. Mia let her dress slide off her sinuous arms as she moved ghostlike across to the floor towards the old Chinese man. They were all instantly mesmerised and silence fell across the party. Max was hypnotised by the slow sensuous movements of her body. Mia knew how to intoxicate all men and twirled on her points, as the tempo increased slowly but surely. She teased with her hands following the curves of her breasts and her slender neck. She pulled a white, translucent, silk scarf across her body and dropped it, floating to the floor. The gold choker round her neck held four gold chains loosely falling to her nipples, pierced with tiny gold rings. As she leant back, cambré, the chains snapped tight and she moaned with simulated sexual pleasure. Ravel's journey to crescendo strode louder now; the party were all stunned; and Max released the safety on his hand gun. The whole orchestra joined the seduction as it moved up, forte, till the sound echoed around the whole of Lake Lefroy.

Even Max didn't hear Daniel take out the two bodyguards, who had been smoking unobservantly by the front door. Suzi stepped over the bodies. Bright red arterial blood still pumping from their heads across the dusty paving. She hid in the bush by the front door as the third heavy opened the door and stepped outside to see what the commotion was about. He found out. She slit his throat with a knife and dragged his twitching corpse out of sight.

Mia caressed her legs and her fingers slid emotionally up her thighs to the silk, covering her virginity. One of the young Chinese went to stand up, but the old man pulled him back into his seat. The music pervaded everything, the hot air, the trees and the men's minds. The tempo increased relentlessly. Mia dropped to the floor on her knees and caressed herself, throwing her head backwards. She had given them the ultimate distraction; they were about to regret.

Suzi burst through the open door and plunged her knife twice into the back of the last guard. He crumpled to the ground behind the sofa. Kilpatrick heard the pain of death and turned around to see Suzi standing with a gun at his head.

"Who the fuck are you!" shouted Kilpatrick.

"Your worst nightmare. Don't move a muscle!" replied Suzi calmly.

One of the young men, pulled a pistol from his jacket and Daniel shot him through the head. He fell into the old man's lap as *Boléro* ended with Mia safely in Max's arms.

"Who are all these people?" asked Mia, shaking with the shock of the surrounding violent dispatches.

"Put the music on again Max, for cover!" ordered Daniel.

"You!" said Daniel, pointing at the old man. "Speak English?"

"Probably better than you sir, but your endeavours are fruitless. There is nothing to steal here," he said calmly.

"I would just like to check, if that's satisfactory with you," replied Daniel cynically.

As *Boléro* rang out again, to shield the sounds of attack, Daniel and Suzi found the stairs leading to the vaults below. The door was locked with a code pad.

"Code please?" Daniel requested from Kilpatrick.

"Fuck off!"

Daniel pointed his hand gun at Kilpatrick's crutch. "Code please."

"You wouldn't dare shoot me." sneered Kilpatrick.

Daniel shot him in the foot. He screamed in excruciating pain, falling to the floor holding the wound; he mumbled the code.

"Thank you; very helpful," said Daniel. "Max, you watch these three and call up Francesca and Marko.

Daniel entered the code and the shiny metal door swung open. He stepped inside and slowly descended the steps, with his gun in his right hand. There were bright lights at the bottom of the second flight and when he got to the first mezzanine, he indicated for Suzi to join him. She then covered him as he made his way down to the base level. He stooped and peered under a supporting beam. There were huge banks of computers lining the walls of the tunnel, until it turned out of view. Apart from the monotonous hum of the server fans, there wasn't another sound, and no sign of human life. Suzi joined him at the bottom of the stairs.

"Looks like the crypto mine we expected," thought Suzi.

"The individual servers look too big for just that?" observed Daniel, "Let's go slowly along the tunnel and see if we can find any sign of life."

They walked tentatively along the bank of servers, on the inside of the curve in the mine, to give themselves some cover. As they proceeded round the bend, the tunnel opened out into a huge cavern, surrounded by a wall of computers, and with a central control desk in the middle. It was manned by three small Chinese, beavering away on their keyboards. A fourth man stood at the far end of the cavern, with a machine gun slung over his shoulder, and a book he was reading in his hands.

"You take out the guard, and I will take care of the other three," whispered Daniel. "Three, two, one Go!" Daniel and Suzi ran out into the light and pointed their guns at the prescribed targets.

The guard dropped his book on the floor, followed by his gun and put his hands in the air, like some old western baddie.

"Hands off the keyboards now!" shouted Daniel at the others. Two obeyed instantly, but one tried to make some sort of key entry. Daniel shot him in the arm and he fell to the floor.

"Away from the computers!" instructed Daniel, and the two remaining Chinese pushed back on their office chairs, so they were clear of the desks.

"She hurt, badly, I help!" shouted one of the Chinese men.

"Stay in your chairs or I will shoot you."

"She my wife, please?" pleaded the man, with tears in his eyes. "I help you, if I can help her. I no gun."

Daniel walked up to the crumpled body on the floor and pushed it on its back with his foot. It was a girl, and blood from her arm was oozing through her shirt.

"I help, please she will die."

"OK but you do anything slightly Chinese and I kill her."

"I no understand?"

"Just get on with it," said Daniel frustratedly.

The man knelt next his wife and took her in his arms. *"Are you hurt badly my darling, Quinyang?"* he asked in Mandarin.

"Only speak English," ordered Daniel.

Whilst Daniel had sorted his captives out, Suzi had retrieved the gun from the guard and cable-tied him to a computer cabinet and stuffed a wadge of paper in his mouth as a gag.

Daniel pointed his gun at the husband. "Who is head man here?"

"Me, I am computer expert. I get you lots of money. Transfer straight to your bank, if you let us go," he stuttered in broken English.

"Is your wife, OK?" asked Daniel.

"I have bound the wound with handkerchief. She needs a doctor now."

"As soon as I have my money, you can get a doctor."

"I show you now, please," he said moving towards the keyboard. Daniel thrust his gun in the Chinaman's face.

"Back off, or your wife will die." The man, looking terrified, obeyed and returned to his sobbing wife on the floor.

"Are you OK to watch over this lot, whilst I go and get Marko and Francesca?" Daniel asked Suzi.

"Yes fine, all under control."

Daniel retook the stairs and went back to the terrace. Kilpatrick was sat on the floor nursing his foot, wrapped in a white linen serviette. The Chinese boss and his remaining young assistant were sitting serenely on a sofa and Max was sitting opposite, holding his gun in their direction. Mia had covered her modesty in a rug and was sitting at Max's feet, holding his leg tightly.

"Any sign of F and M?" asked Daniel.

"Not yet. Is everything under control down there?" replied Max.

"Yes, one guard, regretting he met Suzi, two Chinese computer guys and one wife, who I unfortunately shot."

"I will kill all of you," muttered Kilpatrick, unrealistically. "You have no idea what you are doing. This is way out of your league."

"I think Mr Kilpatrick meant to say that if you leave us alone, we will pay you handsomely to be on your way," said the old Chinese boss pompously.

"How much is handsomely?" asked Daniel, in a serious tone.

"How does 1 million Australian sound?"

Mia gasped and looked up at Max, "That's a fortune, can we go now?"

"Not quite yet, I think," said Max smiling at Daniel, "I think we will hold out for a few dollars more."

"I loved that film!" said Francesca, as she came through the door with Marko, who shook hands with Daniel. Francesca went straight over to Max and kissed him, rather too generously, given the circumstances.

"Can we keep the slave?" Francesca asked, looking at Mia at his feet.

"Can we concentrate on more urgent matters in hand," ordered Daniel. "Marko can you come downstairs with me and we will have a preliminary look around."

The old Chinese man looked up suddenly, and stared at Marko. "Marko Kharchenko?" he enquired curiously.

"That's me! How are you Mr Shyu?"

"It's a great honour to meet you Marko. How are you involved in this fruitless escapade?"

"Long story Mr Shyu. It all started with a cat. I will explain one day, but if you'll excuse me, I have some money to put into a good cause."

"Your reputation precedes you sir, maybe we could work together, to our mutual benefit?" suggested Mr Shyu, pondering whether to change sides.

"That may be possible sir," confirmed Marko, "but let me see inside the Onion first."

"I think you may need the full plate of vegetables to crack this one," smiled Mr Shyu.

"I like a challenge Mr Shyu. We will talk later."

Daniel led Marko and Francesca down the stairs and into the data centre. They walked past all the racks, containing the processors; Marko was intrigued by the set-up.

"It's very impressive, Daniel. It's not a cryptocurrency mine as such. They are processing enormous amounts of data here, but not making bitcoins or other stuff. It will be interesting to get into it."

When they got to the control desks, Daniel introduced Suzi and the three Chinese. Marko immediately sat down at one desk and typed a few keys.

"Mm, interesting," said Marko thoughtfully.

"What does that mean?" asked Daniel.

"Well… it's in Chinese for a start," laughed Marko. "Francesca, can you do a quick search on that terminal over there; see if you can get into the dark web and see any recent transactions."

"How long do you think it will take to get into the accounts?" asked Daniel naively.

"Anywhere between an hour and a thousand years!" said Marko seriously.

"Great; can't these guys help?" asked Daniel pointing at the Chinese, waiting impassively in their chairs.

"They could if they wanted to, but I fear they don't, and if we trust them near the keyboard, we could be locked out for good."

"Well, I'll go and get some sandwiches and cups of tea then," said Daniel, feeling useless, "Keep an eye on them Suzi; I'll go and check upstairs."

Daniel proceeded back up to the terrace, where Kilpatrick was still clutching his bloody foot. Mia was still clinging onto Max's leg. And Mr Shyu was still looking inscrutable.

"Max. Is all OK to call in the second wave?"

"Looks good to me," replied Max, stroking Mia's hair to comfort her.

Daniel called Jondi to give the all-clear for Charlie, Anne Marie and Nzinga to drive up to the ape house.

"We think the coast is clear, but tell them to keep their wits about them for stray vermin."

"Have you neutralised all the Chinese?" asked Jondi.

"As far as we know?"

"I'll call the chopper in then, and come up with Charlie and the others. I can't sit it out here and do nothing. OK ladies, we are good to go," instructed Jondi, "Magazines in your guns, but safeties on for now."

"Are Daniel and Suzi OK?" asked Charlie.

"Seem to be, so far. Have you got all your kit Nzinga?"

"Yes. Good to go. The sooner we can get the tranquilisers in the gorillas, the less stressed they will be."

* * *

They drove stealthily up the drive, by-passed the main house and parked outside the barn where the apes were imprisoned. Jondi went in first and checked the place was clear and came back to the door.

"God, it stinks in there! I'll keep guard out here in the fresh air, whilst you three sort out the wildlife."

Nzinga ran through the door and up the line of cages. Charlie and Anne Marie stood by the barn door in horror at the state of the young gorillas, isolated in their barred prison cages.

"Can you see Didi?" called Charlie up the barn.

"Yes, she's in the last cage at the top, but she's seriously dehydrated and I'm not sure she will make it. A couple of the others are in a serious way too. Can you two wrap Didi in the towels in my bag, and I will dart the older ones that are too dangerous to handle."

Charlie and Anne Marie ran up to the top of the barn and unlocked the barren concrete-floored cage. Charlie climbed in and wrapped the towel around Didi. She was too weak to resist and she could hardly keep her head erect. Charlie passed her out to Anne Marie.

"You poor thing. I hope Daniel kills all the bastards that did this to you!" cried Anne Marie, stroking Didi's head. "If he doesn't, I will!"

"Nzinga, have you got any fluids in your bag?" asked Charlie, used to looking after dehydrated lambs and calves, abandoned by their recalcitrant mothers, in the remote pastures of Wensleydale.

"Yes, in the big side pocket. Tube her first and make sure she swallows the tube. Only give her fifty millilitres of fluid to start with. If that doesn't work, I will give her some intravenously, when I have finished the darting."

"She's quite cold, Nzinga." observed Anne Marie. "What can I do to warm her up?"

"OK, can you sit on the bales Annie and cuddle her like a baby, to keep her warm, whilst Charlie helps me with the other two sick ones."

"I'm feeling quite maternal," smiled Anne Marie, holding Didi inside her jacket next to her breasts.

"I never thought I would hear those words coming out of your lips!" joked Charlie, lightening the mood a little, and being pleased to be actively involved in the rescue at last.

"OK, that's all the darting done," said Nzinga. "Let's have a look at Didi... God she is so thin! She was too young to take off her mother when she was stolen and the idiots have not been giving her the right milk substitute. Her eyes are very anaemic. I will give her a shot of multivits and glucose to boost her up a bit, till we get back to the plane. I've got some special milk for her there. Do you want to pass her to Charlie for bit, Annie, and you help me with some of the older ones."

"I'm glad you sedated that bloody chimpanzee, that screaming was driving me mad," said Jondi, who had ventured inside the barn to see what was happening.

Chimpanzee youngster

"I've never been this close to a chimpanzee before. They're amazingly similar to some of the people I have to deal with!"

"That's not funny Jondi. They are beautiful creatures and never have an evil thought, unlike some people in this world," reprimanded Nzinga, fiercely protective of her charges. "Hold this one," she said, thrusting a baby gorilla into Jondi's arms.

"Thanks, my boss will never believe this!"

* * *

Daniel made his way back down the stairs and he found Marko and Francesca in a huddle over one of the computer screens.

"Are you making any progress?"

"Be quiet" said Marko aggressively.

"Sorry. I only asked."

Daniel wandered over to Suzi, who was keeping guard on the Chinese.

"What's happening?" whispered Daniel.

"I am not actually sure. Francesca said something about Cipher Block Chaining in Mode 8 and IDEA chips, whatever they are?"

"Oh, I thought of that too!" joked Daniel.

"I think they are trying to decrypt a last block of cypher text because the resultant data is XOR'd with the previous block of cipher text to recover the original plaintext," suggested Suzi.

"I thought, that's what they would do!"

"When you two have finished the amateur techy babble," exclaimed Marko, "we have made some progress. We have got into the hot wallets they're using to transfer the crypto from China to the various Australian ministries, investment banks and universities."

"Can you print a list off of the wallets and where the money went?" asked Daniel.

"Print!" exclaimed Marko. "I will send a file to Seb and he can forward it to you in whatever primitive format you want."

"Thank you," replied Daniel, sheepishly. "Any sign of the big stuff?"

"Might need Mr Shyu to get at that."

"I'll fetch him. I am sure he will be delighted to help!"

* * *

Daniel went up to the terrace and found the second young Chinese man dead on the table. Mr Shyu was sitting upright with his arms crossed.

"What the hell happened, Max; why did you have to kill him?"

"Max didn't. I did," interrupted Mr Shyu calmly.

Daniel was mystified, "Explain please?"

"I have developed an exit strategy. Do you need me downstairs?" he smiled.

Kilpatrick was still moaning about his injured foot. "I don't know what the fuck is going on here but you bastards will all regret this when I tell Beijing." He shouted hopefully. "They will hunt you down and kill you all, wherever you are in the world."

"Max, keep an eye our abusive friend here. Is Mia OK?"

"I am fine, thank you Daniel, Max is wonderful," whispered Mia, looking up adoringly at Max.

"I know Mia, everybody thinks Max is wonderful! Come on Mr Shyu lets go and enlighten Marko."

Daniel indicated for Mr Shyu to go down the steps first and they walked along the mine to the control area.

"Marko, my friend, how are you getting on with my labyrinth?" asked Mr Shyu.

"Interesting Mr Shyu, I loved the SNMPv3."

"I bet you still cannot access the cold wallets. But I have a suggestion."

"Go on." said Marko intrigued with his peer.

"I will show you the key to the algorithm if we can share the proceeds fifty-fifty."

"I agree, but if you try anything dubious, I keep it all," confirmed Marko.

"I am not sure I am happy with this," interrupted Daniel. "Francesca, what do you think?"

"We cannot get in without him. It's a huge amount of money. I think it's the only option, anyway."

"OK, I agree," confirmed Daniel reluctantly.

Mr Shyu sat down serenely at the keyboard, next to Marko, and started pressing keys at a lightning rate. The screen filled with undecipherable hieroglyphics and they went on and on as he entered more and more passwords, to access the secret depths of his own personal dark web. Finally, the last door was opened and the figure of US$2.3 billion sat in the credit balance.

"Is that what you were looking for?" Mr Shyu smiled.

Marko was looking worried as Mr Shyu hit the last key and the balance started to decrease at $10,000 per second.

"Get him away from the keyboard!" yelled Marko. "Francesca, quick try and stop the seed key in that chain, he's split his blockchain and is diverting the money somewhere else."

Daniel put his gun to Mr Shyu's head. "Stop the transfer now or believe me I will transfer your brains to the floor."

"If you do that you will get nothing," said Mr Shyu calmly. "I will give you a small fee at the end of the transfer."

"Francesca, what's happening?" asked Marko, frantically trying to block the process.

"I'm nearly in. There's a fault in the algorithm which is slowing me down."

"Where's the money going?" asked Daniel.

"I assume his private wallet somewhere. Could be Nigeria. Good place to hide illegal money. Just give us some space!" asked a very stressed Marko.

"OK sorry. We can't lose everything having got this far," sighed Daniel.

As the minutes ticked by, the money pile slowly diminished. Daniel paced up and down, and then, suddenly.

"I'm in!" shouted Francesca. "I've cracked the XOR encryption."

"Transfer suspended!" sighed a relieved Marko. "Brilliant job Francesca."

"How much have we lost?" asked Daniel.

"We haven't actually lost it. It's just somewhere else. About US$10 million," informed Mr Shyu proudly.

"Can you transfer the remaining bulk to Sebastian's account in Cayman, so we know it's safe," asked Daniel.

"Have done, apart from my £2 million sterling!" replied Marko

"When did you do that?"

"Now!" laughed Marko hitting a key with gusto.

"What about my master's money in South Africa?" Francesca asked with a worried expression on her face.

"It's all gone," joked Daniel. "You will be on the run for the rest of your life!"

"That's not fair!" she protested, after everything I have just done for…"

"Only winding you up!" interrupted Daniel. "I will ask Seb to clear your debts with the South African mine bank account, if you give me the details. And you better get the currency right this time!"

Francesca gave Daniel a rather passionate kiss, much to Suzi's disapproval, who was still guarding the Chinese captives. "What are we going to do with this lot?"

"Cable-tie the others to their chairs and Jondi's men can sort them out. I'm sure Mr Shyu will be a valuable asset to AUKUS at Pine Gap.

"So, you all work for the Australian government?" suggested Mr Shyu hesitantly.

"No, more like *Animal Farm*!" proposed Daniel referring to George Orwell's classic novel where the animals take over running things from human beings.

"Very funny. What about this lady you carelessly shot?" asked Mr Shyu.

"It wasn't careless; she deserved no less. In any case it was a perfect shot, disabled but not dead. I would have killed a man, in the same circumstances."

"Very chivalrous!" sighed Mr Shyu.

"Are you all right down here Suzi, if Marco, Francesca and I, go and see how the others are going on? I'll sent some of Jondi's team down to take over when the Chinook turns up."

"Yes, I'll be fine. They can teach me some Chinese!"

Daniel, Marko and Francesca climbed back up the stairs to the terrace, where Max and Mia were surrounded by dead Chinese in pools of blood. Mia was now sitting on Max's lap and he had his arm around her, in a slightly more than friendly fashion. Kilpatrick was still slumped on the sofa nursing his foot and uttering expletives with every other word.

"I have decided I am going to take Mia back to Sydney to see her father," said Max. "Can you manage without me on the trip back to Africa?"

"Of course, we owe Mia a great deal. Look after her Max and send her details to Seb, so he can top-up her bank account."

"Thanks Daniel, give my love to the others and I hope you get Didi back safely." Max stood up, put his arm around Mia and they walked slowly down the steps to go back to his house.

"Go on, take your filthy whore with you. She was a useless dancer anyway!" shouted Kilpatrick to Max and Mia.

Max turned around, pointed his MP7 at Kilpatrick and shot him once between his red, drink-soaked eyes; he fell back on the sofa stone dead.

"Some people have no culture!" said Max equably.

"Saved me a job," said Daniel. "I'll be in touch."

As Max disappeared down the path with his arm around Mia, Francesca looked at Daniel.

"I guess that's the end or our brief affair!"

"I think you may be right Francesca, but I have a job in mind for you, in Africa, and I know just the right man for you."

"Mmm tell me more." she said, happy to move on to her next conquest.

"He's called Bomani!"

* * *

The characteristic drone of the twin-rotor Chinook gunship grew lounder and louder as it skimmed across Lake Lefroy with it lights blazing, like some supernatural Noah's Ark. It hovered over the lawn, next to the barns and came to rest in a hurricane of leaves and dust.

"Where's Jondi?" shouted the first SAS trooper as he jumped out of the helicopter.

"Over here!" replied Jondi, and she briefed him on the situation. He instructed six of his colleagues to run to the house to relieve Suzi of her charges.

Charlie, cuddling Didi, ran into Daniel's arms and kissed him passionately.

"Will we always have a baby gorilla between us!" laughed Daniel.

"There always has been so far!" smiled Charlie. "I love you, my darling; you've done a brilliant job to get poor Didi back."

The baby gorillas and chimpanzees were all carefully loaded into the Chinook by Nzinga and Francesca, with Marko helping to strap the crates down. Daniel helped Charlie on board, with Didi still in her arms. Anne Marie leant out of the Chinook's door as the giant rotors built up to speed.

"Where's Suzi?" asked Annie, panicking she would be left behind. "We can't go without Suzi!"

Just as the wheels left the ground, Suzi arrived breathless and leapt through the open door of the Chinook. Anne Marie, smiling, caught her hand and pulled her into the seat next to her. For a fleeting moment they looked at each and nearly kissed, but the door slammed shut and Didi was on her way back to Africa.

Baby Mountain Gorilla

"*If we do not do something to prevent it, Africa's animals, and the places in which they live, will be lost to our world and her children forever.*"

– Nelson Mandela

EPILOGUE

Tsavo National Park – Kenya – East Africa

Three years later

"Good morning your royal highnesses, my lords, ladies and gentlemen, may I welcome you all to this opening of The Institute for the Inheritance of Life. My name is Nzinga and I have the honour to be the director of this new, world-leading centre for conservation.

The building of this magnificent, futuristic Institute has only been possible because of the enormous generosity of its benefactors. We are honoured today with the presence of Prince Fahd of Saudi Arabia, who has been intimately involved in the development of this project.

"And with the director!" whispered Daniel into Charlie's ear.

"Be quiet!" smiled Charlie.

"This Institute works in partnership with the new Wildlife Research Centre in the AlUla mountains in Saudi Arabia, where they are doing amazing work on the DNA profiling of endangered animals, especially the iconic Arabian leopards. We are very grateful for the support of Prince Fahd and his country.

"I would also like to thank the amazing generosity of Anne Marie Macmillan for financing the new satellite monitoring programme that is protecting wildlife across Africa. These satellites beam images, twenty-four hours a day, to university students around the world so they can watch every inch of the National Parks of Africa and report any attempts at poaching or abuse, to our dedicated Wildlife Protection Service.

"My next 'thank you' goes to a gentleman I will just call Dimitri. He was killed whilst on a secret mission to protect the world from modern cyber warfare. His work was hugely successful in protecting this planet for the future of our children and the donation of his considerable resources to this project are a wonderful tribute to his kindness and generosity.

"Finally, I would like to thank our main sponsor of this amazing conservation project, who wishes to remain anonymous."

Charlie squeezed Daniel's hand and smiled.

"He was born in Africa and has spent his whole life working to protect the creatures that we are so lucky to have, as our fellow inhabitants of this planet. Without his tireless efforts and unending enthusiasm this Institute would not be here today.

"Your royal highness, my lords, ladies and gentlemen, I offer you a very warm welcome to The Institute for the Inheritance of Life."

The audience, of over 500 people, rose to their feet and their enthusiastic applause and cheers, filled the room with hope, happiness and tears of joy.

Nzinga walked over to Fahd and formally shook his hand for the cameras. He took her in his arms and kissed her for the first time in public. The press were ecstatic and the photos would honour every publication around the world, ensuring the future of the project.

Charlie hugged Daniel, with tears trickling down her cheeks. "I am not sure what his brother will think!"

"I think he might have worked it out by now!" laughed Daniel, just as someone tapped him on the back. He turned around to find Jondi, heavily disguised in a blonde wig and dark glasses.

"Hello Daniel, remember me?"

"How could I forget you Jondi. How are things in sunny Australia?"

"We are all fine thank you; my superiors send their regards. They were just wondering if there was any money left over, from our little goldmining expedition?"

"I think Mr Shyu got most of it. Have you asked him?"

"He says that you got most of it!"

"I suppose it comes down to who are you going to trust then. A lying, cheating Chinese criminal or an honourable English gentleman! Anyway, I got you the list of every single organisation he was sponsoring; I am sure that was the most valuable thing to come out of it. In any case, it wasn't actually your money, it belonged to the Chinese government and I haven't heard from them!"

"My superiors said you might say that, but it was worth a try!"

"Can I offer you a job instead?" Daniel smiled.

"Tell me more!" said Jondi, returning the smile.

Charlie walked over to Nzinga and gave her a hug.

"Well done darling, that was a lovely speech."

"I was terrified, I could hear my voice shaking. I didn't know he was going to kiss me at the end!"

"We are all just so glad you two are happy together. You have done a fantastic job here. The architecture is so amazing and the views of the Tsavo landscape are as magical as ever."

"Mummy, mummy come and see the baby gorillas! They are so cute! Please?" pleaded the two little girls.

"OK, OK I'll come and look," grinned Charlie. "Sorry Nzinga, I think I am needed."

"It's fine. Have they ever asked you, why they are a different colour?"

"No, they live in a very multicultural world. I suppose one day I will have to explain who Aunty Annie and Aunty Suzi are, but for now they are just happy to have us all."

Charlie showed her twins the baby gorillas and explained why they had been rescued, but they were soon off to see the baby white rhinos with Max, who had also flown in for the opening.

Charlie wondered back through the wonderful irrigated gardens, planted with all the vegetation needed by the animals at the Institute. She found Daniel sitting on his own having a quiet moment of reflection.

"Are you OK darling?" she asked.

"I was just thinking of Elizabeth and how proud she would be of everything we have achieved for the children of Africa,"

Charlie put her arm around his shoulder and wiped a tear from his cheek.

They sat for while in the warm sunshine, enjoying the tranquillity of the gardens and their love for each other.

Anne Marie and Suzi, who were walking through the gardens holding hands, strolled up to Charlie and Daniel and sat next to them.

"We've been thinking," said Anne Marie hesitantly. "We've decided that we would like a baby of our own this time and were wondering if we could borrow Daniel again?"

"Of course, Annie, after everything you have done for Daniel and me. We can never thank you both enough for having the twins for us. You'll be happy to help, won't you darling?"

"You know me – happy to go with the flow!"

A Snowflake in the Furnace

The vultures fly, their prey to die
Hyenas 'neath acacias lie
The worst examples of mankind
Think they have the world to hide

But Templar Knights do more than talk
Encampment of Redemption York
To cleanse the world of evil folk
With sword and gun and more bespoke

Release those souls for years oppressed
By shadows of the passed depressed
Luminescence from catharsis
Pathways from eternal darkness

The mountains, meadows and the dunes
Alive with creatures and their tunes
The complex web we must conserve
Our children's children do deserve

Not Bible, Vedas or Koran
Nor any other sacred plan
Can save us from our mortal ways
Unless our planet fills our days

Our world is just a speck of dust
It's breathing plates and air we trust
Destroy the balance of this place.
And then we're gone without a trace

Landscapes of Love Trilogy

PHILIP TYLER

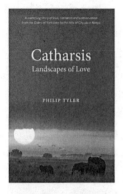

Catharsis, opens the Landscapes of Love trilogy and follows the complex relationship of Charlie, Daniel and Anne Marie and how their lives evolve together, as they battle the poachers across the vast plains of East Africa.

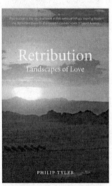

In *Retribution* their sensual relationship intensifies as they investigate a royal kidnapping in the beautiful landscapes of Saudi Arabia and take on the Russian hackers in the Ukrainian border lands.

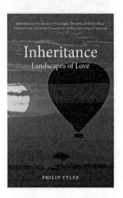

Inheritance is the finale of the Landscapes of Love trilogy. The triangle of love and passion between Charlie, Daniel and Anne Marie reaches a climax, as they track down the real money behind the baby gorilla poaching, in the baking heat of the gold mines of Western Australia.